I0677260

A DREAM OF NEON FIRE

Robert William Harms

TZ3 Publishing

Copyright © 2020 Robert William Harms

All rights reserved

The characters and events portrayed in this book are fictitious.
Any similarity to real persons, living or dead, is coincidental
and not intended by the author.

No part of this book may be reproduced, or stored in a retrieval
system, or transmitted in any form or by any means, electronic,
mechanical, photocopying, recording, or otherwise, without
express written permission of the publisher.

ISBN-13: 978-0-578-69027-8

Cover design by: Robert William Harms (Belmont)

Printed in the United States of America

*For Beth, Mike, my parents, Tommy, JP,
and everyone else who has supported my
art and writing over the years.*

CHAPTER 1

Ian

The spotlights momentarily blind my eyes. My heart is racing faster than it ever has before and I'm doing all in my power not to start shaking. Looking down, my eyes focus as I see my well-worn boots tied up tight. The leather is cracked and split. They've been with me since the beginning and now, this, the end. Bouncing back and forth, the mat gives under my weight. Below that I can feel the spring of the ring floor shift.

The ring is brand new with beautiful red, white, and blue ropes. The canvas, a light grey, not yet stained with blood. The lights all around the ring make it nearly impossible to see the crowd. I was told in the locker room that it's sold out but I can't see anything beyond the first row. Their shouting and screaming is so loud that it has just become one indiscernible sound. An ever-present static, like a broken television, clouding up my ears.

He enters the ring. The static increases to a piercing, sharp, tone like a needle stabbing me through the head. A sea of camera flashes engulfs everything in a brilliant white light. The clacking of shutters adds to the overwhelming nature of everything that is before me.

Suddenly, things seem to be moving in slow motion. He is jumping around. Shouting in my face. His hot breath dances off my nose, his spit splatters off my cheek. He's gesturing and posturing. A true showman. The crowd is going wild. They've all counted me out already. Just some bum for the future champ to beat. A notch in his inevitable title belt.

Clenching my fists tight I can feel the leather of my gloves creak. Everything I have done to prepare for this is about to come to fruition. Never before have I ever been so determined to give everything I have to stop someone. But will it be enough?

The bell rings and my muscles tense. Then a wave of euphoria flushes through me. A calm, peaceful moment. My vision becomes precise. Nevermore focused. All of my senses feel heightened to superhuman levels.

This is it Ian. Nothing is going to stop you now...

The fight has been long and brutal but now I have him in the corner. I'm blasting him with lefts and rights. I've lost all control over myself and my hands are moving all on their own. I feel as though I have left my body and I'm watching the carnage from the front row.

All the damage I have taken in this fight is now meaningless. Pain, anger, joy, hatred, all my emotions are gone and it's just him and me.

His face is shattering. With every punch I can

feel another bone in his body break. Blood spraying into the air and on to me and the referee. His arms fall to his sides, limp. He's not even trying to defend himself anymore. A sick feeling grows inside of me. A feeling that I can't quite describe. Almost as if I'm looking over a cliff and a voice in the back of my head is saying "jump".

For a moment my eyes lock on to her. Sitting in the crowd all by herself. Her face awash with excitement and sorrow. So many emotions on display at once. Tears streaming down her cheeks. She always looks so beautiful and tonight is no exception.

My love. My Gloria.

This is for you.

One final blow.

A right hand so hard I feel like I could have punched through a concrete wall.

Through my hand, and up my arm, I feel his skull crack.

He crashes down onto the mat.

Time slows to a snail's pace.

My heart feels like it's about to leap out of my chest.

The referee starts his count.

Each number echoing off a beat of my heart.

It has become clear what I have done.

The crowd is in stunned silence.

He's not getting up.

Not now.

Not ever again...

CHAPTER 2

Officer Carmine - 1968

We approach the old and dilapidated tenement in our cruiser. The rattle of some unknown object, dangling just under my seat, annoys me just as much as ever. I should get it checked out by someone in the motor pool but for some reason never do. It's a hot and sticky night. A godawful stink permeates the air. It's like all the collective body odor of the city is lingering like a haze, so thick you can almost see it. My shirt is clinging to my back and it doesn't matter how many times I adjust it, it slaps right back into place. Fidgeting in my seat I can feel the sweat starting to collect in my pants.

The windows of our car now have droplets of condensation forming because of the intense humidity, almost as if the car itself is sweating. The rookie in the passenger seat wipes his furrowed brow. I just realized I can't remember the damn kid's name. I'd been calling him 'rookie' all day. I was told he was good when he was in the academy but I hardly got that from the way he carried himself around me. He checks his sidearm repeatedly as if it would suddenly leap away from his hip. Cranking down the window he takes a big deep breath as if he hadn't taken one in days. The damn kid looks like he's about to start hyperventilating.

I can remember my first day on the job. I was wet behind the ears myself but hardly as tense. Of course, my first day didn't involve something as dangerous as tonight.

Stevens. That's his name!

Shaking in his seat he attempts to steady himself and mutters something under his breath. I pretend not to notice. Part of me desperately wants to reach over, open his door, and kick him to the curb. He'd probably like that.

As we roll up some undesirables clear the sidewalk. Mostly working girls, dressed in their hot pants and high boots, and hoodlums. Drug addicts and the like. They scurry into the darkness like rats. This is a popular area for those lost souls.

We are meeting with the rest of our team outside the building. A tip came through the hot-line that big-time drug dealer Oleg Taran was held up in one of the apartments on the tenth floor. We had been tracking this guy for months and this was the first real lead that we had gotten. Every other lead that we had went as cold as a witch's tit. If true this would be one of the biggest busts in Lochland history. I know I wouldn't mind having another medal of recognition on my shelf. It would look really nice hanging next to my bowling trophy.

I park the car and almost in the same instant the rookie, I mean Stevens, leaps out. He's puking his guts out into a trash bin. What a wimp. What's next? Is this guy going to piss himself? I certainly hope not. That's the last thing I need. I consider arguing with Sgt. Phillips to leave him behind but go against my gut.

"What a sorry state of affairs we have over here. Shape up, rookie!" Sgt. Phillips commands.

Flanked by Officers Daigan, Crenick and Marsters, Sgt. Phillips with his big thick mustache and broad chest steps up. Daigan is prematurely balding and severely self-conscious about it. He never takes his hat off. Crenick is about thirty pounds overweight but he's an excellent shot and Marsters, well, he's the ladies man. If I were to believe everything he says, then he's bedded hundreds of women. I don't believe him.

I'd been working with these guys for years. We had taken down several top syndicates in the area and we were getting a bit of a reputation. Sarge was looking for some new blood since Crenick is close to retirement age. That's how we ended up with Stevens. He's supposedly good with a gun. Checking his sidearm again I notice his long blonde hair dangling out the back of his hat. I know it's the sixties but this guy needs to cut his damn hair.

Stevens takes off his hat and runs his fingers through his hair. He seems to be regaining his composure. I see Daigan looking on with jealous eyes and have to stifle a laugh.

"Alright boys, here's the scoop. We've got Taran held up in Apartment 10B. Supposedly he's got some other people in there with him so this needs to be by the book. We must consider him, and anyone else in there, armed and dangerous. I'm going to be point on this one. Daigan, Carmine, and myself will go up the front steps. Crenick, Marsters, you two up the back fire escape. Go through the window of apartment 10C. It's abandoned from what we can tell but stay sharp. Meet us in the hallway in front of 10B. Rookie you go with them and stay in the back. I want no mistakes. Once we are in the apartment I want no false moves. Fire only if necessary. We need to get this guy into custody so we can get him talking. There could be innocents in there too so be careful. I can't stress this enough. I don't want any innocent blood on our hands tonight. You got it?!"

We all nod in silent approval. Sgt. Phillips gestures with his hands and we move. Crenick, Marsters, and Stevens disappear into the alleyway to the side of the building. The Sarge, Daigan, and I approach the front of the building. The place stinks to high heaven, and that's on the outside. I can almost taste the stale cigarettes and cheap booze. It's so potent that as we gracefully walk up the front steps I almost gag. I've been in tons of buildings just like this, stained carpets, wallpaper peeling, unknown substances splattered on the walls, but somehow this one stinks worse than them all.

The front door opens easily enough. In the lobby there's a completely collapsed elevator shaft. The tile floor is cracked and discolored. I wonder, was this place was nice once upon a time? I think about the people who probably once lived here. Good, decent, hardworking people just trying to get by. Now look at it. A safe harbor for the scum of the earth. Better to level the whole neighborhood than to watch it rot.

Sgt. Phillips leads as we go up the stairs. We go slow, taking our time not to create a fuss. Creaking under our feet the stairs feel like they are going to collapse. Why would a big-time player like Taran want to stay in a dump like this? I suppose it's low profile, but still. Feeling something squish under my foot I decide it's best not to look.

The door to apartment 8A opens and a bald, drunken, fat, businessman type stumbles out. Lipstick smeared on his face and neck, his pants barely pulled all the way up. Seeing us he freezes faster than a deer in headlights. Daigan waves his gun in a 'go back inside' gesture. A hand with cracked, ill-painted fingernails reaches out and grabs the businessman by the shoulder. As we pass by I get a glimpse at a middle-aged woman with deep bags under her eyes and sloppy makeup. Her body language says to me that she's high as a kite. I'd be lying if I said I didn't look at her body. A fantasy passes through my mind. I'm not proud.

On the ninth floor a man is sleeping in the hall. I'm not sure if he lives here or if he's homeless or what. He's dressed in a disgusting, ratty suit with a big stain on the ass. I try to tell myself that he must have just sat in something. He must have just sat in something. I hold my breath. Clutching at a half-drunk bottle of whiskey like his life depended on it, his hands look skeletal and brittle. Daigan kicks him just to make sure he isn't dead. He barely responds with more than a grunt and then we move on.

Finally, on the tenth floor, after what felt like the longest walk of my life we meet up with the rest of our team. Crenick is in the lead with Marsters and Stevens behind him. Stevens is pouring sweat. It's hot, but not that hot. I don't believe I've ever seen anyone sweat so much. His uniform has giant pit stains. It's like someone sprayed him with a god-damn hose. For Christ's sake. I catch a whiff of some nasty smell. I wonder for a second if it's Stevens. I check my own armpit and determine quickly that it isn't me.

I feel a moment of haziness. Looking up I see a thick cloud of smoke hanging just above our heads. The cheap lighting flickers. Not enough for a strobe effect, but enough to be truly annoying. A faint buzzing noise rings in my ears. Marsters stops himself from coughing. Blinking my eyes rapidly I try to regain my composure. Daigan pops his hat off to wipe away sweat revealing his enormous bald spot.

Sgt. Phillips knocks on the door. I clench my gun hard for just a moment. There is no response. Trying again he knocks even harder. We all wait with bated breath. I can just barely make out some talking from the other side of the wall. It sounds like a man and a woman. Confusion fills their voices. My stomach turns.

"This is Lochland Police. We know you are in

there, Taran, and if you don't come out here with your hands up by the count of three, we're going to bust this door down!"

Through the wall I hear what sounds like something getting knocked over, and scared voices muttering. The sarge counts...one...two...three!

With all the force of his 250lbs the Sarge kicks the door in. Acting as if controlled by pure instinct the rest of us, guns cocked and ready, follow in behind him. My eyes scan the room back and forth, back and forth.

Gaudy floral themed furniture.

Cheap carpet stained and marked with cigarette burns.

Tiny television with big, rabbit ear, antenna.

Oddly shaped coffee table.

A mirror with remnants of cocaine.

A man in his mid-twenties stands in the middle of the room. A loose button-down white shirt and bell-bottom pants show his athletic build. A thick curly mop of brown hair sits atop of his head. He's rather tall, easily in the mid six foots. On his chin a patchy goatee. Beads of sweat trickle down the sides of his face. He is holding a .38 in his right hand. He isn't confident. It's almost like he's never held that thing before. He looks scared. Truly scared.

This is not Taran.

I don't know who the hell this is. Some low level enforcer? Just a regular old street dealer? Who the hell is this guy? My mind opens up with a book full of mugshots. I can't pinpoint this guy.

Our guns are drawn and poised to fire. On the couch behind the man is an attractive young woman dressed in a silver, sparkly, party dress. She quickly wipes a dab of cocaine off her nose, stands up, and goes to the man's side. Her big blue eyes are wide and she is clearly frightened out of her mind.

Our tip was bad. This is a mistake.

"Don't move!" Crenick screams. "Don't you move a damn muscle!"

"Drop the gun! Drop it!" I find myself joining in.

Out of the darkness a child appears. A young boy no more than eight. He is dressed in Flintstones pajamas. A big goofy image of Fred right in the middle. In bold letters it says "yabba dabba do!". Rubbing his eyes he pushes long brown hair out of the way.

"Mommy? What's happening?" He says in a quiet and confused voice.

Marsters points his gun at the child instinctively. The man reacts quickly and points his gun at us. The woman leaps at the child and hugs him tight. The boy begins to cry.

"Drop the damn gun now!" I yell

It's too late.

No going back.

A scream so loud it feels like my eardrum explodes. It takes me a minute to even comprehend what I have just witnessed. The rookie... That goddamn bastard. He jumped the line and filled that man so full of lead he would sink to the bottom of the Barrington River. His face looks like a week-old hamburger. If I had a softer stomach I'd be about ready to puke.

Daigan is slumped over, he took a bullet of return fire. I know I should be worried about him but that damn bald spot is all I'm looking at. I turn and scan the room. The woman is screaming. The most horrific scream, like the wail of a banshee. She holds the man tight in her arms on the floor. They are both covered in blood. I feel something hot on my face. Touching it, I pull my fingers away revealing blood. Not my own. A pool of it is slowly forming on the floor. It creeps inch by inch towards my feet.

The child. My God, the child. He is standing there. Blood, and God knows what else, splattered on his face. His expression is emotionless. His eyes wide. A piercing blue. I'll never forget that look for as long as I live. Staring at him I feel a chill roll down my spine.

Marsters has the rookie on the ground with a knee in his back. Stevens is yelling that he's cool but I don't believe it. None of us do.

Thinking back to the car I wish I had followed my instinct and kicked him out. Even earlier at the station, when he tossed me the keys to the cruiser and missed by a mile, and he was shaking like a leaf in the wind, maybe then I should have said something.

Sarge is screaming. It's all just nonsense.

White noise layered over a horror show. Crenick cuffs the woman. He's reading her her rights. She's not listening. She's crying and screaming and sobbing. I don't even know what is going on at this point. I'm moving around like a zombie.

Who are these people? What have we done?

Crenick pulls her past me. She looks me dead in the eyes. My heart sinks.

I look at my gun. Truly look at it. A device created only for death...

I toss it to the ground in disgust.

I look back at the corpse of the young man Steven's just killed.

This is not Taran. I don't know who the hell this is.

I find myself checking on Daigan.

He's ok. Just a flesh wound.

He asks about his hat.

CHAPTER 3

Ian – 1980

She loves this. She loves walking in this park. Our hands intertwined like a twisted slinky that can never be fixed. We've done this probably a hundred times, and we'll probably do it a hundred times more, but she never gets sick of it. I go with her because I know it makes her happy. She tells me the sunshine and clean ocean air will do us good. I honestly couldn't care less. I mean it's a park. You've seen one you've seen them all. There's grass. Trees. Maybe a fountain or two. I know she loves this because of this one specific spot. The spot we always go to. At sunset the sky becomes an amazing shade of pink and you can see the whole city looking one way and the bridge and ocean the other. I drag my ass up this hill again and again for her. I curse to myself as my knees ache and my back twitches. The only thing in this life that's worth a damn to me is her. I'd do anything if it meant her safety. My Gloria.

Our hands release as Gloria reaches the peak of the hill. Her curvy body silhouetted against the sunset. I remember the day we first met. She was so scared. I didn't even know her but I risked my life anyway. It wasn't until after that I realized how beautiful she was. She is so voluptuous she could have been a model. I couldn't believe she would even consider dating me, let alone marrying me. My ugly ass. Busted nose, bags under my eyes. No redeeming qualities in the looks department other than a decent set of muscles. It's not like I had any money either.

"Isn't it beautiful here, Ian?"

She turns to look at me. Her long black curly hair waving in the wind. A smile so bright it could light up a room. A black, floral print, sundress bends as the wind blows. She touches her stomach. Her big round baby bump. Inside is our daughter, Rona, waiting to be born. How did I get so damn lucky? I don't deserve such a woman. I don't deserve a nice life.

I moved to Bella Cruz five years ago because some idiot told me the sun and palm trees would change my opinion on life. I guess they weren't an idiot. If I hadn't come here I wouldn't have met Gloria. I'd probably be punchy, lying on a friend's couch, stinking drunk and pilled up out of my mind, counting beer bottles just to pass the time. I definitely wouldn't have a gorgeous wife and soon a family. I wouldn't have ditched the bottle. I wouldn't have stopped the pills. I wouldn't have given up the fight game. I'd be alone or in the bed of some prostitute. Spending every last dime I had wasting my life away. Just like I was doing before. Just like what I deserved.

"Ian?"

"Ian?"

"Mr. Dempsey?"

1985

I can't think. I can't breathe. I can't move. I can't do anything. The smell of bleach and ammonia and who knows what else assaults my nose. I'm choking. I'm choking on nothing. All I can see is cheap tile floors and my beat-up sneakers. I'm looking at it but I don't see it. I don't see anything at all. Everything fades to black. The darkness is overwhelming. It fills my body up to the brim and spills over into eternity.

She's dead. I repeat it to myself over and over again but it still doesn't feel real. She's dead. They are both dead. My beautiful wife and daughter are dead. Car accident. Rona. My sweet daughter. Her chubby cheeks and adorable laugh. Thankfully she got her mother's looks. But that's gone now. That's all gone now. They tell me they didn't suffer but how would they know? How could they know?

Damn! Damn! I repeat it over and over again until it becomes all I hear. It's like the beat of a tribal drum bouncing around inside my head. Damn. Damn. Damn! I feel the most intense anger I have ever felt. It feels like my blood has turned to lava and my skin is about to burst. I clench my teeth so incredibly hard I feel a molar break. My hands are shaking uncontrollably. Veins popping out from under the skin like tendrils. I turn them over and see blood trickling from my clenched fists.

Suddenly, I'm back six years ago. I'm sitting on a hard wooden bench in a filthy locker room. It smells like sweat, beer, buffalo wings, and literal shit. Gloria is sitting next to me. My hands are wrapped in tape and covered in blood. Lumped at my feet, my boxing gloves are split and in ruin. My face is a wreck. Nose smashed. Ribs broken. Sweat pooling on the floor beneath me. Gloria is telling me it's going to be ok. Her gentle fingers glide down my back. My one comfort in this world. Her soft voice echoes in my head. "It was an accident" she says. Deep inside I know it wasn't. Never before have I ever wanted to hurt someone so bad. See them plead for mercy and have me not give it. I couldn't stop myself. He couldn't stop me. No one could. I was God and death all at once. Someone tells me he's dead but I already knew it. It's ruled an accident, but it wasn't.

I snap out of it, stand up, and start smashing things. First a chair, then a table. The doctors try to restrain me but they can't. I don't want to hurt them but I do anyway. I knock out some poor schmoe's teeth. I put a giant hole through the wall. I grab a guy and toss him through a plate-glass window. My hand is broken and I don't even care. Gloria is gone. Rona is gone. Nothing matters anymore. I am alone. Just like I deserved.

I deserved this...

I'm sitting in a jail cell. My arm in a cast. I can't feel anything. I might as well have been in the car with Gloria and my sweet, sweet Rona. I should have been. I should be dead too but I'm not. Why the hell am I alive but two innocent, beautiful, souls are dead?

They only give me a few days in jail given the circumstances. They say I lost control. I didn't mean it. My wife and daughter had just died. The guy whose teeth I knocked out even came to forgive me. He was a youth pastor just trying to calm me down. I had to stop myself from laughing at his goofy ass toothless smile. I should feel bad for him but I don't. He should have known better than to try and stop me.

I deserved worse.

I deserved much, much worse.

I think of that son of a bitch. Lying in a pool of his own blood. Face smashed to oblivion. Drawing his last breath as I stand over him. What a horrible way to go. My lungs are afire and all I can feel is pain like white-hot needles being jammed into every single pore. The crowd is in stunned silence as I'm declared the winner. The winner of what?

It's ruled an accident...but it wasn't.

I envy him now. He will never know the pain inside of me. The pain of your heart exploding inside your chest and yet you still live.

He's laughing at me.

In the end... he won.

CHAPTER 4

Alex – 1980

My coach tells me this is my time. My mom tells me this is my time. My dad tells me this is my time. My time to be great. My time to show the world all I can be. My dad can't help it. He's Japanese and grew up in a strict household. His parents forced him to work all day and all night to succeed. He's a doctor. Just like his parents wanted. He moved to America just like his parents wanted. Whatever they said he did. So he says and I do. I guess it's just how things are sometimes. When I was little I showed potential as an athlete and now all my dad talks about is the Olympics. I'm not sure we've ever really had a conversation about what I really want.

So here I am. Standing in a leotard. My face caked in makeup. My hair pulled so tight in a bun I can feel every inch of my scalp. Thousands of eyes on me. But I can't see them. At this moment I am blind and deaf. The smell of perfume tickles my nose. My nostrils flare. Finally focusing I can hear my dad screaming.

"Alexandra! This is your moment!"

"Next up, from Lochland City New York, Alexandra Faye-Darling!" The announcer says.

I stand at attention. My arms to the sky, I signal I'm ready. Eyes are clear. Toes pointed. The soft texture of the mat squishes under my feet. I dash across the floor and go into my first pass. Round off full twist to double front. I fly through the air so high I feel like I'll never come down. Landed. The crowd erupts. I dance into my next position. Wowing the crowd with my awesome dance moves. I stick out my butt and pretend like I'm pouting. The crowd giggles. They are in the palm of my hand. I tumble and tumble and flip and flip. The crowd is behind me. Their cheers are like fuel in the engine that is my body. I haven't even broken a sweat. Smiling like a spotlight, I push in my cheeks like dimples and I can hear the crowd make a collective "aww".

Candice Marks, my top competition, becomes visible to me. She simultaneously looks angry and sad. Worried and furious. Her parents are poor. She's come from nothing. She's an amazing gymnast. My equal in every way but tonight she blew her balance beam routine. They say she won't make it to the Olympics now unless I royally screw up. Only one of us can go.

I go through my second pass. Double twisting double back. My landing is off by a bit. I know the judges are marking me down for that. I play it off like no big deal. Dazzle them with my smile. My big stupid grin and freckle filled face. I get that from my mom. A red-headed Irish woman. She's so carefree. She just wants me to be happy. How she ended up with my dad I'll never fully understand. Being a half

Asian half ginger has been a bit of a blessing. I definitely stand out.

Now that I'm done mesmerizing the crowd with just how damn cute I am it's time for the finale. I run full blast across the mat. Lungs on fire. Palms sweaty. I know what I have to do. Round off. Full twist. Back to front. In mid-air I think of Candice. Tears in her eyes. I know she wants this and I know what I want...

I'm laying on my back staring up at the lights. The crowd lets out a collective groan. I can almost feel my father's disappointment. It's like a heavy blanket tossed on top of me, but then I hear a voice.

"I love you, baby!"

It's my mom.

I stand up and pose. Arms in the air. Tears streaming down my face. I frown. I bow. The crowd claps and cheers anyway. They don't want to hurt the feelings of a seventeen-year-old girl. I leave the mat. I bypass my coach and go right to Candice.

"You deserve this."

I hold her tight, so tight I can feel her sadness fade away like a dream you try to remember hours after awakening. We are both crying. My tears are as fake as Candice's mother's press-on fingernails. Her parents rush to her and embrace her. They are so happy. Seeing them that way makes my fake tears evaporate and I can't help myself. I'm smiling. Dreams can come true.

It's the award ceremony and because of my colossal flub I actually got third place. I can't believe I ended up placing below Carmella Jones. That girl's a twit. Stuck up rich bitch. I ignore her just like I normally do. We exchange hugs and kisses like we actually like each other. She mutters "slut" under her breath. I just smile. As they are announcing the awards Candice and I hold hands. Carmella tries to play it cool but you can tell she's furious. Everything about her is fake, from her bleached teeth to her bogus blonde hair and that nose job she tried to pass off as a skiing accident. She'll probably go and starve herself for a week over this.

The MC hangs a bronze medal around my neck and hands me some flowers. I feign crying once more but inside I'm ecstatic. By the next qualifier I'll be too old for the team. Now I can stop doing what my dad wants and do what I want and he can't force me. I can finally live. My dad, my mom, my coach. They were all right. It is my time.

I hang up my medal with all the others in the display that my dad built years ago. I'll probably never look at it again. A great big pile of metal, ribbons and plastic. It's time for me to look forward and not back.

Under my bed is my secret collection of comic books. My mom buys them for me. My dad doesn't approve of such things. I grab one of my favorites. The Apparition. I jump on my bed and start leafing through the pages. I've heard rumors that The Apparition is real. That these comics are based on true stories. I hope they are true. God, I hope they are. I want to live in a world of heroes. I flip to the best page. My favorite page. A big splash of The Apparition standing tall over a thug. It says "Evildoers beware! The spirit of justice will haunt you!". It's so corny but I absolutely adore it. His costume is so colorful. He's a tower of muscle but he's wearing a red and baby blue outfit. Hardly a great disguise if he was prowling the alleyways at night.

I read through the rest of the book as I hear my parents arguing in the next room. No surprise really. It's the same old same old. My dad is livid. He's saying stuff like "wasted potential" "what will she do now?" and she's saying "just let her be happy". God bless my mom. She tries. I've kinda learned to drown it out. In my head all I hear is music. I'm sure my dad won't be talking to me for the next month... or year. Finally things quiet down as I lay on my bed staring at the ceiling. I hear a rustling and look to my bedroom door. A cookie on a plate was slid through the gap at the bottom. Picking it up I see my mom put a note underneath.

"Keep dreaming of Neon Fire. Love, Mom."

As I take a big bite out of that sweet chocolaty goodness I go to my desk. I open the drawer and pull out a crude drawing. I was never very talented as far as art goes. It was a superhero character I made up when I was little. It says on the top in big letters "Neon Fire". The drawing is of a woman in a purple leotard with spiky hair. It looks so terrible. You can barely tell it's a woman. Placing it down on the desk I look out the window at my fire escape.

On the roof of our building I stand at attention and raise my hands to the air.

"Next up, from Lochland City New York, Alexandra Faye-Darling!" I say to myself.

I dash. Round off. Full Twist. Back to Front. Landed with perfection. The crowd goes wild. I dance around like an idiot and smile. Smile smile smile.

Plopping down on the edge of the rooftop I look out into the city. A landscape of apartments, skyscrapers, and everything you could dream of stretches for as far as the eye can see. I can hear sirens wailing. Beneath me the police are in hot pursuit. The flashing lights from the cop cars reflect off the windows and fill the air with red and blue light. All of this is like a symphony being played only for me. Closing my eyes, I think about The Apparition. He's jumping from rooftop to rooftop. Swinging from a rope. Launching a grappling hook. Busting criminals left and right. The mayor of the city hangs a medal around his neck. His powerful leg holding down some bank robber. The whole city in unison cheers for him. The protector of justice. The hero to every man, woman, and child.

Butterflies fill my stomach and my heart feels like it grows three times larger.

It's no longer The Apparition in my fantasy. It's me.

My eyes open.

Everyone was right.

It is my time now.

CHAPTER 5

Billy – 1973

Walter. What a little baby. Always whining about his mommy. "I want my mommy!". Jesus Christ shut the hell up! Doesn't he know we are all orphans here? Dipshit. I can't take it. My mom was gutter trash and you don't see me crying about it. I can hear him every single night from his bunk whimpering like a little whiney baby. I'm trying to sleep but he just has to cry. It's like he can do it on command. Lights out, he cries. It doesn't help that he's three years younger than me and almost my size. It makes him look like even more of a little bitch. Are they giving him growth pills or something? Is he some kind of messed up science experiment? Wouldn't surprise me based on the other kids I've seen come and go from this hellhole.

I've made up my mind. Today in the court-yard me, Tim and Greg are going to silence him. I'm not sure if I should kill him or just send him to the hospital for good. I need my damn sleep and all his blubbering is driving us nuts. I thought he'd come to grips with his situation but it's been months. They transferred him here from another orphanage because he was too much trouble. I guess none of the women there wanted to deal with him anymore. The constant crying and sniveling. I heard he even wets the bed. I'll be doing everyone a favor. They'll thank me. Even hold a feast in my honor. Three cheers for Bill "The Silencer of Annoying Pests".

It's noon. The sun is right overhead but it's unusually cold. They let us out in the courtyard for a couple hours a day to get our exercise but most of us just sit around smoking cigarettes and talking about girls. Nobody really watches us except for some half-witted obese slob named Otis. There's a basketball court with a bent rim and no balls. No balls. Just like baby boy Walter. There's also some kind of jungle gym for the younger kids but it's all rusted and gross. Chewing gum stuck on practically every surface. Every once in a while one of the kids might go down the slide but for the most part it seems they just play tag or some ring around the rosy bullshit. All they do is kick up dirt and it pisses me off.

I'm talking to Tim about how I looked up Mrs. Levinson's dress the other day and saw her hairy bush. He doesn't believe me. Screw him. I know what I saw. She's not so hot but as far as the women who work here go, she's the tops.

Walter walks out of the cafeteria and sits on the stoop. Look at him. Feeling sorry for himself. That overgrown doofus. He looks like a big baby with that shaved head. They cut off all his hair when he made the mistake of leaning on the jungle gym and got a huge wad of gum stuck in it. Just the sight of him pisses me off. That bitch.

I take out a cigarette and light it. Me and the boys pass it around each taking a couple of drags. My eyes always on that little bitch Walter. Greg is telling me something but I'm not really listening. Taking one final drag I toss it to the ground and stamp it out.

Tim slips me a bottle he smuggled out from the cafeteria. I used to play baseball before I got dumped here. I was a pitcher. They tell me I'm better off. You know, not in a house with a drug addict whore of a mother. At least when I was with her I could play baseball.

Throwing the bottle as hard and as fast as I can it collides with Walter's head with pin-point precision. The sound it makes is a hollow thunk followed by a crash as the glass shatters into a million pieces. I feel a sense of joy that I can still throw with the best of them. He falls over onto the ground holding his head. I signal to Tim and Greg and we move as one. We surround him as he kneels on the ground crying like the little baby that he is. I mean he's barely even bleeding. Just a cut on the side of his big, stupid, head.

"What's the matter, wuss? You gonna cry? You gonna cry for your mommy?" I say.

Walter gets up to his feet. He's gritting his teeth and his eyes are filled with rage. I notice for the first time that his eyes are a piercing blue. He clenches his fists like he's fitting to do something. Shaking in his boots he begins to turn a bright crimson red, blood oozing from the wound I just created. It streams down his forehead and over his eye and down his cheek forming a bead on his chin. The droplets fall to the ground creating what looks like one of those inkblot tests the doctors had shown me.

"You gonna do somethin'?" I challenge him.

"I'll kill you." Walter says.

"I'd like to see you try."

Walter lunges at me with pure fury but is grabbed by Mrs. Levinson. She holds him around the waist and pulls him away.

"Walter stop that! Stop right now!"

He struggles in her arms. Wailing and screaming, he continues to thrash around. He's like a wild animal. I'm laughing at how stupid he looks, like he's some kinda retard. He knocks her glasses off her face. Then he bites her, hard, on her chest. For a second I'm jealous of him. She drops him immediately and tumbles to the ground. Tears beginning to form in her eyes. The way Walter springs to his feet reminds me of a snake, coiling, getting ready to strike.

"Walter!" She proclaims in astonishment.

I must have been distracted because the next thing I know I'm on the ground. My head throbbing and bleeding. Walter had decked me so hard I blacked out for a second. Jesus, what a punch. I'm seeing stars. Then I feel it again. My mouth starts bleeding profusely as I spit out teeth. Tim and Greg have run off and left me here. What a bunch of wusses. Great friends they are. I'll get them back for this betrayal. The pain comes again. This time it's my nose. I try to get up but those fists keep coming. Putting my hands up in a feeble attempt to defend myself doesn't go well as Walter quickly grabs ahold of my fingers and snaps them.

I think about this kid in my neighborhood growing up who died. He hit a beehive with a stick. He got stung so many times that his body just gave out. We would make fun of him on the playground. Saying things like I bet he looked like a pile of rotten meatloaf. I remember thinking about how he was such an idiot.

My eyes are swelling shut but I can just barely force one open. Walter is standing over me poised to strike. I know he wants to kill me. I hope he does. I've never been in so much pain. I just want it to stop. My fingers are bent every which way. My teeth are like crushed rock candy in my mouth.

Walter rears his hand back. I find myself counting the seconds. One, two, three, four, five. How much longer do I have to live? Looking past Walter and into the blue emptiness above I notice not a single cloud in the sky. I think about my mommy... My mom. Dead in a ditch somewhere. I'll be with her again soon. Maybe they'll let me play baseball in hell.

I wake up in the infirmary. My head is all bandaged up like in that movie the invisible man. I'm so numb I can barely feel anything except my mouth feels like a giant open sore. I take my one undamaged finger and feel around but most of my teeth are gone. It's just a wet, warm, hole. That makes me think about Mrs. Levinson... That thought doesn't even comfort me now.

One of the nurses comes in. She tells me I'm going to be blind in my right eye but the good news is they have a dentist ready to help me once I'm healed up. Great, at least I'll be able to eat solid food again at some point. For some reason I find myself asking about Walter. They tell me he's ok. Sixteen stitches in the side of his head, his hands are broken and he's got a concussion, but he'll be fine.

They also tell me that he just got word yesterday that his mother, who was locked away in prison, was killed in a riot.

Tears slip from my eyes.

The nurse asks me why I'm crying.

I think about that stupid kid with the beehive.

CHAPTER 6

Ian – 1985

It's raining again. Why does it always seem to rain when I come to visit you? I park my car in the usual spot and walk my usual way. Down the dirt path, past the mausoleum and then up the hill towards the creek. I picked this spot out because I thought you might like it. You can see the ocean on a clear day and the sunset is the perfect pink that you loved so much. But it's not like that now. It's raining. Again. Because of course it is. It always rains when I come here. Why would today be any different?

Standing here talking to you like I usually do, sobbing like a baby like I usually do. I miss you two so much. My Gloria. My Rona. My beautiful ladies that made all that was wrong in my life go away. Even on the toughest days when I'd get home from work you would be there to greet me with a smile and hug. Shower me with kisses. I was the luckiest guy in the world. Now what am I? I would read Rona stories at night before bed. Her favorite was about a princess who saved a knight from a fiery dragon using her golden hair as a bow. For the life of me I can't recall its name. I think so hard but it won't come to me. Rona wished she had blonde hair like the princess in the story. Gloria even promised we would dye it for her someday. That day never came. My sweet Rona with her beautiful brown curls.

"Gloria, what do I do? What do I do without you?"

I kneel down and clean off their headstones. I can't let them get too dirty. You deserved better than I could give. Now you're dead and I'm still here. What is left for me? I place flowers down and kiss the ground above you. I lose it. I fall over in shambles. I can't stop crying. My Gloria. My Rona.

I'm at work. I'm wearing this stupid uniform. Selling stupid TVs. I feel dead inside. I can't even pretend I care anymore. Customers ask me questions but I'm just going through the motions. Yes, that's a nice one. Oh I've heard good things about that one. You should buy this one. Have I told you about the extended warranty? For just a few dollars more you could upgrade your package. Have you considered surround sound? Have you thought about homicide? I would be a willing victim. I'll even provide your weapon of choice. No? Just the TV? Ok. Never mind.

Checking out at the grocery store I realize I bought too much again. They say old habits die hard. I still buy Rona's favorite cereal. The one with the unicorn on the box and all the fake marshmallows. Then I eat it and try my best to hold it together. When you buy for three and hate wasting food things don't go so well. I looked in the mirror this morning and looked simultaneously fat and skinny. My muscles are fading away and a big gut is starting to rear its ugly head. Rubbing my face I notice I haven't shaved in days, maybe weeks. I look absolutely horrible and I wasn't at all good looking before. Now I'm borderline a side-show freak.

At night I lie alone in bed. I reach out for you and you aren't there. I can't stop myself. I grab the sheets and cry. You'd think after a few months it would get better but it's only gotten worse. With every passing second it gets worse. And worse. And worse.

Sleep is no comfort. The nightmares never end. My sweet girls lying on the slab. Their bodies cold and lifeless. I wake up screaming.

Losing all track of time I'm welcomed at work with a pink slip. Big deal. I didn't want to work there anymore anyway. The manager is a total asshole. I wanted to snap his neck like a twig a few times. Skinny prick. The other employees pretend to be sad. Wish me luck as I'm walking out the door. Like that's going to do anything.

I take my last paycheck to the bank. Clearing out all the funds I have, I close my accounts. I won't need them anymore. On the way home I stop at a liquor store and buy enough whiskey to kill me ten times over. I can tell the clerk wants to say something, but he doesn't.

Back at home I drink myself into a stupor. I'm crying and babbling on incoherently. Looking at a photograph of the three of us together I lose it altogether and start screaming and throwing stuff.

There's hardly a piece of furniture I haven't destroyed a this point. It's not long before the police are at my door and I'm in the drunk tank again. It's pretty bad when the officers start to remember your name.

"Hey, aren't you Ian Dempsey?" Some drunk asks.

"Yeah, so what?" I slur.

"I saw you fight. That one fight, you know? Against 'The Baron' Aaron O'Shaunessy. That was... brutal. I've never seen a massacre like that. I heard he died. Absolutely goddamned brutal man." The drunk shakes his head. "He must have done something to really piss you off."

A memory flashes in my mind and is gone in an instant.

"Yeah, must have..."

It's ruled an accident...but it wasn't.

The next morning they let me out and tell me not to do it again or this time I'll be sorry. They told me that last time as well. I wander the streets all day. No place to go. No one to see. Nothing to do. No reason to live. I pop into a bar and drink myself stupid. Some slut at the bar asks me if I want to party. She's halfway hot and I'm in no position to resist. Turns out she's a professional. Next thing I know I'm having sex with her in some nasty apartment doing cocaine off her chest. My head is swimming. I can't tell what's left and what's right. The room is spinning with no sign of stopping. The pleasure I feel is drowned out by the pounding in my head. It seems like she's having a good time. I don't even care. I don't even know why I am here.

When it's over she asks for a couple hundred bucks. Giving it to her as I leave she kisses me on the lips. The taste of menthol cigarettes explodes into my mouth. I wonder how many men she's been with. How many disgusting perverts have had her? She grabs my crotch and tells me to come back any time. I did. Three more times.

It's been days I think. I look and smell like garbage. There are stains on my clothes from I don't know what. What day is it? Wednesday I think. I can't for the life of me think straight. Too much booze and drugs. Looking in my wallet I see that I'm flat broke. Now I remember. I went to see that girl again last night, Candy, and she took the last of my money for something I can barely even recall happening. Tossing an empty bottle of whiskey into a dumpster, I head to my final destination.

It's a long, arduous, hike and my knees ache and my back twitches. This was your place... Our place. I look out across the water as the sky turns a beautiful shade of pink. Perfect timing. Probably the only thing to go right in my life over the past year. I guess God, if there is a God, has a sense of humor.

I approach the ledge of the lookout. It's a long way down to the water. Long enough. I teeter on the edge. The warm summer breeze kisses my cheeks. Closing my eyes I think of Gloria. Her gentle fingers gliding down my back. Her whispering in my ear telling me everything was going to be ok. I think of holding Rona when she was a baby. God, she was the most beautiful thing I ever saw. She coos and I laugh. I never laugh. She could make me laugh.

"Gloria. I'm sorry."

I leap off the edge. The fall feels like an eternity. The wind blows sharp in my face and feels like razor blades. The blue ocean waves below me look like a beautiful painting in a museum. Everything is frozen in time. I'm flying and for an instant I feel something inside of me for the first time in almost a year. Happiness maybe?

Gloria. My Gloria. She's so gorgeous. I can feel my hands on her body again just like when we were younger and making out in the back of my car. Her lips press hard into mine and at that moment I was in heaven.

Gloria. My Gloria. She's trapped under a collapsed building. She's calling for my help. I've never seen someone so scared. I didn't even know her but I risked my life anyway.

Gloria. My Gloria. She glides her gentle fingers down my back. She tells me I can be anything I want, do anything I want, be who I want to be.

Rona, My sweet Rona. She tells me that she wishes she could have seen me fight. She tells me I'm her hero. I hold her so tight I think her tiny little head is going to pop off. She laughs and laughs. Her curly brown locks bouncing back and forth. Gloria tells her she can dye her hair blonde someday just like the princess in that story. A day that will never come.

"Brave Elysee and Her Magical Golden Hair." I read the title to her.

Aaron O'Shaunessy. He's lying dead in a pool of his own blood. The referee raises my hand in victory. The crowd is silent. I just stare at him laid out on the ring mat. I stare so hard that he ceases to even look human to me anymore. His toothless mangled grin still laughs at me. That cocky disgusting laugh.

I don't regret what I did.

Not for a single second.

Gloria turns to me.

"Isn't it beautiful here, Ian?" She asks.

She touches her round baby bump. Inside our daughter, Rona, waiting to be born.

Life begins and ends in an instant.

CHAPTER 7

Bram

This old ship is about to fall apart. Hell, I'm falling apart. Nothing I do will stop that from happening, that's for sure. I turn off the motor and head out onto the deck. It's a beautiful day. The air is warm and the breeze off the water is as sweet as can be. It's just about sunset. The sky turns a brilliant shade of pink. It's almost like the sky is on fire. A neon fire that stretches on and on as far as the eye can see and these old eyes have seen quite a few things.

Sitting on the deck I scratch at my thick heavy beard. It's pretty coarse from all the salty sea air. Leaning back in my chair I just listen to the wonderful sounds of rushing water. A bird chirps in the distance. The horns of other ships echo across the water.

This year I'll be seventy years old. Where did the time go? You can't stop it, that's for sure. So many friends of mine are gone. I should have been dead a hundred times but here I stand. Still alive and kicking. My memory isn't what it use to be but all things considered I'm doing just fine. Just fine indeed.

Looking out in the distance I can see someone standing on the top of the cliffside. It's too far away to tell if it's a man or a woman. They are all alone. Just like me. They leap off the cliff. A moment frozen in time. For a second I'm in shock but then instinct kicks in just like old times.

I rush to the wheel and fire up the motor. I pray that whoever it is they survived the fall. I slam the throttle down and my old boat leaps forward. Come on, come on. We can make it!

"Come on you old piece of junk! We've got a job to do!" I scream and laugh at the same time. The engine roars!

I stop the boat right around where they should have hit the water. Scanning left, then right, searching for any signs of life. Without hesitation I grab some rope off the deck and tie it around my waist and then the railing. Diving into the water with more grace than I should have at this age, I swim with all my strength. It's so dark but I can just make out a body slowly sinking to the bottom. I kick my legs almost to the point of exhaustion. I reach out and snag something. I'm quickly running out of breath. I have to hurry or their fate will be mine as well.

We break the surface. Taking a huge breath I start swimming for the boat. My arms are starting to give out so I use the rope for leverage. I can't tell if he's breathing or not. Dragging him up onto the deck I feel a sharp chill from that ocean breeze. Even though I'm shivering and soaking wet the work isn't done yet. Checking him for a pulse I realize he's in dire straits. I begin performing CPR. Two breaths, fifteen compressions. Two breaths, fifteen compressions. Come on, man! Wake up! I try once more. No response. I slam my fist hard on his chest and as if some kind of miracle just occurred he begins coughing up water. Thank God. I wipe the water off of my brow as he leans over the edge of my boat and pukes his guts out.

He's just sitting there on the deck looking out across the water with a thousand-yard stare. The sun is starting to go down and he's holding the towel I tossed him for warmth. I'm sure he didn't want to live. Most people who leap from high places don't. I stole something from him so I understand why he isn't being so pleasant to me. He hasn't even spoken a word yet, let alone made any kind of eye contact. Approaching slowly I sit on the bench opposite of him.

"That was quite the fall. Best be more careful while standing on such a ledge. I'm sure you wouldn't want to have an accident like that again." I say.

He looks at me with the coldest eyes I've ever seen. He's a disheveled mess. Shaggy brown hair, cold brown sunken in eyes, ratty-looking beard, and a distended stomach. As far as I can tell he's in his mid-thirties. Something seriously went wrong in this man's life. I try prying again.

"Name's Bram. As in Abraham. But you can just call me Bram. Like Bram Stoker, that Dracula fella. Did you ever see that movie? The original I mean. With Bella Lugosi?"

God, I embarrass myself.

"Yeah. I've seen it." He replies.

"Oh good, good. I like that movie. So yeah, name's Bram. I didn't catch yours though, unless your name is 'yeah, I've seen it'?"

He chuckles. I guess I'm getting somewhere. I'm out of practice, been on this boat for way too long all by myself.

"Ian."

"Well nice to meet you, Ian, I'm Bram."

I have said my name five times. I think he knows what it is by now. He must think I'm senile. Just a doddering old codger. A coot. I adjust my cap a few times and try to play it cool. Not too many times. Jesus, Bram, get it together.

"Thanks for saving me back there. From, uh... my accident." He says.

"Oh. Yes certainly. No Problem. No Problem."

In honesty I haven't had so much excitement in years. Reminds me of old times. Back when things were different. The image of a beautiful woman in a revealing black dress enters my mind. Her long, sharp, fingernails dance across my shoulders. She whispers in my ear and my thoughts get scrambled. I can still remember that wonderful perfume that left me so intoxicated. A voice snaps me out of it.

"So where is this boat headed?" He asks.

"I don't have a destination. I let the water tell me where to go. Been doing it this way for years. For the most part it's a peaceful life. I can take you back to shore if you'd like."

"No. I know this is going to sound weird, but would you mind if I just went with you for a while. A peaceful life sounds... nice."

I am accustomed to strange things. I've definitely seen more than my fair share but in reality I don't even know this guy who just tried to kill himself. I must have been silent for a while because he responds to me as if I answered.

"That's ok, just drop me off wherever."

I think about it for a few more seconds. I've known some of the best and worst people who have ever lived. I don't get the evil vibe from this guy. Troubled? Definitely. But I might be able to help him. Remember helping people? It was kinda your thing.

"Sure young man. I'd be glad to have you aboard!" I say as I leap on to my feet and posture like I used to back in the day. "Join me and the adventures of The Wandering Spirit!"

He asked to come along. No need to act like a used car salesman.

"Thanks. And, you know, thanks for saving my life again. I don't know what I was thinking."

"Thinking what? Accidents happen. Next time look where you are walking!"

He chuckles again. Playing it off like an accident has really defused the situation. We both know it wasn't but maybe I can convince him it was.

"Do you need anything from home? Need me to stop anywhere before we continue on? You might need some earplugs, I tend to drone on nonstop. I think you'll be begging to get off this boat sooner than later." I'm trying too hard to be funny but it seems to be working.

He looks longingly off the bow of the boat. The sun is almost completely set. What little light that is left silhouettes him against the orange and pink sky. Something about this guy reminds me of myself. Years ago I found myself at a crossroad but with no one to show me the right way. I wonder if I made the right choice to walk away and live on this boat. Maybe I can help this boy. Truly help him. One last person to save. I think I still have it in me.

He turns to me. Half of his face is lit the other half in darkness.

"No. There's nothing left for me here." He says with a hint of sorrow in his voice.

"You'll probably need some clothes. Just a thought." I say.

He smirks. I return to the wheel. The ocean air fills my nose and I feel alive again.

"Just like old times." I say to myself.

Firing up the engine I ease the throttle. Over the roar of the engine I can just barely make out something Ian says.

"Gloria. Rona. Goodbye..."

CHAPTER 8

Ian – 1986

Awaking in the cabin of the boat, I let out a gasp. Some kind of nightmare that I can't quite remember. I place my feet on the floor and get my bearings. I have definitely developed sea legs. Being on a boat with a crazy old man for over a year can do that to you. Standing up I can feel my knees aching. I rub them as if that will actually do something. It never does. I twist back and forth to crack my back. A series of loud pops follows. Reaching towards the sky my shoulders crack. I take a few steps from my bunk and look in the mirror. My beard is nearly a foot long now. My hair tied back in a messy bun. I look healthier than I have in a long time but I've gotten pretty skinny. Eating out of cans and fresh fish (which I've learned to tolerate) has changed me. I look at my arms and notice that some of my muscle has returned, but if anyone who saw me years ago saw me now they wouldn't recognize me. Turning my attention to the window I realize I have no clue where we are.

I exit out onto the deck of The Wandering Spirit and see that we are just outside a city. Huge skyscrapers and derelict tenements are accentuated by a dense cloud of smog. It reminds me of a nightmare version of Bella Cruz. Open sewers run off into the ocean. The smell is quite unpleasant. I'm not sure anyone is fond of the smell of raw sewage. There are so many sounds happening at once that it all blends together. Cars, trucks, music playing, people chattering, the water rushing around the boats. A big ship blasts its horn. Bram is sitting in his usual spot tugging at his huge white beard. His dark, tan, skin shining in the warm light. He's wearing that white tank top again and his favorite hat. That thing has so many holes in it I'm not sure it still qualifies.

"Good morning, Son. Sleep well?"

"Not especially." I reply. "Where are we?"

"Lochland City."

"Do you plan on docking? I noticed we are low on some supplies."

"We probably shouldn't. This is a bad place, Ian."

"What happened to 'wherever the water takes us'?" I reply.

"This place is the dumping ground of humanity. Crime, poverty, drugs. You name it. I grew up here. Nothing's changed. I left for a reason. Too many bad memories." Bram states very matter of factly.

I can tell by the look on his face that he's serious. I don't want to put pressure on him. I've never been here before. Growing up on the other side of the country Lochland City was only something I ever heard about in the news or was talked about in history class. It was once called the most dangerous place to live on earth. Somehow I always thought that was just hyperbole but the look in Bram's eyes tells me it wasn't. I wonder what happened to him here that makes him so anxious. I've never seen him like this before. Usually he is so confident.

Back when I was a boxer I dreamed of making it here. A lot of big fights went down in this city. Millions of dollars on the line. Big Kane Vorhees vs Darling David. George Jackson vs Allan McDonald. Unfortunately, or fortunately, Ian Dempsey never was on the big marquee. Before I met Gloria it's all I ever wanted. I sacrificed so much for it. My health, relationships. All for nothing in the end.

Gloria.

Rona.

I haven't thought about them for a long time. Is that a good or a bad thing? I don't know. Why am I thinking about them now? Stop. I haven't thought about a woman or sex in a long time. It's like the fall knocked those desires right out of me. I'm different now. A better person I think. It's hard to tell. What is better, really?

Gloria...Rona...

Stop.

Gloria's gentle fingers gliding down my back. Rona's chubby cheeks and bouncing brown curls. Gloria tells me I can be anything I want, do anything I want, be who I want to be. Old feelings come rushing back into my mind like a tidal wave. Gloria's curvaceous body lying on top of me. She smiles at me through her long curly black hair. She's so warm and soft. My hands grab her sides. Rona is just born. I'm holding her in my arms. She coos. I laugh. I never laugh. Gloria touches the side of my face.

Stop. Stop it now.

"Ian!" Bram yells. "Where the hell did you go?"

"What do you mean?"

"I've been talking to you for like five minutes and you haven't responded."

Jesus. What is happening? Have I really been sitting here lost in thought?

"This place is bad, Ian. I told you. Bad memories." Bram laments. "If you stay here too long it will infect you. It seems like it's already started."

Is it really that bad?

Gloria.

Rona.

Stop.

CHAPTER 9

Officer Carmine – 1986

I'm sitting here in a puddle of my own piss. I pissed myself. I'm a disgrace. They say this can happen when you're scared and I'm as sure as can be scared. I don't think I've ever been this scared. I'm also angry. So goddamned angry. A string of obscenities is flowing out of me like never before but it's all pomp and circumstance. I know I'm screwed.

I tug at the wire that holds my hands behind my back. I can't break free. My wrists are starting to bleed. Feeling the wire cut into my arms is far less painful than the embarrassment I feel from pissing my pants. I was a police officer for thirty hard years, but here I am tied up and pissing my stupid pants. When they find my body I only hope they don't mention it in the paper. I can just see it now. Officer Jack Carmine, a decorated policeman and upright citizen found murdered, lying in a puddle of his own piss. They say you crap yourself when you die. They'll probably put that in the paper too. Sarge would be laughing at me but someone got his ass last year. We busted so many dealers and peddlers and pimps it's no surprise that someone would be after us now. With Sarge there were no witnesses.

His head was crushed. His wife was a victim of being in the wrong place at the wrong time. Her neck was snapped. A clean break. I'm pretty sure it was a mercy killing. I had a drink for them and thought "better them than me". Karma is a bitch it would seem.

I finally look up again to see the agent of my death. A huge hulking beast like I've never seen before. We busted all kinds of steroid heads and speed junkies over the years but this guy is like something out of a science fiction novel. He's got to be six foot five and at least three hundred pounds of solid muscle. His arms look like a road map with bulging veins everywhere. Biceps are bigger than my head. It's like he's an experiment gone wrong... or *very* right.

This whole time he hasn't said a goddamn word and that makes this even worse. He beat me within an inch of my life and tied me up without saying a single thing. I did what I could to defend myself, but my gun was locked up and I couldn't get to it in time. My punches and kicks did little to slow him down.

Who is he and what are his motives? Thoughts rush through my mind. Old cases. Old busts. I can't think of anywhere a guy this size was involved. There were some huge dudes, but they were mostly fat-asses. He must be a hired gun. A hitman sent to take us all out. I haven't talked to a lot of those old guys in years. I wonder if they are ok. The only reason I even knew about Sarge is because he still lived in this godforsaken city. It even made the paper.

"Who are you?" I shout.

He doesn't respond. All I hear is his heavy breathing behind that disgusting mask. It's like a distorted skull. Cracked porcelain with a terrible grimace. The eye sockets, a hollow black void with nothing behind them. I try to stand but he easily holds me down. Such power. I struggle but can do nothing. What little strength I had has left me.

"Please. Give me peace. Tell me who you are working for. Why are you doing this?"

He places his hands on the sides of my head and starts to squeeze. I think about how I'm happy I never married. I never had any kids. I was married to the job or so they say. No one will miss me. There will be no wife lamenting her immense grief. No children grubbing over my pension. Maybe. Just maybe someone will have a drink for me.

Stevens. Whatever happened to that bastard?

The pain increases rapidly. I can actually feel my skull starting to cave in. The sound is horrific like an old creaky door, rusted to shit, in desperate need of some WD-40. His fingers dig into my scalp and the warm blood trickles down the sides of my face.

I try to speak but it's slowly becoming slurs. I can't get out a complete sentence and now my words aren't making any sense at all. It's just gibberish.

I was a good man. I thought I was a good man. I stole some money. I had sex with prostitutes. I gambled. But I never locked up any innocent people. Did I? We were right, weren't we? I never hurt anyone who didn't deserve it. Did I? So many faces and names flying through my mind. It's too much to try and take in.

My thoughts...
Confused...
Try. Try to remember.
Try. Remember.
Remember.
Blue. Eyes...
I hear a loud pop.

CHAPTER 10

Gina

Remind me to, like, totally, kill the guy who recommended this bar. This place is full of creeps and smells like vomit. Becky is drunk out of her mind so she is having fun at least. She orders another drink but I snatch it away from her and chug it. She totally shouldn't be drinking this much and I don't want to end up with her in the ER again. Spending a night in the hospital is a total no go for me.

"Bitch!" she yells over the blaring music with a smile on her face.

She wanders out onto the dance floor with her arms up in the air looking to party. It's not long before a swarm of guys are all around her. Loving the attention, she dances as one guy grinds her from the front and another squeezes her ass from behind. One of her tits pops out of her dress and I swear it's, like, five minutes before she notices. I swear, like, totally, if we didn't grow up together I'm not sure we'd be friends.

The drink I just chugged has given me a serious buzz. I pinch my nose and rub my eyes. The neon lights in the place are really starting to aggravate me. On stage the live band, Patient Zero, is playing. It's just two guys with synthesizers. One of the guys looks like a two-dollar Zorro knock off and the other, like, totally has a bucket on his head. The vocals are so produced I can't even make out a single word of what they are saying. It's got a kinda catchy beat though and I find myself tapping my foot and bouncing my head.

"Hey beautiful. You looking to party?" A voice comes from over my shoulder.

Turning to look, I see it's a moderately handsome guy with a stubble beard and the total Miami Vice thing going. He's wearing a blue sport coat and a neon pink t-shirt underneath. He smiles and it's not unpleasant to look at. He slides me a drink but I know better than to drink it. I pretend to take a sip.

"Thanks." I say as I pretend to be aloof.

He moves in closer. I can tell he works out. He's not really my type, I'm not so much into muscle guys, but I'll see where this goes. Maybe I was wrong about this place.

We talk for a few minutes. He tells me he's in real estate. If I'm looking he can get me a good place just uptown. When he tells me for how much I nearly choke and I dump the drink he gave me onto his pants. Either this guy is for real or he's totally a poser. He doesn't even get mad about the pants. Playing it totally cool he asks the bartender for a towel.

"Hey, you wanna dance?" He asks me.

I probably would have said yes anyway but after spilling my drink on him I kinda feel like I owe him one. What's the worst that could happen?

"Sure." I grab his hand.

Taking him out onto the dance floor we start to get into the groove. It's easy to tell he likes me. Turning my back to him I feel him sliding his hands where he wants them. Giving in to the music, and his hands all over me, I find myself actually starting to have a good time. He moves his hands and starts to try and unbutton my top. I bump him away from me and turn back to face him. He's got a big grin on his face. I use my finger to gesture for him to, totally, come over. We grind for a few more minutes. I even let him kiss my neck a few times. Looking up at the flashing neon pink and blue lights I hear the song come to an end.

Leading him back over to the bar I tell him thanks for the good time and we exchange numbers. I mean, what the hell, he seemed nice enough. Gavin is his name.

I finally remember I should be babysitting Becky. Scanning the club I don't see her anywhere. I ask Gavin and he just shrugs his shoulders. Disappointing Gavin, I leave him at the bar as I search the dance floor. She's not at any of the tables and she's not dancing with anyone. I half expected to find her dancing on a table with her top off.

First I check the women's room. She's not there. I dread what I might see next. I push open the men's room door. There she is, half undressed, sitting on the counter. There's a mirror with remnants of cocaine next to her. Her eyes are closed and she looks like she might be passed out. Some creep is on his knees snorting cocaine off her thigh. I push him out of the way.

"Back off, creep!"

"Hey, what's it to you, bitch? We're just having some fun! Ain't that right, Jessie?"

"Her name's Becky, dickwad!"

Shaking and slapping her I get her to come to.

"Come on, babe, we're out of here." I tell her.

"Ok Gina, I...love you." She slurs.

Helping her off the counter we begin to exit the bathroom.

"Bitch!" The creep yells.

Ignoring him, we leave the club. Out front, Gavin asks me if my friend is alright. I tell him she's fine and I'll give him a call sometime. He smiles and goes back inside.

"Gina, let's go back inside too. I want to keep dancing."

"That wasn't dancing."

Waving down a taxi I toss Becky into the back seat. I tell the driver her address and toss him a couple bucks. At this point my buzz was gone and I was about ready to call it a night. As the taxi speeds away I take a big breath. It is unusually chilly. I consider getting a cab for myself but I kinda like the cold and totally need the exercise. I need to burn off those drinks and the crappy finger foods I just ate. Hoofing it downtown I really regret wearing these shoes but I'm totally not going to go barefoot on these streets. Looking down I see all kinds of gunk, crusty stuff, and God knows what else. Yuck!

Coming to an intersection a few blocks from my place I'm startled by a sudden voice.

"Spare any change, Miss?"

My eyes are drawn to a homeless girl. Her face caked in filth. Huge, coke bottle glasses. A ratty old beanie on her head. Her clothes are all tattered rags. She has this sweet look about her though and *it is* a cold night. Looking in my purse I decided to give her a crumpled five-dollar bill that I had drawn on. I figured she wouldn't care if the former president suddenly had big goofy glasses.

"Here you go, honey."

Handing it to her, her face lights up with joy. She says thanks to me a million times over and even tries to hug me. That would, totally, be too much.

Continuing my walk home I feel a sense of pride. I feel really good about myself. What a nice thing I just did. I probably made that girl's day. Totally her month!

I know it's late, but it's eerily desolate. Not many people out and about. One car has passed me by in the last five minutes. I'm only a block away from home but the sound of footsteps behind me sends a chill up my spine. Quickening my pace I hear the footsteps increase in speed as well.

Hop Sing, the Chinese restaurant I order from all the time, I'll just pop in there. I take the corner quickly and break the heel of my shoe in the process. Tumbling to the ground I bash my knee hard on the concrete. It's not long before I feel the warm blood beginning to pool.

"Need some help, lady?" A voice comes from nowhere.

Looking around quickly I can't see that well under the street light. I can just barely make out three silhouettes. One of the shadows comes into view. It's the creep from the bar that was all over Becky. His hair is blonde, wet and curly. A leather jacket and jeans top off his wannabe greaser look. The top button of his pants is open.

"Oh no, I'm fine." I say to try and get him to leave.

His friends move into view. Its almost like they are carbon copies of him. All dressed in leather with varying haircuts and builds. One of them is really skinny with sunken-in eyes. He gives me the creeps the most. The three circle me. This is, totally, not good.

"Sid, I think she's hurt." The skinny one says.

"Oh yeah, Cutter, I think she needs some medical attention." Sid, the blonde, replies.

"Maybe she needs a physical exam?" Cutter replies.

"Or maybe just a deep cavity search?" The third one says while grabbing his crotch and humping at the air.

"Really, I'm fine, you guys can just go on your way." I say as I start to get up but my knee hurts so bad I can't manage it.

"But why would we leave a helpless young thing like you out here alone? It's dangerous. You wouldn't want to run into some kinda hoodlums, would ya?" Sid says.

My mind is rushing a mile a minute. I don't know what to do. Frantically I look around anywhere for help. I consider screaming my lungs out. Maybe someone would come. Maybe not. Noticing Cutter fingering a knife on his belt makes me reconsider screaming.

"You know what? You guys are right. What will a helpless girl like me do without a couple of strong boys to take care of me?" What the hell am I doing?

"Now you are seeing things clearly." The unnamed one says.

"Speaking of seeing things clearly, Puke..."

Great, his name is Puke.

"...Do my eyes deceive me or is this chickadee a smoking hot piece of ass. She's got some tight little body on her and look at her face all painted up nice." Cutter exclaims.

Puke starts to undo his pants. A tuft of black pubic hair becomes visible. I'm embarrassed but I'm looking at it.

"I can think of something I'd *love* to paint her face with." Puke says as he slides his hand down the front of his pants.

The punks move in a little closer. Puke's crotch is mere inches from my face. I can smell their collective body odor and to say it's unpleasant would be the understatement of the millennium. Suddenly, I realize I've been gripping my broken off heel this whole time. The veins in the back of my hand bulging from how tight I've been squeezing it.

"Now boys, I don't think I can handle you all at once." I'm totally disgusted by myself at this point. Even just feigning interest in these guys is, totally, turning my stomach.

Puke takes his... piece... out of his pants. I can't believe what I'm about to do.

"Me first, you slags!" Puke says.

With all my might, with every ounce of strength I have, I drive the sharp end of my broken heel right down into Puke's foot. Thrusting my bodyweight down I feel the heel go through the top of his canvas sneaker and into the flesh beneath. He lets out a yelp so loud the other two cover their ears. Completely ignoring the pain in my knee I'm already a few yards away running full sprint. My two hundred dollar stilettos a casualty as I left them behind. My bare feet slapping at the concrete, I pray I don't step on a needle or something else sharp. I try to yell for help but no sound is coming out. Hearing the guys behind me in hot pursuit, I make a rash decision. I'm only seconds away from home but if I go there they'll know where I live and if they don't kill me now they might come back. That's it, the alley by my house, it leads to Hop Sing. They are open late. I can get there. I know I can.

Darting down the alley I don't think I have ever run so totally hard in my life. I can feel the hot blood trickling down from the wound on my knee and I don't even care. I have to get away.

Oh... No.

Running full force into a chainlink fence, the sudden realization that I might be dead soon hits me like a brick. I forgot that this alley was a dead end. A loading and unloading area. I'm totally a dumbass. There's a door to my right. I bang on it over and over again. Screaming for help as loud as I can I see a light pop on in one of the apartments above me. An old lady looks out briefly. I wave and scream at her. She turns the light off. Bitch. Rotten old bitch! It's too late. The three are only a couple feet away from me. I don't know what to do. Looking all around me for some kind of weapon but there's nothing but trash. I fall onto my butt almost paralyzed with fear. I break a nail gripping at the ground so hard.

"Oh baby. You made a very, very big mistake just now." Sid says.

Cutter pulls out his knife. The dim alley light glimmers off of its cold steel. I wonder, how many women had felt that blade? It doesn't take long before they are on me like a bunch of jackals. Sid slides his hand between my legs. His fingers prying at my underwear.

"She's already ready for us, boys." Sid says as I think of Gavin. "It's a real pity that a fine looking woman like you is gonna die. Before we were just gonna shag you rotten, but now, well, after what you did to my pal, Puke, we're gonna kill ya. But first..."

"Oh, God. Please no." The words struggle to

come out.

My panties are torn away. Sid tosses them to Puke who rubs them on his face. Closing my eyes tight I try to think of anything but what is about to happen. I hear the zipper of Sid's pants as he puts his hand over my mouth. A song my mother used to sing to me comes to mind. I see her at the end of my bed touching my feet and singing that song. What were the words again? Something about little pigs or a big blackbird?

"What the hell?"

I open my eyes just in time to see a shape come flying out of nowhere. With amazing precision this shape lands a flawless side kick to the head of Puke. He goes soaring into the alley wall and crashes onto his ass. His face is in complete shock. Sid and Cutter turn their attention away from me. A figure stands before us. My eyes focus. It's a woman. Thick muscular legs are sheathed in tan nylon stockings that lead up to a tight posterior. Her upper body clothed with a dark blue denim jacket with the collar popped, rolled up to the elbows with the letters "Ne" spray-painted in white on the back. Her forearms are laced with lean muscle. Fingerless purple gloves accentuate her neon pink manicure. She turns to face us. She is wearing a dark magenta one-piece swimsuit style outfit with black side panels zipped up to a high collar. She is incredibly fit and even through the outfit has visible abs. I'm honestly jealous. A white belt hangs low on her hips. To top it all off she is totally gorgeous. I can't tell for sure but she might be Asian. Thick, black, cat-eye eyeliner and fuchsia lipstick perfectly match her crazy long side-swept purple hair that fades to a light pink at the tips.

Wait...

I know who this is. I didn't think they were a real person but seeing is believing.

NEON FIRE...

"Why hello, boys! You want to play rough? Let's play rough!" Neon Fire exclaims.

My fear melts away. I don't know if it's shock or what but a grin betrays me.

Cutter lunges at her with his big knife but she ducks underneath him by doing a complete split. He whiffs big time and almost falls on his ass. Neon does what I can only describe as a breakdancing move and pops back up and blasts Sid in the face with a kick. Even in the dim light I'm sure I just saw teeth go flying. A couple of white dots soaring into the air, disappearing into the darkness.

Puke grabs her from behind by the hair.

"I got you now, bitch!" He yells.

"Do you?" She retorts.

Cutter has regained his composure and thrusts his knife towards her abdomen. Using Puke as leverage, Neon jumps up and grabs Cutter around the neck with her thick, strong, legs. She then proceeds to flip down and through Cutter's legs causing the two scumbags to collide headfirst. I have to stop myself from cheering. The punks are dazed and holding their heads.

"Damn, my nose is broken!" Puke yells.

Sid pulls a gun. I don't know where he had that thing hidden. It looks like some kind of Saturday Night Special. Neon lays out Puke with a quick one-two combination. She finishes off Cutter with a brutal haymaker that sends a mist of blood into the night air. Sid points his gun at me. My excitement quickly dissipates. I'm hyperventilating. My heart is beating out of my chest.

"Back off or this bitch gets it!" Sid yells as he places the barrel against my head.

Neon turns her attention to Sid now that the other two have been handily dealt with. She doesn't even look like she's broken a sweat. She takes a few steps closer. Her stride is that of pure confidence. Sid cocks the gun. I start praying to myself. Hail Mary... full of grace...

Suddenly, Neon jumps forward like a cat and he turns the gun to her. In a movement so quick I could hardly see it she grabs the gun. It goes off and fires into the wall as she slams her palm into his elbow, causing his arm to bend the wrong way. The bone breaks in a sound I can only describe as snapping wet celery. He falls to his knees before her, screaming in pain. The bone is sticking out through the skin. I gag. He's muttering a string of curses. She picks up the gun and dumps out all the bullets. She tosses it up and over the fence into a dumpster. Sid has collapsed in pain and is attempting to crawl away. Neon takes a few steps and punts him square in the face knocking him unconscious.

Puke has recovered a bit. He's on his knees struggling to get up. He grins and begins to taunt her with his hands.

"Come on, bitch. Come on." He's egging her on.

She strolls over to him and grabs a handful of his hair. Yanking his head back, she gets right in his face. He lets out a whimper.

"I can think of something I'd love to paint with your face." She says as she smiles.

Neon slams Puke's head into the side of the alley wall so hard I hear a sickening crunch. She yanks his head back, his face is covered in blood. Releasing him, he slumps to the ground. He's out cold. Neon has a big clump of his hair still in her hand. As if it meant nothing she blows it into the wind. The hairs dance in the light as they drift and then fade from sight.

"Hey, are you ok?" Neon says as she kneels in front of me.

"Thanks to you I am." I reply.

Up close I can see how pretty she is. Just a hint of freckles peaking out on the tip of her small upturned nose.

"Good. You take care of yourself, Ok?" She says.

"I'll try."

She pats me on the head like a little kid and grins. Then in an instant she's gone. I don't even understand how, she's just gone. The flashing lights of a police car pulling up finally put me at ease.

Three cops come down the alley, guns drawn. They are silhouetted by the lights from their cars.

"Ma'am? Are you alright?" One of them asks as he helps me to my feet.

"Look at these sorry motherfuckers."

"Sir, I think it was her..." The third one interrupts.

It's been a long night and the sun is just starting to come up. I look around and see all the commotion in the police station. So many people running back and forth. Looking in my purse I pull out my compact. Although I look disheveled I try to straighten myself up a bit. Digging in my bag for my lipstick I find a ratty crumpled up five-dollar bill with glasses drawn on Abraham Lincoln's face.

A tear of joy sneaks out.

CHAPTER 11

Detective Tom Hudson

Another long night. I'm getting too damn old for this crap and I'm not even fifty. Melinda is gonna chew me out again when I get home. "Where were you?" "Why didn't you call?" "I was worried sick!". The usual business. I know she worries about me but this is my damn job. I became a cop for a reason. No point in giving it up now. A few more years and I'm set. I'm mostly a pencil pusher at this point anyway. I haven't been on the beat in years. Hanging out in this police station is starting to get to me. The fluorescent lighting flickering. The constant sound of keyboards clicking. Drug addicts, whores, criminal scum always coming in and out of here. There's no end to this crap. Speaking of crap, what is that damn smell?

A big report falls on my desk like the sound of thunder. The coffee hasn't quite kicked in yet so I'm a bit startled. Officer Blankenship stands before me. His wiry ass looking goofy as ever. He called me hot chocolate one time. My backhand straightened him out right quick. Now we're "buds" as he likes to say. We have shared a drink now and again, but I'd hardly consider us best friends.

"What is it Blankenship?" I say.

"Another Neon Fire sighting. The eye witness is in the other room if you'd like to talk to her. She's been up all night so you should probably be delicate."

"Delicate is my middle name!" I say.

Neon Fire. Again. Every time Blankenship hears that name he gets as giddy as a schoolgirl. A grown man with a crush. They keep on giving me these cases. I'm the so-called expert. The chief doesn't want any vigilantes in the city trying to do our jobs. It makes us look like a bunch of "ineffectual halfwits" in his words.

"Ok. Send her in."

I was half expecting some kind of crackhead or some other scum of the city looking to get their name in the paper, but to my surprise a lovely blonde girl enters my office smelling like she spent the night sleeping in a dumpster. I guess I can't rule out crackhead just yet. She's all disheveled and has on Blankenship's jacket. I bet he liked that. Acting all heroic. I bet he tried to put the moves on her or something. Blankenship isn't exactly a man of tact.

She tells me the whole story from beginning to end. And I mean beginning. I really didn't need to know about what she ate for lunch yesterday. Salmon salad with a side of toast. Or that she met some guy named Gavin who looked like the dude on Miami Vice.

"You know, Don Johnson?" She asks.

I take notes, and by notes I mean I doodle a

caricature of Blankenship. I almost laugh at my own drawing.

"Is there something funny?" She asks.

"No no... Please continue." I say placing the drawing down.

Reaching into my desk I pull out a nice cigar. I light it up and sit back in my seat. The old chair creaks and squeaks. I even throw my feet up on the desk for good measure. I know these things might kill me but a man has to have his vices. I take a big fat drag off of it and blow the smoke all over the place like an asshole. Gotta make it stick. I genuinely care if this girl is alright or not, but I made a promise.

"You know those things will kill you?" Gina says.

"Yep!" I take another long drag. "So what you are telling me is that a woman, fought off three armed men? A woman? You have got to be kidding me or have you gone blind?"

"I swear! She was rock-solid muscle. I couldn't believe it myself at first." Gina replies.

"I think you need to schedule an eye exam. Stat. Or a cat scan. Maybe one of those thugs we have in custody knocked you loopy. Are you seeing stars? Hearing sounds?" I say while over embellishing every word.

I snap my fingers in her face like a total jackass. If my mom saw me now I bet she would be so proud. She's probably rolling over in her grave with disgust. I'm sorry mom, but a promise is a promise.

"I'm not lying..." She groans.

I know she isn't.

"Here. Follow my finger." I say.

I wave my finger back and forth frantically. She actually tries to follow it.

"I think you have a concussion!" I exclaim. "Blankenship, Get your ass in here!"

He runs in so quick you would have thought I said she was hooker giving out freebies. The coffee in his hand spills on his shirt. Just another stain to add to his collection.

"Ms. Anderson here requires immediate medical attention. Please escort her to the hospital. That is, if you have the time."

"Oh. I'm definitely free." Blankenship says smiling ear to ear.

"I feel fine!" She scoffs.

"Standard procedure." I retort.

He escorts Gina out of my office and takes her to the hospital to be checked out. When filling out my report I change just enough details to make her account of the incident seem incoherent. I take another drag off my cigar. The ash falls on my lap and burns me.

"Damn!"

I chug down what's left of my coffee. It's hours cold and it tastes like dirt. I wonder if I might have ashed my cigar into it at some point. Looking at the clock I realize I should have been off work six hours ago. I rub my eyes feverishly. Still waiting on that coffee to kick in.

On my desk is a picture of Melinda, my daughter Cara, and me. It was taken at the central park fair. Cara has a big handful of cotton candy. She loves that sugary stuff. She always wants it every time we go to a fair or carnival. Her hands get all sticky and then she always wants to touch my mustache.

Cara is just starting the fourth grade. She's at school right now. The teacher called and told us she's already one of the standouts. She's smarter than I am I bet. I definitely never got any As in school. I was too busy chasing girls or playing football.

Tossing my report in the bin like I couldn't give a crap, and then quickly pulling on my coat, I head to the front door to go home. Blankenship catches me as he's coming back from the hospital. Great.

"On your way home, bud?"

"Yep. Bud!" I grin like an imbecile and give him a big thumbs up.

Goofy ass Blankenship.

I can't wait to see Melinda. Touch her warm skin. She's gonna be pissed but that will fade quickly. She never stays mad for long, and once she's calm I'm going right after her big fat ass.

One of the thugs from the incident last night is being moved. Tony has him in cuffs.

"I'm telling you, it was a huge guy! A man! I swear. You think a girl could do this to me? Come on! You can't believe anything that broad says! I never touched her!" The thug yells.

"Oh shut up. No one cares what you think, lowlife." Tony retorts.

I catch my appearance in the reflection off the glass in the exit door. Man, do I look like a steaming pile. I try really quickly to make myself look presentable. I straighten my tie and fix my collar. I run my fingers over my mustache a few times just for good measure.

"Good enough." I say to myself.

Popping into my car I fire up the engine. It sputters but then roars to life. It's a little chilly this morning so I crank on the heat. Before long I throw it into drive and head out.

Like vampires, the scum of this city cowers away from the sun. During the day time you might think Lochland is actually a pretty nice place to live.

At the intersection of North Main and 32nd street I happen to peer down an alleyway. There I see a young girl, dressed in overalls and a backward cap, spray painting something on the wall. Her hands move quickly and efficiently. This is clearly not her first time. The pink spray paint settles into something recognizable and the kid runs off. In large letters it says:

"Believe in Neon Fire!"

I smile.

"Oh... I believe."

CHAPTER 12

Ian

Sitting on my bed in the cabin I'm suddenly jerked to the floor. What the hell just happened? I rush out onto the deck. Bram seems just as befuddled as me. He's looking around frantically. Lifting his hat, he scratches his head. He looks over the side of the deck.

"Bram, what happened?" I ask.

"Oh Jesus. We've run aground." He says.

Looking over the edge I see that we've definitely hit the rocks.

"I'm sorry, my boy. I dozed off in my chair." He says.

"I'll hop out and take a look." I say.

"I was just about to suggest that." He says.

Jumping out into the shallow water the cold liquid rushes into my shoes. Giving it a cursory glance it seems like all is ok. No substantial damage. No giant hole to worry about. Just some scratches in the paint.

"Why don't you try and give it a push?" Bram yells from the deck.

Digging my feet in hard to the rocky soil beneath me I push against the side of The Wandering

Spirit. It begins to move. I take a big deep breath and push again. I hear the scraping as the boat slides off of the rocks. Because of the momentum I quickly end up in waist-deep water. It is so damn cold that I am starting to shiver. Noticing that the water is filthy, a piece of trash floats by me. It's a wrapper for some kind of pastry. "Taste E Treat" it says on the label.

Rona loved those nasty things. It was a yellow cake, covered with green frosting, with yellow sugar stars and filled with what I assume was supposed to be cream. I ate one once and immediately got a headache. How kids eat that kind of crap I have no idea. I know that I used to eat stuff like that too. Twinkies and Ho Hos. Getting older can really change your taste buds I guess.

I must have been lost in thought because The Wandering Spirit is now at least fifty yards away and I'm just standing here in freezing water holding a piece of garbage. I must look like some kind of lunatic.

"Hey Bram! Bram!" I yell as I toss the wrapper away.

Getting no response I swim over to the shore and hop out of the water.

"Bram! Come back!"

Bram walks out onto the deck. He throws me a backpack. Kneeling down I open it up. It's all my stuff. In the bottom is a key with a note. The note has an address scrawled on it.

"It's time to move on, kid!" He says.

Kid. He always called me "kid" or "son" even though I'm thirty-five years old. I guess he is old enough to be my dad and that's all that matters. Thinking of that makes me realize that he was more of a father to me this past year than my real father was my whole life.

"Bram! What the hell do I do?" I ask.

"Live!" He laughs and gives me a wink.

Bram goes back to the wheel and fires up the engine. I watch as the ship disappears on the horizon. I'm going to miss that old bastard. He was such a kook.

The sudden realization that I am alone in a city I've never been in before hits me like a tidal wave. I stand there staring out across the ocean for a long time contemplating my next move. I haven't been alone in a year and the last time I was it didn't go so well.

Finding a public restroom I change into some dry clothes. My shoes will have to remain wet for the time being. I really should have taken those off before jumping in the water. Look before you leap as they say. That is something I've never been too good at. I'm very impulsive. Reactive. Emotional.

Gloria was often my guiding light. She could help me calm down in a matter of minutes. Without her, without Bram, I'm not sure what's going to happen. Here I am alone in a big city I know hardly anything about. I remember hearing that they have good hot dogs. It's a big thing apparently.

Chomping down on a hot dog I'm delighted

to not be eating fish. I hate fish and I never quite got used to it. Looking in my wallet I come to the realization that I definitely need to find some source of income and quick. The few bucks that Bram and I had earned from doing odd jobs here and there was close to gone. I'll worry about that later.

Pulling out the key Bram gave me, I ask the hot dog vendor if he knows where 138 North Harbor Road is. He gives me a bunch of convoluted directions but assures me it's not too far. He says I should just take a cab. My financial situation does not dictate that I can take a cab so I'm going to hoof it, plus I need to get my land legs back. I'd been walking like a zombie for the last hour and drawing unwanted attention to myself.

Walking the city streets I'm in awe of how big some of these buildings are. Giant glass towers stretching into the sky. Bella Cruz was a city but not like this. Constantly bumping into people on the street I'm met with cold suspicious glances. There are so many people here. All going about their busy days, heads looking down at their feet. The smell of car exhaust and the sounds coming from every corner assaults the senses in an endless barrage.

Hearing some synthesizer music I find myself wandering into an alleyway. A small courtyard is hidden between the buildings. A group of three kids has a big piece of cardboard laid down on the grass. They are taking turns breakdancing. On the wall behind them spray-painted in huge letters it says "Believe in Neon Fire!". I wonder what that means?

Spending a few minutes watching, one of them stops to speak to me. A girl in her mid to late teens. She's got on baggy pants, a loose shirt falling off one of her shoulders cut to show off her midsection, and a backward cap.

"Hey Captain! You want in on this?" She asks pointing to the cardboard.

"Captain?" I ask in return.

"Yeah, like a ship captain, you wanna dance with us or what?"

Oh. Right. The beard and my hair tied in a bun. It's easy to forget what you look like when you're not looking in the mirror daily.

"I could never do something like that." I reply.

She approaches me and grabs my hands. Her skin is soft and her touch is gentle. I can't remember the last time I held a woman's hand. She starts moving me to the music.

"See! It's easy. Just move your body to the music."

I start to laugh. I really don't know what I'm doing. I barely even danced at my wedding.

"Now you got it!"

The next minute or so I bob back and forth while the girl is moving her hips effortlessly.

When the song ends she gives me a love tap on the face and I say farewell. We all share a laugh. This city is bad? Are you sure about that Bram? Maybe things have changed since you were last here. Those kids seemed pleasant. Far better than the group I hung out with as a kid. We thought breaking windows was a good way to pass the time.

Confused and wandering, I accidentally run into a large man. Easily a head taller than me. Long hair tied back in a ponytail. Despite looking burly he is surprisingly apologetic.

"Sorry man, I didn't see you." He says.

"It was certainly my fault. I don't know where I'm going."

"Well, where are you off to?" He asks.

"Uh...138 North Harbor Road."

"That's simple. Head down West street." He gestures. "Then when you get to Memorial Boulevard take a right. Then it's the third left. You can't miss it. It's right on the water."

"Thanks! You're surprisingly helpful."

"Are you new in town or something?" He asks.

"Uh, yeah. Just got in. A friend of mine is lending me his...apartment." I say.

Quickly I realize I'm not sure what this address is. For all I know it could be a storage locker or a garage.

"Are you looking for work? There's a dock not a mile from that area. I work there. I could get you a job if it's something you are interested in." He tells me.

This man's friendliness I find refreshing and simultaneously odd. I've met quite a few big men in my life when I was fighting an none of them were half as nice. Part of me wonders if he's hitting on me.

Nah. It can't be. I'm too damn ugly. Although I do notice he has very stunning eyes.

"Thanks so much. You really have been helpful. What's the name of the job? I'll be sure to check it out."

"It's East Coast Shipping. Just ask for Daigan. That's me."

"Well, thanks again, Daigan. I'll be seeing you around. Name's Ian, by the way."

We shake hands and part ways. His hand was huge, like twice the size of mine. I'd hate to be on the receiving end of a punch from him.

I can't be far from the place. I'm on Memorial Boulevard. Passing a club I notice that it's dusk and starting to get a bit chilly. Looking into the window I see people dancing. Their bodies almost moving in slow motion. The club is illuminated with neon lights and I can hear the blasting techno music from the street. There's a line out the door to get in. It must be a popular joint. The sign out front reads "Tech Noir".

"Move along! We don't want any homeless people lurking around here!" The bouncer yells at me.

Some attractive women in line laugh at me. I must really look bad. Being on a boat for a year with a crazy old man can warp your perspective I guess. I thought I was looking pretty decent compared to how I looked before, well, right before my "accident". Why Gloria ever fell in love with me I don't think I will ever truly understand.

It took longer than expected but I made it. It's not an apartment but a little waterside cottage built into the side of a hill. It's two floors with a balcony sticking out the front facing the water. It doesn't look like it's in the best of shape. The blue exterior paint is chipped and falling off all over. Several of the windows look as though kids, or whoever, tossed rocks through. I guess there are still kids like I was out there. Sliding the key into the lock I have to exert a large amount of force to push the door open. It must have been warped from the ocean air. Part of the molding around the door breaks away with ease.

Inside is a disaster. I don't know if someone was squatting or hooligans just ransacked the place. The walls are painted with graffiti and most of the furniture is busted. Cobwebs and dust cover everything else. The downstairs is just a small kitchen and dining area. The stove, which I think is gas, doesn't work. The refrigerator is warm and stale smelling. Thankfully no rotting food. A steep set of stairs, well, more like a ladder, leads to the second floor. Upstairs has faired better. A bed with a mattress still intact, a couch, a desk up against the wall. There's a really old TV with the screen smashed in. I guess whoever was here didn't think it was worth anything otherwise they would have stolen it.

Going to sit on the edge of the bed I stop when I notice semen and other various stains on the sheets. My best guess was some teenagers were using this as a love pad. I yank the sheets off the bed and toss them aside. The mattress itself seems reasonably clean so I plop down. Looking at the ceiling I notice huge cracks in the drywall. The pattern makes me think of a painting I once saw in a museum Gloria took me to. It was supposed to express the artist's anger towards society or something. I never quite understood modern art. When I was younger I loved western comics. Cowboys and lone gunman. That was art I understood.

Sliding open the glass door to the balcony I look out across the water and deep into the orange and red sunset. Leaning on the railing I think of Gloria. It looks so different here but somehow the same. Her long black curly hair bouncing, her black dress bending as the wind blew.

"Isn't it beautiful here, Ian?"

Old wounds start to open.

Stop.

The sun creeping in through the doorway wakes me. Sitting up on the old mattress I rub my eyes. I'm confused for a second but then I remember where I am. Spending the next couple hours checking the place out I discover a generator outside. The gas is almost empty but I'm able to get it going. It seems like it's the main power source for this cottage as no power lines are going to it. Scouring the cupboards I find some old can of olives. My stomach groans and my contemplation ends with it. They pass the sniff check so I eat the whole can. I can't say it was the best meal I've ever had although I did find it more appealing than eating that raw squid Bram gave me once. Never again.

In the bathroom I discover, to my amazement, that the water functions. After an initial spray of rusty water it turns clear. I let it run for a bit and then take some in an old glass to drink. My mouth was really parched so that hit the spot. It still tasted a little chemically but I'll most likely survive. If those ancient olives didn't kill me I'm sure a bit of rusty water won't either. The shower stall works as well. The water only gets lukewarm but that's good enough for me. An old bar of soap I discovered under the sink does its job.

Using a straight razor from the medicine cabinet I shave off my beard and cut my hair short. In the mirror I see someone I don't recognize. My face is thin and my cheeks hollow. I've never been this skinny before. I guess I didn't notice always being around Bram who was smaller than me in both height and weight. The beard helped fill out my face too.

After getting dressed I head out to the East Coast Shipping Dock to see about that job. Money was soon to be an issue and a man needs to eat. Daigan was right. It was only about a ten-minute walk from the house. Knocking on the office door I'm greeted by a loud "come on in!". Inside the tight office a fat man in a button-down shirt sporting a serious case of male pattern baldness waves me in. He's screaming at someone on the phone about money.

"Now you better ante up or I'll break your

legs! You got that?!" He slams the phone down. "Mothers, you got to love em. So what can I do for you, you haggard-looking fellow? Let me guess, looking for work? You look like the type. This place employees all the dregs of humanity! If you're willing to work I'm willing to pay. It's as simple as that. Now the pay ain't great and you're sure as shit not getting any benefits, but you get to be outside all day! Fresh air just as good as going to the doctor, I say." He beings coughing for a solid minute straight. "Where was I... ah yes. You want to work? I'll warn you, it's not fun stuff, but you get to be outside. Did I mention that already?"

The phone rings and he quickly grabs it. He gestures at me with his finger like 'wait a minute'.

"Hello? Yes? You're talking to him! What the hell do you want? Ah, not that shit again! Get the hell outta here! I don't give two shits. Send in the papers and I'll sign them. It's as simple as that! You got it? No. No. No. No. No. I said no. Are you some kinda halfwit? N. O. Listen with your goddamn ears will you? No. Ok. Yes. Yes. Yes. That's fine. Ok. Ok. What? Screw you too!" He slams the phone down which sends his coffee flying. A splash of it just barely misses my face.

He gives me a look like "what the hell are you doing here?".

"Um. Daigan sent me." I say.

"Ahh. Yes. That big mother! He's been working here for years. He's a good hand. I trust him. Dad was a cop or so he says. I got a couple of cops on my payroll if you know what I mean. Strike that. I didn't say that. Don't repeat it."

He throws some paperwork at me.

"Fill out these forms. It's as simple as that. Five bucks an hour. It's an honest living. When can you start?" He asks.

"Um, now?"

"Good good. Go out on the dock. Ask for Eric. He'll show you the ropes. Simple as that. You got it?"

I nod as I fill out the paperwork.

Out on the dock I ask for Eric. He's a strong-looking black guy. Shaved head and a goatee. Red tank-top and jeans with holes in them.

"You ever work on a dock before?" He asks.

"No, but I did live on a boat for a year." I reply.

"Look man, this job is pretty simple. Stuff comes in, stuff goes out. We don't handle any of the paperwork we just move the stuff. Shifts start at five AM and end at two PM. It sucks and it's hard labor but it's all the work guys like us can get."

"Guys like us?" I ask.

"You know, ex-cons, uneducated folk." He replies.

I don't argue with him. I spend the rest of the day tearing my hands open pulling on ropes and lifting crates. Eric was right. Stuff comes in, stuff goes out. Looking for Daigan I don't see him anywhere. I ask Eric about him.

"Daigan? He keeps to himself mostly. Said he had some personal shit to deal with. He's been out more often than not lately. His mama's sick or something. I don't know how he could help pay for any of her bills working at this place. He must have some kind of side gig breaking people's legs or something." Eric tells me.

By the time I get home I'm totally exhausted. I pass out on the bed face down.

About a month has passed. Time has flown by. It's now late September. Working at the dock has been killing me, although it has given me a purpose. Something to force me out of bed in the morning and to move around. Move around like a zombie, but still I'm moving. Better than standing still. The more time I'm alone the more those old thoughts seem to start creeping back in and that isn't good. The work keeps my mind occupied.

I've barely touched the cottage. It's still in need of some fixes but at least now I can afford gas to fill up the generator. Hot showers have made this whole situation more bearable.

It's Sunday. My one day off a week. I really need to find a different job. I've told myself that every day and yet I'm still working there. I decide that today is the day that I'll finally clean up the place and get rid of all the trash. The only thing new I have bought is sheets for the bed. The mattress is lumpy and uncomfortable but it's currently not worth the expense to replace it, especially when I'm too tired to notice how terrible it is on most nights.

After what feels like hours go by, and ten trash bags later, the place actually looks halfway decent. Noticing how much dirt is on the floor I realize I need to buy a broom. In the corner of the room is a desk half covered by a dusty sheet. I don't know why I haven't done anything with it yet. Yanking the sheet off of it reveals a large desk with drawers on both sides and a chair. On the wall above the desk is a pretty risque poster. It's a topless woman. Her ass is in the air with a string polka dot bikini bottom on. One of her arms is covering her nipples and in her hand is a bottle of beer. There's a catchphrase. It says "Bottoms up!". Whatever the company was, the label has been torn away. Trying to move the desk I can't seem to get it to budge. It's bolted to the wall for some reason. I go through the drawers but it's nothing but junk.

The poster makes me thirsty amongst other things. Returning from the kitchen I pop open a cold one and sit in the desk chair. I spend an unreasonable amount of time staring at the poster. Although it is old and faded the woman on it is very attractive. I feel like I've seen her before but I can't quite put my finger on it. Maybe she was in an old nudie book I had as a teenager. The more I look at it, the more I'm sure that's it. I definitely spent several nights under the sheets with her. Leaning back in my chair it springs to mind.

"Ms. Autumn '65!"

One of the chair legs snaps and I fall on my ass. My foot flies up underneath the desk and kicks it hard. My leg is throbbing with pain because it's somehow bolted to the wall and my kick didn't even move the damn thing. A weird wiring noise suddenly catches my attention. A panel in the floor under the desk shifts out of place all on its own revealing a passageway of some sort. As curious as curious can be I slide under the desk ignoring my potentially damaged leg. Just on the underside is a cleverly hidden button. I press it and the passageway closes.

"Well what do we have here?" I say to myself.

Pressing the button again the passage reopens. I can't see very far but it appears to be a slide heading down somewhere.

"Where the hell does this go?"

There was nothing outside the cottage that indicated a basement or anything. Maybe it was a laundry chute or it was used for dumping coal or garbage and had been closed off on the outside. I know I should look before I leap but something in my gut told me I'd be fine. What is life without risks? I remember Bram telling me over and over to look before I leap.

I leap.

Tumbling and twisting down a long metal shaft I can't see where the hell I'm going. The fall feels like it takes minutes, like I'm moving in slow motion, but it was only seconds. Crashing down on my butt I am welcomed by a pitch-black void.

"Hello?" I shout into the nothingness. It echoes back.

Where the hell am I? In a silent prayer to myself I desperately hope I'm not stuck in some old garbage dump. Getting to my feet I feel for anything around me. I find a cold stone wall. Taking baby steps and cautiously touching anything I can find I eventually come to some kind of electrical panel. Flipping the switches, against my better judgment, I hear all kinds of electrical noises fire up. Huge over-head lights come on in a giant white flash and I'm momentarily blinded.

When my eyes focus again, to my astonish-ment, I find myself in some kind of man-made cave. To my left is a computer station with multiple displays. On the center display is a single blinking dash mark. It reminds me of one of those command prompts you see in the movies. Gliding my fingers over the keyboard they get a thin coat of dust on the tips. No one has been here in a long time. I've used a computer once or twice before but I'm not sure what I'm supposed to do. Out of pure instinct I hit the return key.

"Welcome back, Sir!" A female electronic voice greets me.

"Hello?" I say back. There's no response. It's a computer you idiot.

"Mother?" I try one more time, thinking of the movie Alien.

Yet again there is no response. I hit the return key once more.

Giving me a startle a large panel opens up with several enormous glass tubes built into the wall behind it. One of them is empty. The middle one has an outfit on display. Its a goofy-looking baby blue and red superhero outfit, for a lack of better term. It reminds me of the old comics I used to read and carnival strong men. It looks well worn and used. Damage marks from gunshots and knives are present in almost every area of the suit.

To the right of it, in the final tube, is a gray, black, and red outfit. The bodysuit section is gray with black trunks on the outside and a black utility belt. The boots are black and the gloves are red. Well, more like a maroon. It has a long maroon cape that touches the ground that sits around the neck. As for the head, its a full face covering mask with a fixed angry look to it and maroon accents going down across the eyes and around the back. The eyes are white lenses. On both arms and the right leg are maroon straps like I had seen before in books about spartan warriors. It honestly looks both silly and scary. I can't put it to words. A plaque at the base of the tube reads "Prototype". Clearly it has never been worn.

On the opposite wall is a large panel that seems like it should move out of the way but it won't budge. Touching what looks like a sensor, a screen lights up that says "Access Denied". I wonder what could be hiding behind this wall.

What have I stumbled upon?

What is this place?

So many thoughts go rushing through my mind.

It comes to me like a bolt of lightning hitting my head. A sudden and shocking revelation. Bram lived here. This has to be his stuff. So many things that Bram had alluded to over this past year suddenly make more sense. He told me that he used to "help people" for a living. I figured he was a firefighter or police officer. The man moved around the boat like some kind of Jolly Roger. When we would dock you should have seen him swinging from the ropes.

The man is instantly likable. A real good guy. When we would be in port he would talk to strangers like they were his best friend. So many smiles. He would call everyone "brother" or "sister" and he genuinely meant it.

This seventy-year-old man dove into freezing cold water with a rope tied around his waist and pulled a random stranger out of the water. Someone he had never met. Someone he couldn't have cared less about, but he did it anyway.

That was me.

"Bram. You son of a bitch."

CHAPTER 13

Inhuman Monster

Red and orange tones rise and then fall. The cracking and popping of the burning timbers is music to my ears. Its glow illuminates me. The shadows play a carefree game across my face. I am envious of the power it holds. Raging, engulfing. A never-ending hunger for destruction.

I put my hand in the fire. My flesh is searing. The pain is white-hot and blinding but I do not and will not retract my hand. I will not falter. Holding it there for as long as I can I see the boils begin to appear. This pain will become their pain. I repeat it like a mantra. My pain will become their pain. All that I have suffered will be given back tenfold. The fire blazes in a hypnotic dance. Its warmth embraces me. I feel its power pulling me in. I wish to be engulfed by its beauty. When the pain feels overwhelming I steady myself and I press on longer. Soon there is no more pain at all, only pleasure.

The fire is my one true love. Her warmth caresses me. Holds me closer than any person ever has. Her strength gives me strength.

Pulling my hand from the fire I stare at its red and seeping flesh. The hairs on it carry the flames like a beautiful candle. The light reflects in my eyes. Wisps of smoke lift and fight with each other into the air. I breathe it in.

Happy.

I feel happy.

CHAPTER 14

Ian

This locker room stinks but it's an old familiar smell. It's the smell of sweat from desperate men. I slipped the promoter a ten to get me a fight on the card. I think he would have taken less. I'm fighting some guy who goes by "The Tarantula". I toss my bag down on the ground and a cloud of dust is kicked up. It contains that prototype outfit I found in Bram's cave.

I haven't fought in years and for a second I wonder if this is a good idea or not. Winner's purse is a hundred bucks. From what I could tell the crowd was only a handful of people and on the flier I didn't recognize any names which is probably good, I'd prefer to go unnoticed.

The locker room is filled with men of all races. Some just fought, others getting ready. In the corner one guy is praying. I think he is speaking Italian. The locker room walls are plastered with torn up old fight posters and centerfolds. The concrete floor is cracked and stained with blood. Half the lockers are busted and one of the fighters is complaining that the shower doesn't work.

Knowing they won't let me fight in the full

getup I only put on the bottoms. They fit pretty well considering they weren't made for me. Bram must have been quite muscular back in the day. I slide on the black trunks and secure the leg straps. The boots are too small though. I should have tried them on ahead of time. I push my toes in but the leather is too stiff and will not budge. I can't wear these. One of the fighters who just fought, sitting across from me, being checked out by the doctor, has black high-top boots like the ones I used to wear.

"Hey, what size are those?" I ask him.

"Twelve? Why?" He replies as the doctor applies a cold compress to his cheek.

"You want twenty bucks?" I ask.

I'm lacing up the boots and they fit almost perfectly. I stand up and bounce back and forth. They are already broken in. They're perfect. Going to the mirror I shadow box. A feeling from long ago grips my gut. My pulse quickens. A bead of sweat forms on my forehead. A smile appears on my face. An expression I thought I had forgotten.

"Dempsey, you ready?" My appointed corner-man asks.

He ties up my gloves and tapes over the laces. I slap them together a few times. The leather makes a loud banging sound with every hit. They feel good. Sturdy. Ready for the fight.

"Are you actually wearing that getup?" He asks.

"You damn right!"

Walking out to the ring they don't play any

music just the sound of glasses clinking and old men coughing can be heard. Passing me on the way to the ring is the guy who lost the last fight. His face is a swollen mess. He pulls a towel over his face to hide his shame. A feeling I knew all too well, once upon a time.

Up ahead stands the ring. It's barely off the floor and the ropes are loose. Several of the turnbuckles are missing and the thick smell of fresh blood kisses my nose.

In the ring across from me stands "The Tarantula". A skinny looking Hispanic kid with a crooked nose dressed in Mexican flag trunks that look like hand-me-downs. His trunks are splattered with blood. Is it his own or one of his past opponents? I'm not sure on the legality of this fight since I'm pretty sure I outweigh him and I bet I'm fifteen years his senior, easy. Back in the day I would have easily cleaned this kid's clock but it's been too long to get cocky. Staring deep into his eyes I can tell he's hungry. I remember a time when that was me. He bounces and raises his fists to the air. Gesturing to the crowd he receives a lone cheer. That's better than I got. When they announced me you could have heard a pin drop.

The referee calls for the bell and that sound I used to know so well echoes through this dive bar's high ceilings. He rushes at me with a head full of steam. He strikes at my midsection over and over again. For a little guy he packs a punch. I shift my weight and get out of the corner. Throwing a haymaker he hits me right in the nose. Blood gushes. It trickles down my upper lip and into my mouth. Tasting it I feel alive again. The old moves come back to me. Step, pivot, strike. I blast him with a right hand that sends him straight to the mat. His eyes wide with shock. The referee counts to seven before he gets up. We dance, exchanging a few blows, but then the round comes to an end.

Sitting down, my appointed cornerman starts giving me advice. He's way younger than me and far less experienced. His advice is complete trash. Giving him a dead-eye look I stand up for the next round. The lighting is dim, the canvas is torn and stained, the air heavy with smoke. I'm home again.

Tarantula busts my ribs up good but I'm not hurting for real just yet. I throw a series of punches that all whiff. Get it together, Ian. You're better than this. I try to focus. It's been too long and you're getting old. Tarantula lands a few blows to my head. Wake up you dumb son of a bitch! I close my eyes for only a moment but a bad memory rushes in.

"The Baron". Aaron. Aaron O'Shaunessy. That piece of crap. Lying on the mat in a pool of his own blood. Teeth all knocked out. Face looking like a pile of hamburger. You got what you deserved.

It's ruled an accident...but it wasn't.

I'm back in the fight. My hands move like someone else is controlling them. Left. Left. Left. Right. Left. Right. Left. Body blow. Body blow. Uppercut. Tarantula is on the mat again and the ref is counting. I look at him and I see Aaron. He's laughing at me from his broken toothless face. He blows me a kiss.

The ref counts ten and I'm declared the winner. The crowd gives a mild reaction. Half of them are drunks. Some guy tosses a ticket to the ground, curses, and storms out. Helping Tarantula to his feet I tell him it was a good fight. He doesn't speak English but he tells me "Gracias". How humble of him. I can't say I was the same way when I was his age.

Afterward, in the locker room, I give him my winner's purse. Between that and his loser's share he made one hundred and forty dollars. Not a bad wage for two rounds. Gushing, and repeatedly thanking me, I push him away. I don't care about the money. That's not what this was about. The doctor comes in and tosses me a bag of ice. Holding it over my face the cold feels painful and great at the same time. Sweat trickles down my back and the thought of Gloria's gentle fingers returns.

She tells me everything is going to be ok.

CHAPTER 15

Gloria – 1978

Those old familiar smells. Right after a fight this place fills up like nobody's business. The BARe Knuckle is a hot spot since it's right across the street from the North Bridge Gym and Fight Club. Ian and I frequent this place. Good chicken wings and for the most part good people. I don't even mind the warm, flat, beer. The walls are littered with old fight posters and the air is filled with the voices of old fighters telling old stories. The bartender, Big Mac, is a retired pro who once fought in a lower card match in Lochland City. He takes every opportunity he can to talk about it. He lost, but he tends to leave that part out. Every time a wet behind their ears fighter comes in he takes them under his huge arm and tells them the story like it's some well-kept secret. They listen because they want to respect him and learn from him. Maybe one day they too can lose in an undercard fight in Lochland City. A young guy comes in the door with wide eyes. It's not long before Mac leaves the bar and is on him. I laugh to myself.

Sitting next to me is my darling Ian. His left eye is black and he has a bandage on his chin from it getting busted open the night before. One advantage of having a nurse for a girlfriend is I can take care of a lot of his minor wounds right at home. He goes to take a swig of his beer but instead chugs it down. A skill I definitely don't have. I usually just take a few sips here, a few sips there. I'm not a heavy drinker. Gliding my fingers through his shaggy brown hair he closes his eyes and smiles.

"I love it when you do that." He says.

Ian thinks he's ugly. He tells me all the time. And while not conventionally handsome, he's got that rugged look and charm that I find very appealing. Plus he's got these big brown doe eyes that could melt steel. If he wasn't there on that fateful day I'd be dead. It just so happens that he ended up being an amazing man, and I would have fallen for him no matter what he looked like.

"So when's your next fight, babe?" I ask.

"Two weeks. Against Aaron O'Shaunessy." He replies.

Aaron O'Shaunessy is a hot up and comer. He is an undefeated southpaw fighter. In fact he's in the bar right now over in the lounge area. He's got quite the entourage around him as well as some beautiful women. He's a pretty boy, wears a lot of jewelry and fancy clothes. Diamond stud earrings top off the whole look. Claiming to have come from nothing it's hard to imagine that now. He flips up one of the girl's skirts revealing she has no panties on. His boys hoot and holler. She acts ashamed but falls right into his lap. Grabbing ahold of her ass he pulls her in and they start making out. Meanwhile he has his hand on another woman's breasts. A real play-boy, that one.

"More drinks!" He yells. "Big Mac! Get us some more drinks, my man!"

Big Mac rushes over with a tray of beers so fast you'd think he just got called to the principal's office. After placing them down Aaron tosses a wad of crumpled up money at him. Mac clenches his fist but picks up the money and walks away. Mac is an old-timer, and behavior like Aaron's is heavily frowned upon.

"Back in my day fighters were also gentle-man." He'd lament.

"Hey Jimmy, you like what you see?" Aaron gestures at the girl sitting to his right.

She's maybe twenty, wearing a short white bob wig. I can't tell if she is shy or if she just doesn't really want to be here.

"Hell yeah, I do!" Jimmy replies.

"Baby, how about you show Jimmy a good time." Aaron commands.

Jimmy puts out his hand and the girl goes with him to the bathroom, but not before Aaron slaps her hard on the butt. His boys laugh, cheer, clack their glasses together, and all share a drink.

Suddenly, I realize I'm scratching a hole through my nylons and tapping my foot. I haven't had a cigarette in hours and I need one now. Ian hates that I smoke but I'm trying to quit. I promised him I would quit. He stopped using pain killers for me. It's the least I could do.

"Babe, I'm going to get some fresh air." I say to Ian.

He knows I'm lying. I can tell from the look on his face. He knows that fresh air is code for a cigarette break. I'm down to only three a day. Starting next week I'm going to try for two.

"Ok baby, I'll be here waiting for you. Want another drink?" He asks.

I nod. He smiles. Even with his slightly crooked grin he lights me up inside like no one else has before, or most likely will again. He's my one and only.

I'm still waiting on the ring. Ian said that when he was done with boxing, he'd buy me a ring. I don't hate that he boxes, but I do worry that one day he might get knocked down and not get up. He lost a fight about a month ago and couldn't see out of his left eye for a few days. I was honestly scared. He tells me that all he needs to do is get that one big fight and he's done. I'm supportive but I know they don't give out big purses to fighters with 15-13 records, especially not in Bella Cruz. Beating Aaron would be a big deal, the winner's purse is the biggest he's ever fought for, but I'm not sure he has what it takes. Aaron is stronger, younger, and has more time and money for training. I would never tell Ian these thoughts that I have. I love him so goddamn much. I know he can be anything he wants to be. The first time I saw him fight he fought with such passion. I sometimes wonder if I've made him weak. Most of his losses have come since we've been together.

Outside of the bar I take in a big deep breath of that sweet fire. I tap the ash and it falls like a snowflake fluttering down to the ground. I take another drag and watch the bright red cherry glow against the darkness of the alley. My lungs fill with smoke and I can feel that gentle buzz that I'd come to love.

"We need to break up." I say as I hold the cigarette out in front of me. "It's not you, it's me."

It's a nice night, not too cold or hot. It had just rained so that magical smell still lingers in the air. Catching a glimpse of myself in a puddle I see my curly black hair is a bit messy. I fluff it up and flip it over to one side showing off my neck. I unbutton the top button of my blouse. I want to look sexy for Ian. I quickly dig through my purse and find a small bottle of perfume. Spraying a little on my wrist I dab it onto my neck. I hike my skirt up a bit showing off my legs. I take a final long drag off my cigarette.

Going to put my cigarette out a voice interrupts me.

"Hey baby, would you mind if I took a drag off of that?"

It's Aaron. Alone. He comes into view under one of the overhead lights. He smiles at me. His perfect teeth glisten. His fire engine red hair looks almost black in the alley light. I feel my body tense up for some reason.

"Sure, it's all yours." I say as I pass him what remains of the butt.

He takes a couple quick drags.

"I'm Aaron. What's your name?" He asks.

"Gloria." I reply.

He isn't even hiding that he's checking me out. I try to nonchalantly pull my top up a bit to cover my cleavage.

"So, Gloria, why is a smoking hot woman such as yourself hanging out in bar like this?" He asks.

I'd be lying if I said I wasn't a little bit flattered. He is a very handsome Irishmen and the accent is like icing on the cake. But still, there is something about him giving me a weird vibe. I reply without an ounce of subtlety.

"I'm with my boyfriend. He's a fighter."

"Oh, you have a boyfriend? I see. I see. He's a fighter too?" He replies while stroking at his chin.

"Yeah, Ian Dempsey."

The name instantly clicks in his mind. He smirks.

"Oh! You mean that chump I'm going to beat in two weeks."

This conversation is over.

"If you'll excuse me." I say as I go to go back inside. His hand grabs my arm.

"Look baby, let's be serious here. He's a zero and I'm the real deal. I'm going to be the heavyweight champ in less than a year. My manager is taking me straight to the top with no stops. Pedal to the metal. Understand? A hot piece of ass like you needs to know which man to be hanging on." He says, oozing with pure ego.

I yank my arm away and blast him across the face with a slap. The sound echoes off of the alley-way walls and up into the crystal clear moonlit sky. He turns back to me with a bloody lip.

"You like to play rough huh? I like that!"

Suddenly, I'm against the wall. His alcohol ridden breath fills my mouth as he forcefully kisses me. Trying to knee him in the balls he grabs my leg and slides his hand up my skirt. Somehow I get my hands between us and I'm able to push him back a few steps.

"Get the hell away from me!" I scream. "You're not a man!"

I give him another slug to the chin. He easily shakes it off.

"Not a man? I'll show you a man." He replies.

He rushes me and although I try to hit him with my purse he's too quick. My head bashes off the stone wall behind me and things get blurry.

I'm on all fours with my face down in the muck. A metallic flavor rushes in and causes me to gag a bit. It's my blood. I feel my skirt being forced up and my underwear being pulled down. Hearing the sound of a belt buckle coming undone I scream as loud as I can.

"Help! Help! Help!"

"Shut your bloody mouth, bitch!" He says as he yanks my head back with a hand full of my hair.

He bites my ear.

The door to the bar flies open and with tears

in my eyes I see Ian. He doesn't even say a word. He rushes in and punches Aaron right in the face. A tooth goes flying into the night air. I'm able to roll over and pull my underwear back up. They are straight-up brawling. Ian grabs Aaron's shirt and pulls it over his head and starts punching him repeatedly in the gut. Aaron gets out of his shirt and lands some blows of his own busting open Ian's chin again. Aaron slams Ian into the side of a dumpster. Grabbing at his lower back Ian is in pain as Aaron punches him in the ribs. Ian headbutts Aaron cracking his nose, he screams.

"My face. My goddamn face!"

Aaron is pissed now and goes back on the assault. The two exchange a few more blows before a couple of Aaron's people spill out from the bar.

"What the hell?" One of them yells.

They pull Ian and Aaron apart. Aaron grabs a gun from his friend's belt and bashes Ian over the head with it. He couldn't even defend himself because his arms are being held by one of Aaron's cronies. Ian falls to the ground bleeding from the back of his head. I crawl to his side.

"Babe, are you alright?" I ask.

"Yeah, you?" He asks.

He shakes it off like nothing happened although I can see the rage in his eyes.

"In two weeks, you're dead meat!" Aaron says as he gets his shirt back on. "Let's get the hell out of here. Get the girls too. I need to blow off some steam."

"Boss, you're bleeding." One says as he points out Aaron's nose.

Aaron wipes the blood off on his shirt sleeve.

"I'll be seeing you again real soon." He says.

He blows me a kiss.

The three of them leave, walking off into the darkness, hopping into a limo out front. I look to Ian. His fists are clenched. The veins in his hands and forearms look like snakes trying to bust out from under the skin. His eyes are on fire with such hatred like I've never seen before.

"Two weeks..." I can hear him muttering to himself.

Back at home I help patch up his wounds. He barely says anything to me the next two weeks other than that he loves me more than life itself. If he's not at work he's in the gym training. While going through his dirty laundry I find a bottle of steroids in his gym bag. Part of me wants to say something but I don't want to make things worse. Ian admitted to me early on in our relationship that he had used them in the past. I just worry about his safety.

It's the night before the fight. Ian has been sitting in the living room silent for hours. He didn't even touch his dinner. He hasn't touched me in weeks and I'm worried that he sees me as damaged goods. Aaron never got all the way and I've assured him of that but he doesn't even want to talk about it. I love him so much. I don't want him to leave me.

Walking into the living room I've put on the

slip that he loves. I've done my hair and makeup too. Approaching him on the couch I try to act sexy and aloof. He doesn't even look at me. He's just staring at the wall. I have to make him look at me.

I mount him and start kissing his lips. At first he doesn't respond much but when I slide my slip down and push my breasts up he can't help himself. His lips greet my nipples and then he bites. I love it when he does that. Painful bliss. His powerful hands grip my waist.

"I love you, Gloria." He says.

The next morning I wake to find myself alone. On the dresser is my ticket to the fight. Ian is nowhere to be found in the apartment. All of his fight gear is gone. I call down to the gym. Derrick, the club manager, tells me that he hasn't seen Ian. I'm starting to get worried.

Using my ticket to get in I find my seat easily enough. Front row center. I don't think I've seen a fight with such a big crowd before. It's amazing. It's hot inside the building from all the bodies. People chattering about the fights. It seems no one is giving Ian a chance in hell. I regret all the thoughts I had about him losing. Putting out bad energy into the world. He deserves better than that. He can and will win... I hope.

Several undercard fights happen but I'm not exactly interested. My worry and fear is becoming overwhelming. I need a cigarette. My heels are tapping on the floor and it must have been pretty loud because the woman sitting next to me asks me if

I'm ok. I give her a quick "yeah" and then go back to worrying. Twiddling my fingers and counting the seconds like minutes, time seems to have ceased moving.

It's finally time for Ian's fight. Ian enters the ring and goes to his corner. He turns to the corner and shakes the ropes. He turns back to center and in this harsh overhead lighting I see just how muscular he has become. Deep cut abdominals and huge thick arms. His body covered in a roadmap of veins. His eyes, they look dead. I want to scream out to him but I catch my tongue.

Aaron enters the arena with big fanfare. Entrance music and surrounded by an entourage, he's yelling and cheering, hyping up the crowd. They return the favor. He's the clear favorite. Looking back to Ian he still has that dead look in his eyes. He's staring out across the ring like he's staring into the void. Butterflies appear in my stomach.

Aaron enters the ring as one of his cronies holds open the ropes. He dances around throwing punches in the air. The crowd cheers. He gets in Ian's face. Ian doesn't even react. I can just barely make out...

"You're gonna die boy!" Aaron yells in his face.

The referee separates them. The ring announcer rattles off the rules and then their names. When Ian is announced there's a mild swell, when Aaron is announced the crowd goes ballistic. He is the home town boy after all. Ian is originally from the pacific northwest, not southern California.

The bell rings and the two meet in the middle. To say it's a slugfest would be a huge understatement. I think I have never seen such a fight. Within a minute it's divulged into a brawl. The ref gets between them several times. So many wild, rabid punches. Both of them are busted open by the time the bell rings to end the first round.

I'm not breathing.

The bell rings for the second round and Aaron starts strong. He's more focused. Landing body blow after body blow. I can feel Ian's ribs cracking. Ian backs off and spits blood in Aaron's face. Aaron lets out a stream of obscenities. The two clash again. Ian lands a brutal overhand right which knocks out Aaron's mouthpiece. The ref breaks it up and gets him a new piece, but Ian is like a rabid dog. He's back on the attack. He lands three consecutive blows to Aaron's head. Going for a fourth the bell rings to end the second round.

My heart is beating out of my chest.

The crowd is losing their minds.

My ass is barely touching my seat.

The third round starts and things get dirty. Aaron slips in a headbutt and Ian is dazed. I can't help but let out a yelp. The ref starts accosting Aaron and Ian sucker punches him in the kidney. The two grab each other and land dirty shot after dirty shot. It's getting brutal. Both of them look like they took a bath in blood.

I'm so worried that I feel like I have left my

body.

Ian lands a right hook that sends Aaron into the corner. Ian rushes in and lands a devastating barrage of punches. Blood and sweat spray into the air like a mist. The crowd is cheering but slowly fall silent. All that can be heard are Ian's punches echoing off the rafters. It's hard to tell but Aaron doesn't seem to be defending himself. He's taking blow after blow full on. Suddenly, I realize his trunks are snagged on the ropes, holding him up. A lone voice cries out to stop the fight. Ian isn't stopping. Aaron's face looks like rotten ground beef. All swollen and gushing blood. The ref finally pushes them apart. Aaron slumps to the ground like a sack of bricks. The ref begins his count. An eternity passes in that ten seconds. Ian stands over Aaron, breathing heavily, his body doused in sweat and blood. The ref raises his hand in victory but his eyes are locked on Aaron. The crowd is in stunned silence.

Ian spits out his mouthpiece on to Aaron's lying body.

The ring is suddenly rushed with people. It's absolute chaos. In all the blurry aftermath I manage to sneak my way back into the locker room.

Ian enters. I've been waiting for him. I tore a hole in my nylons again. The light behind him casts his body in a dark silhouette. He's almost unrecognizable. He's swollen, bruised, and covered in blood. Some not his own. He collapses onto the bench. I quickly sit next to him. I pull him tight to me showering him with kisses. The blood is staining my dress but I couldn't care less. I'm panicking and I don't know what to do. I help him get his gloves off. He puts his big strong hands around my face. He looks me in the eyes and I fall in love all over again.

"It's all over." He says. "This was the last one."

Sitting beside Ian I gently caress him. My fingers glide down the center of his back and I can feel him starting to relax. An official comes into the locker room. He says a whole lot of things but the only thing that sticks is that Aaron is dead.

It's ruled an accident...but it wasn't.

"Well Dempsey, here's your payday. Don't spend it all in one place." The promoter says. "This was a big victory, son. You should look into getting a manager."

Under his breath I can hear the promoter talking to the official as they walk away.

"You ever see a fight that brutal?"

Ian tears open the envelope. Inside is a check for fifty thousand dollars.

On the way to my car we have to push through a crowd of people shouting and screaming. Cameras going off left and right. Between the shouting and the camera flashes I'm becoming extremely disoriented. Ian grabs my hand and helps me back down to Earth.

"How does it feel to kill a man?" Someone shouts.

Finally security gets involved and helps us away from the crowd.

I feel the immense urge to smoke. So much

has happened and I can't seem to wrap my head around it all other than I know I love Ian. I want to marry him and have a family. I stop suddenly.

"What's wrong?" He asks.

His face is completely swollen up. One eye is permanently closed. His lip is five times its original size, and yet he takes the time to ask me what's wrong.

I pull a pack of cigarettes out of my purse. Drawing one cig out with my lips, my hands are shaking so violently that Ian needs to help me with the lighter. Before it's lit I see things so clearly.

"I don't need these anymore."

My hands steady. I take the cigarettes and toss them in the garbage.

That night in bed he holds me close. Closer than he has in a long time. He tells me how much he loves me. That he would do anything to protect me.

Ian...

He asks me to marry him.

I say yes.

CHAPTER 16

Alex

"Order up!" I hear yelled from the kitchen followed by that all too familiar "ding ding" of the bell.

Rushing over to the counter I'm greeted by two plates. Bacon and eggs on one, a stack of pancakes on the other. It's busy as hell this morning and I know I'll be right back here for more plates in a matter of moments.

Balancing the hot plates on one arm and two cups of coffee in my other hand I deftly maneuver around another waitress and a couple of customers coming in. Table five. Two trucker types. Big beer bellies topped off with baseball caps. Placing the plates down I catch one of them trying to look down my shirt. I pleasantly smile.

"Is there anything else I can get you?" I ask.

"Everything looks great, sweetheart." The one on the right replies.

Sweetheart, honey, sweetie, baby, babe. I'm used to it by now. Walking away from the table I hear one of them say "she's pretty cute for a gook." It doesn't even bother me that much anymore. In this get-up my Asian heritage barely shows. I'm surprised he even noticed, although he's got his ethnic slurs mixed up. Thick black rim cat eye glasses and a long red wig with bangs, plus my adorable freckles, usually throw people off.

Damn this wig can get itchy. I'm scratching under it again.

"Hey, Ms. Faye-Darling! Wake up!" My boss Sheila screams.

Oh damn! I dozed off leaning up against the wall. Again. Long night, what can I say? Scrambling, I apologize and assist my next few tables. Some families and more single guy types. The tips are solid for a Wednesday. Nothing really of note happens which is the way I like it. I like being unknown. Unremarkable. Every once and a while I'll get a guy trying to hit on me but that's it. I don't wear any makeup and I attempt to make myself look as frumpy and unappealing as possible. Aside from wearing fake teeth or gluing on a giant fake scar I'm not sure what else I could do to not get "the eyes". The uniform is thankfully not all the flattering in any way and has a long skirt to hide my sculpted legs. What can I say? I'm proud of those babies. Unfortunately I can't really hide my mixed heritage and some guys are really into that.

Speaking of guys, I haven't really had much time for dating and it's really difficult to hide who you really are when someone else is in your life. There was a busboy that worked here a few years ago that was pretty cute. We had sex a couple of times. He kept wanting to play with my hair and I was terrified my wig would fall off. I wouldn't really say that was a relationship though. He never saw me fully nude and we never actually went out. We never even kissed. Talk about awkward. He was younger than me. A senior in high school. He was just so happy to get some action he didn't really ask any questions. Before that it was James, my high school boyfriend. We made love almost every day the summer after we graduated but he went off to college and I didn't. That was all she wrote. Last I checked he's married with children. I don't exactly miss sex. My life is far more exciting now anyway.

During my break, I always listen to the police radio. I bob my head and pretend like it's music. My fellow waitress, Tamara, blabs on and on to me but I'm not listening at all. I'm nodding as if I give a damn about her boyfriend or where she's getting her nails done or how much her bikini wax costs. Although I do get my legs waxed at a place she recommended so I guess she isn't entirely useless. Somehow she has managed to make this hideous uniform look sexy. It helps that she's very well endowed. She puts those puppies to work, literally collecting double my tips. This morning I saw her lean forward and press those things on the countertop right in front of some old guy. He looked like he saw a goddamn ghost. I swear the table moved up a couple inches. The tip she got was more than the bill. If you got it, flaunt it I guess.

Sheila tells me I did a good job today but to get a good night's sleep. If I fall asleep again she's going to suspend me. An empty threat that she repeats almost every day. She's a good, well-meaning woman. When she first hired me I still had my natural hair. Between my auburn hair, vaguely Asian features, and cheeks full of freckles she was confused by my name.

"Alexandra Faye-Darling? Where's that from?" She asked.

"Well, my dad is Japanese and my mom is Irish. When he moved to this country he wanted to sound less ethnic so he changed his name. His last name sounded close to Faye so he just changed the spelling. My mom is a tough one, she didn't want to change her name so they eventually agreed to hyphenate." I replied.

I guess that was more than satisfactory so she said "oh" and nodded.

At the end of our shift the night crew comes in. Tamara, Angelo (the only male waiter on staff), and I count out our tips in the break room as we prepare to leave. Seventy bucks. Tamara got two hundred. Even Angelo got eighty.

"Girl, you need to up your game!" Tamara says to me. "You're cute, you can work that to your advantage, love!"

She plays with her blonde hair, which has upward bangs simultaneously with long wavy downward locks, the whole time she is talking. She unbuttons her top about halfway and those ginormous things nearly fall out. Angelo is staring and not doing a good job of hiding it. He once confessed to me that he has the hots for her. I'm glad he sees me as a friend and nothing more.

"Girl, can I ask you something? When you start dating a guy do you make him wear a rubber?" She asks.

I pretend to be in shock.

"Oh, I don't know." I act bashful.

"You don't know? Personally I love it *raw*." She overemphasizes the word raw. "I don't want anything to come between me and my man." She continues as she looks over to Angelo. "It just feels *so good*."

He awkwardly coughs and excuses himself. Poor kid.

"Now that he's gone let's get down to business." Tamara turn towards me.

I shudder to think what that means. She approaches me and I feel my shoulders tense up. Few things scare me in this world...

"Babe, look!" She grabs me by the shoulders and turns me to the mirror. "Look at your neckline."

She begins unbuttoning my top, like hers, but I stop her before she gets too low. I'm decently endowed myself but I wear a tight nylon top to push them down and in. Thinking of that makes me think of the big frumpy old lady underwear I wear to change the shape of my hips and ass. They are padded like a diaper. Surprisingly comfortable.

"You have a gorgeous collarbone. Guys like that." She assures me.

Guys like collarbones? I'd never thought of that. Tamara then takes off my glasses and hangs them on the collar of her shirt. She thinks I'm uncomfortable because I'm shy. I don't know where she had it hidden but she rubs some kind of glitter-filled lotion on my chest. I've seen her wear it before and it really, really, makes her boobs more of a spectacle than they already are, if you can believe it.

She takes a moment to look me up and down.

"Just one more thing. Hold on." She says as she starts digging through her bag.

"Tamara, really, this isn't necessary."

"Oh come on, this is just girl stuff." She pulls out a bright pink lipstick. "You have such plump, full lips. Can't hurt to show them off!"

She comes at me like an attacker with that thing and I jerk my head back so quick my wig nearly falls off. Reminding myself that I shouldn't act too weird I let her put the lipstick on me. Part of me wonders if this is remotely sanitary. I also think about what things Tamara's lips might have touched. She turns me back to the mirror.

"Voila!" She exclaims. "That lipstick is just your shade."

Courtney Barnett "Be Foxy" Hot Mauve # 29651. I have ten sticks of it. If Tamara only knew, what would she think?

I gaze deep at my reflection. With this lipstick on it's hard for me to not see my alter ego which I've buried every morning for three years. Feeling proud of myself I notice just how good of a job I did covering up the shiner I got the other night. While she's admiring her handy work I gently steal that bottle of glitter stuff from one of her dress pockets and toss it in my own.

"See. You're sexy, bitch." She says.

Hell yeah I am.

CHAPTER 17

Masked Man

"Give us all the money and put it in the bag!" I scream as I point my gun in the face of some middle-aged bitch.

She looks like she is going to burst into tears at any moment. This feels like it's taking too goddamn long. I cased this place for a week leading up to this and I know they don't have any security cameras. My partner is in the back trying to get the owner to pop the safe. I'm counting the seconds in my head like minutes. My face is starting to sweat under this good for nothing ski mask. I should have used pantyhose. Damn. What the hell is taking him so long back there. He can't handle a little old man?

Suddenly, I hear sirens in the distance. Shit. The cops. How did they find us so quickly? There's only the clerk and the owner. Like the sound of a hundred glasses breaking at once I hear a gunshot come from the back room. The owner comes stumbling out with a gushing wound in his stomach. His eyes are lit up like goddamn headlights. My partner pushes him to the ground and proceeds to put his foot on his back.

"What the hell are you doing?" I yell to him.

"Piece of shit triggered a silent alarm hidden behind the safe!" He yells.

My partner points his gun at the owner's head and without an ounce of hesitation pulls the trigger. Poor old bastard. His brains splattered all over the tile floor.

Snatching away the duffle bag full of money from the clerk my partner and I exit the corner store. A scream echoes from within. It's the clerk. She's sobbing over the body of that stupid old man. What a waste.

We hop in our getaway car. It's a rusted old piece of junk that I bought at the dump so it would be easy to dispose of. Without thinking my partner slams on the accelerator while I'm halfway in the car and we're off and running.

"You motherfucker! You couldn't wait two seconds for me to close my goddamn door!" I scream in his face. "I just barely got the money in you dumb shit!"

There's traffic up ahead and the cops are right on us.

"Shit! Shit! Shit!" My partner is yelling at himself while slamming his hands on the steering wheel.

I can't believe he offed that poor guy. I've had to kill before but it was purely self-defense. I would never straight up execute some crippled old man. I told him beforehand to leave the guns unloaded. What a dumbass! If we get caught I'm throwing him under the bus.

The cops are hot on our heels. Shit. This is getting close. Suddenly, my partner turns down a street that wasn't part of the planned route.

"What the hell are you doing?" I yell.

"Trust me!" He replies.

"Trust you? Trust you? You just killed that guy for no reason! What the hell's wrong with you?" I scream as I slap him on the back of the head.

"Son of a bitch had it coming. He should have just given me the money!"

I load up my revolver. Leaning out the window I try to aim for the cop car's tires. It is way too bouncy and I don't want to risk hurting any innocent bystanders. I take a single shot and miss. Damn! I slide back into the car.

"We are in deep shit if we get caught, man! You better not mess the rest of this up!" I yell while fingering my gun and contemplating taking another shot.

A mother and child appear on the road ahead of us.

"Look out!" I scream.

My partner doesn't move. This guy is sick. He looks like he really wants to run them down. He's pressing the accelerator.

Without thinking I grab the wheel and swerve the car. We go careening into a telephone pole. With a sudden jerk I drop my gun. It takes me a second to regain my composure. My partner is already outside the vehicle. He better not be leaving me here. I kick open my door and grab the money from the back seat.

"Come on. We have to go!" I tell him as he is standing there just staring.

"Stop or we'll shoot!" A cop yells.

I turn and see two cops, armed with pistols, staring us down. One is older and fat and the other looks young and fit. He might be able to run us down on foot. My partner acting all on his own raises his gun and shoots the younger cop. He falls to the ground quickly and lets out a loud scream. Grabbing my partner by the arm I yank him into a full sprint. We need to get out of here and into hiding right now. The older cop is clumsy. He aims and pops off a few shots but none of the connect with anything but air.

My partner and I dart down an alleyway. It's not well lit and I'm not all that familiar with this area of the city. If we had stuck to our planned route this wouldn't be a problem. Finding a door I kick it in. We rush inside and see it's an old abandoned factory. It's dark and frankly it's giving me the creeps. The place is littered with old machinery draped over with big sheets. The air is thick and dusty. Cobwebs stretching from corner to corner. It's like some kind of rotting machine graveyard.

"Come on." I say as I lead the way.

I'm trying to find a way out. I can still hear police sirens wailing in the background. We're not out of this mess yet. We need to get to the safe house and quick.

A loud pinging sound comes out of nowhere and startles us. My heart jumps and I almost crap my pants. My partner grabs me and we sit for a second behind some kind of piece of machinery that looks like it was used to compress garbage. I'm catching my breath and trying to get my goddamn heart to stop racing when he says...

"Did you hear that?"

"Of course I did you fool!" I reply.

"What was that? Did you see that shadow move?" He asks.

"No, I didn't see anything. Now let's get the hell out of here." I say.

We continue moving through the factory when we come to a side door. It's got a wooden bar on it so I pull it off and toss it aside. It makes more noise than expected when it clangs on the concrete floor. Exiting into another alleyway I really have no idea where we are. I'm probably going to have to risk going out onto the main road to get a better idea of where we are compared to the planned escape route.

"Hey Er..." I cut him off.

"I said no names! You understand?" I reply.

Smacking him upside the head he acknow-ledges our agreement.

"Where are we going?" He asks.

"This way!" I yell with confidence even though I don't know where to go.

We continue down the alleyway. At the end is a fire escape leading up the side of another build-ing. A big apartment complex. If we can get in through a window and down the other side that will be our way out. We'll get to the roof first and hang there until the cops cool it and then we can make a move for the street. I'm sure one of those apartments belongs to a little old lady, or some stupid gimp, and we can silence them quickly.

I nearly crap my pants for real this time when a rat scurries out from a pile of garbage. I accidentally let out a loud yelp. Hold it together man. Trying to play it cool I gesture to my partner to keep going.

"Come on. Let's hurry." He says.

He walks off into the darkness and I lose track of him. A sudden noise makes me grab for a gun that I no longer have. I remember that I dropped it in the car and I'm sure as shit not going back now to try and get it. I'm squinting to try and see in the dark as my partner, screaming, comes flying through the air at me. With no time to react and a heavy thud the two of us collide and fall to the ground. This bastard is bigger than he looks and I got the wind knocked out of me. I take a couple deep breaths.

"Get the hell off of me!" I say.

I push him off of me and then we scramble to get back to our feet. I turn and look into the darkness of the alleyway.

Those eyes...

"You've got to be kidding me!"

CHAPTER 18

Ian

Following the radio I found in Bram's cave I'm up on a rooftop looking down at the street. I feel really cool dressed in this outfit. It's like a strange dream that has somehow come true.

Back at the cave I convinced myself this was a good idea. I put on the whole outfit, cape and all, and stared in the mirror for probably ten minutes straight. Posing and taunting. Shadowboxing. The eye lenses emit a white light and in the dark it's definitely creepy. The outfit is equipped with what I think is bulletproof lining. It's a thick muscle suit that doesn't quite fit right which is unsurprising since it wasn't made for me.

On the belt is a button that I can press to hear the police band radio inside my mask. I press it. For a second there is static but then a voice comes through...

"Suspects are on foot. Two men, approximately six feet tall wearing ski masks. They are armed and dangerous. We have one confirmed casualty and an officer down. Proceed with extreme caution. They were last seen heading north on Delmont Drive." The voice on the radio says.

Delmont. That's where I am. I scan the street below me but I don't see any activity. The lenses in the mask also seem to have some sort of vision enhancer. My eyesight isn't poor but I feel like I can see extremely well with this thing on. Everything is super crisp and detailed.

Suddenly, I see them. Two guys in ski masks. One carrying a large duffle bag. They dart down the alley below me and bust into the building that I am on the roof of. I'm starting to hyperventilate. Am I scared? Excited? What in the world am I doing?

"Calm down, Ian. This is just like before a fight. Take some deep breaths. Visualize your attack and follow through." I say to myself, still trying desperately to convince myself that this was a good idea.

I can't believe I'm doing this. I can back out now and be fine. No one will ever know that you put this thing on and you can go back to being a normal everyday kind of guy.

But you're not...

I open the roof access and enter the building.

Moving along the rafters like a cat I get a view of them. They are moving slowly. I guess they can't see very well. Luckily for me this suit has a light amplification ability so I can see fine in the dark. Bram, you truly are an amazing man. If he built all this stuff on his own he is a certifiable genius.

Oh damn. I accidentally knocked a rusted bolt off the scaffold. It falls to the ground and makes a sharp ping.

The two thugs jump behind some piece of machinery. I can't see where exactly they went. I need to be more careful. Skulking as slowly as I can I find them once again. They open up an exit door, toss a heavy wooden bar to the ground, and leave. Following closely behind I slip out a window onto a fire escape. They are heading down the alley and I can't pursue unless I get to the ground. Quickly looking around I see a wire leading from the fire escape across the alley to another fire escape that connects to the opposite building. Giving it a tug I check to see if it can hold my weight. What the hell am I thinking? I grab the wire tight with my hands and a memory of gym class in elementary school comes to mind.

I start across the wire. Hand over hand trying to be as quiet as possible. With every movement my body tenses. A fall from this height would most likely kill me, or at the very least break both my legs. I'm right above these guys and somehow they haven't thought to look up. The gloves I'm wearing have a strong grip so my fear of slipping off starts to go away. Getting to the other building, my heart skips a beat when I hear one of the guys let out a shout. They've seen me. They must have seen me.

It was only a rat.

Reaching out with my foot I get my leg over the railing and pull myself to the other side. I work my way down the steps of the fire escape, trying to be as quiet and sneaky as possible, and to the street below. Crouching down behind a pile of garbage one of the thugs approaches me. I think about what I'm doing. Truly think about it.

They have guns.

They are murderers.

You're going to die.

You're going to die.

You. Are. Going. To. Die.

Maybe that's what you wanted when you put on this suit. An excuse to get yourself killed. And would that be so bad? Maybe this is it. Maybe this is my time. One final blaze of glory and then it's off to be back with Gloria and Rona.

Gloria...

"You can be anything you want to be. Do anything you want to do." I hear Gloria's voice inside my head. "I love you, Ian."

"You're the best daddy in the whole world!" Rona says as she wraps her arms around my leg. I pick her up and give her the biggest hug. She giggles and the corners of my lips force themselves up.

Popping out as if from nowhere I deck one of the thugs right in the face. The lead shot in the knuckles of my gloves makes his face feel like breaking an eggshell. When I connect I hear a loud satisfying crack. His nose is definitely shattered. I've broken plenty of noses in my time so I know that I'm right. He goes flying back into his friend knocking both of them to the ground. They scramble and get back to their feet. The one I punched is grabbing his face and groaning. Blood streaming from under his hands.

Well... It's now or never.

"Gloria. Rona. I love you."

I step out of the darkness.

"You've got to be kidding me!" The one I didn't hit says.

Without thinking I rush in and blast him with a front kick that sends him into the alleyway wall. I quickly twist around and backhand the other guy.

This is going well. Surprisingly well.

I pounce onto the guy I just backhanded. Rearing back to land another punch my cape gets grabbed by the other guy. He yanks me and I fall onto my back. I've never fought two people before, well, maybe back in the schoolyard but this is a whole different animal. This is getting tricky. Visualize and attack.

Springing to my feet I grab my own cape, and with all my might yank it back causing the guy to come rushing at me. Landing a devastating clothesline I send him to the ground with a heavy thud. His head snaps back against the concrete.

Broken nose guy comes at me. I throw a couple punches that whiff big time. Crap, this guy has a bit of training and I'm not used to moving in this suit. It's heavy and throws off my balance. He rushes at me again and I try to duck but he still punches me in the head. The mask has protection but I still feel the impact. My arms get grabbed from behind. The other guy is holding me back. Struggling, I try to break free. Broken nose guy pulls a gun.

I think back to a night long ago. O'Shaunessy and his goon squad in the alley behind the BARe Knuckle...

"Gloria..."

Oh no.

Oh no.

Ian.

Think.

I push backward and drive the guy into the wall. His head, bashing off the bricks, makes a sickening crunch. Without thinking I turn around to incapacitate him. Two loud gunshots echo through the alleyway. I feel sharp impacts in my back. Tumbling to the ground it feels like I just got hit with a sledgehammer. I can't seem to catch my breath. Taking sips instead of full breaths I reach for my back. Am I dying? The pain is unlike anything I have ever felt. Get a grip, Ian. Remember where you are. Remember who you are. Tough as nails and just as stubborn. Get to your feet now!

Suddenly, my face is greeted with a kick. Blood rushes into my mouth. It's my nose. I guess turnabout is fair play. Rolling over onto my back I look up into a smoggy starless night sky. It's beautiful in its own way. The smog dances with itself, catching the light from the street lamps and cars passing by. I wonder if screaming for help would do me any good. The floor of the alley is cold and wet, or is that my back gushing blood? The pain is an overwhelming pressure like I'm slowly being crushed in a trash compactor. I think of Aaron.

Lying in a pool of his own blood. What a horrible way to go. He deserved it. But now is my come-uppance. They say when a man seeks revenge, he should start by digging two graves...

A barrel is pressed to my forehead. This is it. Just pull the trigger and get it over with.

"Time to say goodnight." The man with the gun says.

Am I seeing things or is there another person with them?

"Goodnight!" A feminine voice commands.

The guy turns and is blasted in the face by a palm strike. Blood and what I think are teeth shoot out into the night air. Suddenly, I'm starting to get my wits back. The pain in my back has gone from sharp to numb.

This is your chance.

As hard as I can I up kick the other guy in the balls. He lets out a huge yelp like a beaten dog. He grabs his balls and starts coughing. He vomits. I know that was dirty but this isn't a situation where playing by the rules will earn me points. He stumbles backward and the woman grabs him around the waist. She tosses him overhead with a wrestling suplex, slamming him hard on his neck on the concrete. Both guys are completely incapacitated.

I'm finally back up on one knee. The pain in my back is still throbbing but I can breathe with moderate ease again. I take several deep breaths. An outstretched hand appears before me. It's very feminine with long narrow fingers and a flawless bright pink manicure. Grabbing it she pulls me up to my feet with an unexpected amount of strength.

She is about a head shorter than me. Looking down I'm greeted with an adorable smile. She's maybe in her mid-twenties and vaguely ethnic. Her face is done up immaculately with makeup. Winged eyeliner, blue eyeshadow, glitter on her cheeks, and bright pink lipstick. Her hair is absolutely wild. It's dyed purple and is crazy long. It's all flipped to one side and slowly fades to pink at the tips.

She's dressed in a full getup. Denim jacket with the sleeves rolled up past the elbows. Purple fingerless gloves. A dark purplish-red leotard with a black trim zipped up to the neck. Her chest is pushed up by some kind of protective breastplate under the leotard. A white utility belt similar to mine hangs low on her waist and her thick powerful legs are sheathed in tan nylons with calf-high white athletic socks with two purple stripes. Black Dr. Marten boots finish off the look. She's simultaneously glamorous and punk rock.

"Are you ok?" She asks.

I'm so confused. I'm just standing here like an idiot in an outfit I found in an old man's basement being talked to by one of the most attractive women I have ever seen. What the hell is going on? How did I get here? My head is absolutely spinning.

"Hey." She places her hand on the side of my face. "Are you ok?" She asks again.

Somehow I find the ability to nod. Something about her smile and the way her hair is flipped makes me think of Gloria, even though the two looking nothing alike. A loud police siren snaps me out of my trance.

"Can you run?" She asks. "Because that's my cue."

I don't think it was so much a question as a request as she takes off running into the darkness. Doing my best to follow after her she climbs the fire escape like it's nothing. It's almost like watching an Olympic level gymnast tackle the bars. Before I know it she's on the roof and out of sight. I'm climbing as quick as I can but the injuries I just sustained, plus the weight of this suit, are making things difficult. Her head pops back over the edge.

"Are you coming or not?" She says with a smile.

That smile.

CHAPTER 19

Alex

Back at my apartment after work I'm in my underwear and dancing to The Psychedelic Furs. I let the music take over and my body moves almost on its own. My eyes close and all I can think about is every possible scenario I might encounter in my nightly romps. The hairs on my arms raise and I feel butterflies in my stomach. The excitement has hit me like a brick. My dancing has shifted into a display of combat techniques. The blood is rushing through me and I feel high. It's almost time. Every night it's like I'm born again.

In the bathroom I tear off this stupid, itchy wig, followed by the hair net. My beautiful purple locks fall down. Pulling out the hairspray I go ape shit on it. Tossing my hair side to side to the beat of the music, I consider wearing it to the left today. Nope. Right. I flip it over and spray the crap out of it. My fingers gliding through it, I push up the front and then slide it down to my shoulder and beyond.

Rolling on my nylons, pulling up my socks, and then zipping up my battle suit I can't help but flex in the mirror. My arms are looking really nice. I'm such a goofball.

Doing my nails I sing to myself "pretty in pink". When they are dry I toss on my jacket and roll up the sleeves. Then I do my makeup. I think a light blue eyeshadow would look good tonight. Eyeliner next. I top it off with bright pink lipstick. "Be Foxy" indeed. Something is missing. I reach into my work uniform and pull out that glitter stuff I stole from Tamara. Dipping my finger into it I rub a small amount across each cheekbone. Then I go a little crazy and put some into my hair. Making a kissy face at myself in the mirror, pursing my lips, I can't help but feel incredibly hot.

"I'm so punk rock."

Flipping on the police radio I crash on the couch with my legs in the air. I put on one boot, and then the other. I listen closely while also crisscrossing and scissor kicking my legs. Pretty boring night so far. Minor traffic violation here, jaywalker there. Come on! Give me something to work with. I want blood!

"Silent alarm triggered. Possible armed robbery at 14th and 10th. Please proceed with caution." The voice on the radio says.

Her name is Devra. Like Debra but with a V. I'd like to meet her someday. I wonder if the image in my head of her is anything like what she actually looks like. People's voices are the most deceptive thing in the whole world.

It doesn't take me long to get to the roof of my building. I saved up a ton of money and hired a private contractor to have a secret exit and entrance built. I chose this building for a reason. It's right in the heart of the city. I can get anywhere and the roof is in a perfect position to see out in all directions. It also helps that hardly anyone lives here other than me. If I hadn't cleaned it up my apartment would be a dump just like all the others. No one wants to live here for a reason. Just some old lady and her billion cats and some sketchy drug addicts, but they might just be squatters. For me, it's perfect. Some nights I stay up just looking out into the city. In the summer all the lights and sounds of the city are like watching a symphony being conducted just for me.

On the roof I think to myself for a second. 14th and 10th? That's on the west side. I take off running. Leaping between buildings like I've done it a million times because I have. I know routes to almost every corner of this city. I practiced for a whole year, planning out dozens of street-less runs. This city is mine. She is my lover. And I won't let anyone put baby in the corner.

Between 13th and 10th the only good way to get to the next street is by jumping on a pretty dodgy flag pole. Coming to it, I leap. My hands grasp it and I feel it snap. If I was only half paying attention I would have been done for. Not so gracefully I snag the ledge of the opposite building. Hopping onto that rooftop I turn back. I'll have to figure out another way to get here in the future since that pole is out of commission. Pressing onward I arrive at the roof of the building of the supposed robbery. I've beaten the cops. Suckers. They wish they had half of my talent and abilities. The city might be crime-free if the force was a couple dozen of my clones. But if that were the case then I wouldn't have the opportunity to have this much fun.

The sirens wail as a cop car pulls up. Only one car? Come on guys. The perps come running out and get in their car. A crappy old rust bucket. Now they're flooring it and I have to try and keep up.

For some reason they wreck their car. They got ahead of me and I missed why. The thugs spill out of their vehicle. I doubt it can still drive wrapped around a telephone pole like that. The cops are right on them with guns drawn. I guess that means my playtime is over. Oh well.

One of the thugs pulls a gun and just as fast shoots one of the cops. The younger of the two, not the old fat one. I think the young one's name is Stapleton. Not sure. Poor baby. The perps take off running. The old cop returns fire but misses, woefully so. Following as fast as I can I track them to Delmont Drive. They are heading north. I need to get across the street. Frantically I look all around me. There must be something for me to utilize. Reaching into my belt I pull out my wire launcher. I haven't used it that much over the years and never a distance this far but I have to risk it. This went from a robbery to a possible homicide. This is serious.

The roof I'm on has a water tower and the

building across the street seems to be solid brick so I should be good. I twist one end of the wire launcher around one of the supports of the water tower. Aiming as best as I can I pull the trigger. The dart goes flying across the street with a soft thwipping sound and imbeds into the brick of the opposite building. No time to test it. I leap up and rush across the wire. One foot in front of the other. The best way to do it is to not look down and go as fast as possible. Basically how I felt when doing balance beam, which, for the record, was my worst event. I'm literally over a hundred feet up. One false step and I'm a pancake. Making it across unscathed I have no time to try and retrieve the wire. I leave it and press on.

The perps head down an alleyway just as I catch up to them. Going to jump down I stop myself as they break into some old abandoned factory. Not knowing the layout I'm hesitant to go right in after them. There are just too many variables. The distance between buildings is only about thirty feet. I make a running leap and land with perfection on the roof of the old factory.

What in the name of?

I swear I just saw a guy with a mask and cape go through the roof access.

My heart stops.

The Apparition. He's real! He's really real! I knew it. I'd been working these streets for years and not once come across another vigilante. It has to be him. I mean, it's gotta be, right? Stop fangirling,

Alex. Remember who you are.

I hang back. I want to see where this all goes.

Carefully, being sure he doesn't see me, I follow behind him. Up on the rafters, inside the factory, I'm just a few steps behind. He kicks over some nut or bolt that falls to the factory floor with a loud ping. Kind of a rookie mistake if you ask me but I guess it can happen to the best of us. He's watching them and I'm watching him. This is so terrifyingly surreal. I'm surprised he hasn't noticed me. A keen sense of my surroundings was one of the first things I developed.

The two thugs exit the building and he follows after them going out through a window that leads to a fire escape. Sneaking quietly I stalk him like some kind of pervert weirdo. Looking out the window I see that he can't get down to the ground from here. I wonder what an expert like him will do?

Ok? He's climbing hand over hand on a clothesline that I'm pretty sure won't hold his weight. They say to respect your elders but he could have just used the ledge of the building, crawled out a little bit, and jumped. It would have been quicker and far less risky.

One of the perps lets out a yelp and our mysterious hero hesitates on the wire. He regains his composure and makes it to the other fire escape. Once he's down on the ground I pop outside and sit on the ledge. My feet dangling in the night air. I'm sure I'm in for a show. If only I had some popcorn.

Hmm... Not quite what I was expecting. He's got some fighting chops but he's really just a brawler. At least he seems to have things under control. One of the guys grabs his cape. See, that's the problem with capes. Anyone can just grab them and use it against you.

He grabs a handful of his own cape and yanks the guy towards him. He follows up with a brutal clothesline. Now that was a great move!

I must have been mesmerized by what I was seeing because I didn't see the gun. Two loud gunshots echo up to my ears. My eyes go wide.

Oh shit. He's on the ground. This isn't good. Come on man! Get up and fight! What's the problem? You're too tough for this!

Thinking back to the old Apparition comics I used to read, there would always be a cliffhanger just like this. Our hero would be in peril only to narrowly escape in the next issue.

Is there going to be a next issue?

This is getting bad. He's not moving. I need to do something and fast or he is totally going to bite the big one. No time to get to the other fire escape, I have to jump from here. I take a deep breath. Eyes focused. I raise my hands to the sky and hear the crowd scream for me.

"Alex! Alex! Alex!" They chant.

The hair on my arms stand up. A chill rolls up my spine. My stomach fills with butterflies and my heart starts pounding.

Every night I am born again.

Leaping into the air I twist and front flip right before hitting the ground. Perfect landing. Ten out of ten. The crowd goes wild. I barely make a sound. The thugs don't even notice me.

I'm so damn cool.

"Time to say goodnight." One of them says.

I grab him by the shoulder.

I grin ear to ear.

He turns and looks at me.

"Goodnight."

CHAPTER 20

Officer Marsters

"We need a bus! We need a bus at the corner of Delmont and 10th! Officer down! Officer down!" I scream into my radio.

In the back of the ambulance I'm putting pressure on Stapleton's wound while the EMT is getting things ready. Hitting a bump in the road I lose my grip. Shit. He's bleeding like a stuck pig. We're both covered in blood. There is blood everywhere. Feeling sweat dripping down my forehead I go to wipe it and accidentally wipe blood onto my face. Damn.

"I'm dying!" He yells.

"No, you're not! You're going to be fine!" I do my best to reassure him but things are not looking great.

Finally the EMT starts working on him and I get a moment to catch my breath. I've really let myself go. Jesus, my gut is bloated out like crazy and I've gotten winded just lifting a donut to my mouth. I should have retired like Crenick. That son of a bitch is living it up in some sweet townhouse. I don't know how he affords it. Must have been on the take. We were all good cops but a man's got to pay his bills. That's why I'm still working and will probably stay on the force until they have to push me out the door.

Seeing the kid bleeding all over the place makes me think about those crime scene photos I saw from Sarge's murder. Got his head crushed by some hired goon. It was one of the most gruesome things I've ever seen and I've seen some serious shit. Asshole deserved it no doubt. He probably messed with someone he shouldn't have.

I haven't heard from Carmine in a while. He was a good guy. One of the best of us. I hope he is doing well.

The ambulance hits another bump and the three of us bounce around like some kind of funhouse. Feeling my pants tear up the back I regret not buying one size up. I wasn't willing to admit to myself the truth.

"Hey, keep an eye on the road!" I yell to the driver. He doesn't say anything back.

Resting my head up against the interior of the ambulance I close my eyes for a moment. I almost dozed off but the damn kid started screaming again. We should be at the hospital any minute now. I've got a microwave dinner and a big glass of beer waiting for me at home. As soon as we get Stapleton's ass secure I'm heading right there. Take a nice long shower and plop down in front of the TV. My favorite show is on tonight. That game show "Who Done it?". I like that hot blonde cohost with the legs that go on for miles.

It feels like it's taking a really long time to get to the hospital. Sticking my face in the window I realize we've left the city. We're on backroads somewhere. All I can see are trees whizzing by and darkness. No other cars in sight.

"Hey, driver! Driver! Where are we going? Saint Maria's was the closest hospital. There was no need to leave the city!" I yell to him.

"Turn around! We need to get to Saint Maria's right away or this officer is going to bleed out!" The EMT echoes my sentiments.

I can feel the ambulance accelerating. The trees are flying by outside the window and have turned into a blur. Turning to the EMT we exchange a confused glance.

"What the hell's up with this guy?" I ask him.

"I don't know." He replies. "Driver, stop right now and turn around!" He yells.

The ambulance continues to increase in speed. We hit a huge bump as we go off the road. I smack my head on an overhanging shelf. Now we are headed through some huge cornfield. The corn stalks slapping against the side of the ambulance sound like thousands of tiny drum beats. With a lack of better options I draw my gun and point it at the driver.

"Stop this bus now!" I scream.

Thumbing back the hammer I desperately do not want to fire. Through the windshield I can see a clearing up ahead with a big tree in the middle. A tree that we are rapidly approaching. The driver paying me no mind whatsoever opens the door and leaps from the vehicle!

"Oh shit!" I yell.

Some time has passed. I don't know how long. Coming to in the wreck of the ambulance, it takes me a minute to get my wits about me. The smell of gas permeates the air. Smoke starts coming in from the cab. Coughing hard, and choking, I scramble to get to the back door. The EMT is dead. His upper body is crushed. I can't even see it. Just his legs sticking out from under the overhead shelf that collapsed on top of him. Stapleton seems in one piece but he's unconscious. He won't last long without help. I need to do something. The door is jammed shut. Slamming my body as hard as I can I'm able to get it open but I tumble to the ground outside. Damn, I threw my back out.

"Ahhh!" I moan.

I struggle to try and get to my feet for a few moments when suddenly something catches my eye. Only a few yards away is what appears to be a very large person standing at the edge of the cornfield. Rubbing my eyes I try to get a better look. His face seems distorted for some reason. I rub my eyes again. I can't tell who it is. Maybe it's one of the farmers from this area. He must have seen the wreck and decided to help.

"Hey! Hey! We need help over here! Call 911." I yell to him.

At first he just stands and stares at me, seemingly ignoring my pleas.

Maybe it's just a scarecrow? Maybe I bumped my head a little too hard and now I'm having a delusion?

Then he starts to approach. That's one big mother. What's farmer John been eating? As he gets closer I can tell that it's not his face that's distorted but he's wearing a mask.

"What's with the mask? It's not Halloween just yet." I say.

Crawling towards him through the muck I'm desperate for help. My back is in so much pain. I'm starting to think I broke it. Suddenly, I smell something burning. I turn back and see the ambulance burst into flames. Stapleton!

"My friend! He's in the ambulance! Help him!" I beg the stranger.

I grasp at his pant legs and try to tug myself up but it's no use.

"Help?" The stranger replies in a cold and low voice.

The ambulance is completely engulfed in flames. If Stapleton wasn't dead before he is now. My only reprieve is I don't hear any screaming. I pray to God that Stapleton was already dead. Poor boy.

Wait until I get my hands on the driver. I'm not going to arrest him. I'm going to put a bullet through his head.

A huge hand grabs me by the throat. What is happening?

"Hey, what the hell?" I shout.

I feel my feet come off the ground as he easily lifts me into the air. All 350lbs of my fat ass. Finally, I get a good look at him. Long dark hair cascades over a strange twisted skull-like mask. It's all cracked, spattered with blood, and sporting a disturbing grimace. The eyes are blank, black, emotionless holes. I can hear his breathing. A heavy deep rasp. His neck is about as wide as my waist and has several huge, pipe-like veins. They are pulsing in a way I find most grotesque. His hands begin to close around my throat and now I really can't breathe. I'm choking and gasping for air. I try for my gun but it must have fallen out in the crash. My holster hangs empty at my side.

"You look cold." A deep disturbing voice echoes from behind the mask. "You are starting to turn blue."

Grabbing at his enormous hands I'm rapidly losing strength and I can't do anything to fight him off. My legs kick fruitlessly. I feel something pop and the metallic taste of blood rushes into my mouth. I would gag if I could breathe.

"Let me help you get warm." He retorts.

Carrying me, as if I were a baby, we get closer and closer to the fiery wreckage of the ambulance. Oh, God. Not like this. Before I can do anything he's holding my head in the fire. The pain is agonizing and unending. I'm praying to go into shock but somehow I don't. The smell of burning flesh is the most disgusting part. It fills my nose as the fire spreads across my body. I'm screaming. I'm screaming and flailing and he's just grinning at me. Through the flames a grinning skull. I pray for a vision of a beautiful woman or sweet angels to come and take me away but all I see is that twisted grimace. No white light. No family calling my name.

My screams have grown silent.

The last thing I see before I go blind is that twisted face.

That last thing I hear is a deep hollow laugh.

The Devil has come to collect his due.

God... Not like this...

CHAPTER 21

Ian

We've been on this rooftop for ten minutes and she's just been staring at me. I wonder if I should just leave or not. Should I say the first word or should I wait? What's the respectable thing to do in this situation? Has this situation ever happened before? Ever? So many thoughts rushing through my mind. This woman just saved me from certain death. I owe her big time. Of all the women I have known, I've never seen one who could easily take out two armed thugs like that. I'm kind of in shock. She's muscular but feminine, hard-edged but delicate. Powerful and yet graceful. Her smile is so bright it could light up a whole room and those baby brown eyes are so warm and inviting. How did she end up doing what she's doing? What series of events lead her to this very moment. I think about how I ended up here and a hole begins to open in my chest.

"So, who are you?" She finally speaks.

I don't know how to reply. Do I tell her my real name? Do I come up with a fake name? I hadn't thought of a name. I probably shouldn't try to come up with something on the spot and say something stupid that might stick. Hell, I didn't think I'd even make it this far. This whole situation is completely unprecedented. Suddenly, I think about the pain from those gunshots. It hasn't taken me long to realize this outfit is bulletproof. The pain, at this point, has changed to just a minor nuisance. I silently thank Bram. He saved me again without even knowing it.

"Hey, did you hear me or what?" She says, getting impatient.

I've just been standing here awkwardly silent. She crosses her arms and starts tapping her foot. Gloria used to tap her foot when she was getting anxious too.

"Look, I can tell you are new to this. When someone asks you a question it's customary to answer them." She says. "It's called being respectful."

Oh yeah. The name. I don't have one. I'm not going to give her my real name.

"Do you have a death wish or something? Going all 'Charles Bronson' are you?" She asks.

Oh, ok. Forget the name. Just move on. Say something damn it!

"No." I reply.

No. That's it. No. That's all you've got? Ok. She's not wrong though. You know deep inside part of you was kinda hoping to die.

"Hey! He speaks. Congrats! You're not a mute!" She jests.

"Thanks for saving my life."

"You're welcome." She says as she approaches me. My heart sinks.

Just come up with some excuse and leave.

"I'm an idiot. I apologize for inconveniencing you. I'm going to leave now." I say like an emotionless robot.

I turn and head for the roof access.

"Hey! Hey! Hey! You're not getting off that easy!" She says as she grabs me and pushes me against the wall.

She is remarkably strong for only being about five foot three. She pushes her finger into my chest. Her face is mere inches from mine.

"I need some answers!" She says.

Her nose has the cutest freckles. I can tell she tries to cover them up although I'm not sure why. The makeup has slightly worn off.

"I'm just a nobody." I say.

"Everyone is someone to somebody." She replies. "Look. I can tell you have fighting experience..."

"Boxing." I reply for some reason.

"Ah... Now we are getting somewhere." She grins. "The outfit? Did you buy it? Make it? Have your butler design it?"

"I found it."

I think of Bram again. Don't mention him you idiot. Why does it seem like you can't keep your mouth shut? You were doing just fine with that before.

"What do you mean, you found it?" She asks with an inquisitive look on her face.

"I found a secret entrance to an abandoned...

room in my house. All of this stuff was in there. Somehow I got this half baked idea in my head that I could handle this and I think it's clear that I can't. This stuff doesn't even fit that well. I don't know what I was thinking so I think it's best we just go our own ways."

"Oh hell no! You're taking me there right now!" Her smile goes ear to ear.

I can't say no.

I'm like a schoolboy with a crush.

What is happening to me?

Back at Bram's cave she is like a kid in a candy store. She's looking at all the devices and gadgets. Sitting down in the chair in front of the computer backward she spins around and reaches her arms over the back of the seat. She starts typing on the keyboard.

"Access denied!" The voice on the computer says.

"I already tried." I say to her.

"Damn!" She says as she slams her hand down on the keyboard.

"Well, don't break it!" I retort.

"Sorry, Dad." She says as she turns back to me. "How did you find this place again?"

"See that slide?" I point to it. "That leads to a trap door in my house. My guess is whoever lived here before me was our mysterious hero."

Don't let her know you know who that mysterious hero is. Bram chose to not tell me. I'm going to honor his silence.

"You know who that was, right?" She asks.

"No idea." I lie, but under this mask she probably can't tell.

Gloria could always tell when I was lying. She said my face moved in a certain way that it was painfully obvious.

"This was the cave of The Apparition!" She says with glee.

I have no idea who that is. I mean, I know who Bram is but I had never heard that name before... Wait. Yes I have. I think I remember seeing comics with that name on it. It's clear to me. That was his superhero name. Superhero? Did I just think that? I stop myself from smirking. I shrug my shoulders as to continue the lie.

"He was a superhero in the fifties. Supposedly took down a huge mafia syndicate. It was reported in the papers, well, the tabloids, but the police denied it all. I knew he was real and this confirms it. This is so freaking cool!" She says. "The comics I had were based on true stories! Maybe not the one where he stopped the mad scientist from destroying Lochland with a giant laser, but the smaller stories."

She is glowing. The way she talks about this makes me feel warm inside. Her happiness is infectious. She hops up from the chair and goes over to the costume hanging in the tube.

"This is the costume I remember from the comics. It looks insanely goofy in real life. How did anyone take him seriously?" She says turning to me. "The one you are wearing is definitely more modern but the 'trunks on the outside look' is so passe."

I thought I looked pretty badass.

"Hey, come here!" She gestures to me. "Turn around."

She grabs the back of my cape and yanks it. The bullet holes in the back made it brittle and the lower quarter easily tears away.

"There you go. Now you're a little more 'you'."

Catching my reflection I see the cape is tattered and scalloped at the bottom giving it an edgier look. She's definitely right. This is more me.

"I wonder what happened to The Apparition? He's got to be retired at this point. Or dead." She says with a hint of sadness in her voice.

"Maybe he's just on a boat, sailing the seas, relaxing the rest of his days away." I reply.

"That's lame as hell! Definitely not a fitting end for someone so legendary." She laughs.

If she only knew.

"When I found this place it hadn't been touched in years but everything was neatly stored. I don't think he left in a hurry. Hopefully he's somewhere nice and he's happy." I say thinking of Bram, his boat, and all the adventures we had.

The year we spent together will forever be with me. His impression reaching out past that even now. Maybe it was his plan all along to have me here. In this costume. Maybe he saw something in me that I couldn't see. He and Gloria, always trying to get the best out of me.

"Ok, so are we going to address the elephant in the room or not?" She says to me.

"And what's that?" I ask.

"You are still wearing the mask."

She's right. I haven't taken it off. She crashes back down in the chair and throws her feet up on the desk. Leaning up against a workbench I consider taking it off, but I don't know if I can trust her. She saved my life but who is she really? Maybe she's an undercover cop and this is all some giant sting operation? Maybe I've watched a little too much cable TV.

"Take it off!" She demands.

"Can I trust you?"

She looks pissed.

"Trust me? I just saved your life you jackass. Plus you can see my adorable face."

She points at her dimples and smiles hugely. I'm still hesitant.

"Oh come on! Are you Tom Cruise? Are you Alec Baldwin under there? No? Then just take the damn thing off."

She does have a valid point. I'm really a no-body. My name was briefly in the news after the fight with O'Shaunessy but that was it. I quickly retired after that to start a family with Gloria. The payday from that fight paid for us to buy a house. That minute of fame I had for killing someone in the ring faded quick, like trying to remember a dream hours after waking. The phone calls stopped after a couple weeks, the paparazzi shortly thereafter. Especially with guys like George Foreman and Muhammad Ali taking center stage. If it wasn't for me people might be saying Aaron O'Shaunessy in the same breath.

"Why don't you wear a mask?" I retort.

"Just not my style, plus it's not like people have a camera in their pocket ready to go. Not a single news report or magazine article has gotten my description even close. Plus, no man I know is willing to admit that they got their ass beat by a girl. Probably wouldn't go over well in prison either. Some of the early reports even said I was a dude! Can you believe that? With a body like this? And this outfit? Come on!"

She stands and poses. Tossing her hair to the side and bringing up one knee, slightly arching her back. Inside of me the embers of a fire begin to glow.

"Is that thing even protective?" I ask.

"You bet your ass it is! The whole thing is made from a lightweight... Hey! Stop distracting me!"

She pushes me playfully.

"Take it off or I'm going to snatch it off your head!" She warns.

Ok. Just do it. You've gone this far. No turning back now. The mask clips into the neck. It's really more like a helmet. Using my index fingers I push in the clips and they release. I grab both sides of the mask and slowly pull it off. There is blood dried on the inside. Based on her reaction I can tell I don't look so good. My nose definitely got busted up earlier. If there is blood on my face it's most likely dry too.

"That bad, huh?" I ask.

"I've seen worse... I've done worse." She replies with a half-smile.

"It's fine. I told you I was a boxer, right? I'm used to that look. I've had my face broken more than once."

She leaves for a second and comes back with a wet towel from the bathroom. Her gloves shoved into one of the pockets on her utility belt. She gently wipes my face. Her face is so close to mine I feel her breath kiss my cheek. She's even more beautiful than I thought. For someone so tough, her touch is gentle and caring. Upon close inspection I can see signs of scars covered with makeup. Her knuckles also show that they have been broken before. Her finger pads are heavily callused as well. No doubt from gymnastics experience. She's also had dental work done. I wonder for a second that if in this line of work she's had her teeth knocked out before. I can't imagine any sane person, let alone a woman, wanting to get into this kind of life.

All of a sudden, my heart is racing. A memory of going to a school dance when I was thirteen years old leaps to the front of my mind. It was the first time I ever touched a girl. Carolynn Jenkins. She had short, curly blonde hair and big metal braces on her teeth. I wasn't even that attracted to her but my hands on her hips were enough to get me aroused and send butterflies into my stomach. That's the same feeling I'm having right now.

"Thanks."

"No problem." She replies.

She sits back down in the chair and stares at me.

"So what's your deal, man?" She asks. "How did you end up dressed in that outfit talking to a strange woman in a cave on a Friday night? I'm sure you must have had some other, less dangerous, things you could have been doing."

"No, not really." I say. "You know that face you made when I took off the mask? I've seen it a lot. From my wife."

Maybe I should have left out the family. Too late now.

"Oh? You're married? Tell me all about her!"

She places her hands under her chin in an undeniably cute way. How do I put this without sounding like a weirdo...

"She's dead."

Good job, Ian. You officially failed at not sounding like a complete creep.

That's the first time I've said that aloud. It felt weird. Why am I sharing so much? Bram saved my life too and I didn't tell him much of anything.

"Oh... I'm sorry." She says trying to sound empathetic.

I don't blame her. She doesn't know me or my life. It's sad when someone dies but if you don't know them it can sometimes be hard to pretend it means more to you than it does.

"It's ok. It was a few years ago."

Is it ok? Am I ok? I haven't thought about it in this way for so long. The image of Gloria and Rona in their coffins makes my heart feel like it's about to tear apart. I grit my teeth.

Stop.

"Can I ask how it happened?" She asks.

I can't blame her for being curious. This is definitely an out of the ordinary situation we are both in.

"Car accident. They were stopped at an intersection. A truck driver, he, just, well, fell asleep at the wheel."

"They?" She replies.

Rona. My sweet little Rona. Her beautiful brown curls. Her rosy cheeks. That laugh that would put me on the moon. My little girl.

"My daughter. Rona."

She is stunned. I'd be too. Some strange man sharing these intimate details of his life. For a second she pauses but she hops up on the workbench next to me.

"My mom's dead." She says. "She got breast cancer. They found it too late. There wasn't much the doctors could do other than make her comfortable. I was devastated... She was the only one who truly believed in me."

"What about your father?" I ask.

"He had a complete break. We were never really close and I guess he just couldn't handle it all. After she died he just left. I think he went back to Japan but I don't know. I was a failure in his eyes so there was no reason for him to stay. He'd given up."

"I'm sorry to hear that."

I think of my own father. He was a good, but heavily flawed, man. Worked himself to death. He died at just fifty years old from a heart attack. He only said it once, but when he was drunk one night after I won a fight he told me he was proud of me. My mom now lives up in Canada somewhere. I haven't spoken to her in years. We just grew apart. She never even met Gloria or Rona.

"Look, we are getting somewhere." She says with a smile. "How did you meet your wife? Give me the short version. I don't need the 'I never saw someone so lovely'."

"So...I was fighting at a carnival. I fought Big John Calloway. He was a big redheaded guy. Like six foot three with a mean right hook... Anyway it was a second round knock out. One of my first big wins. Afterward I was taking a walk around the fairgrounds. Checking out all the booths. It was a big deal in that town. All the local vendors would set up tents. It was mostly just hand made crafts and stuff like that. She was working at the snack shop, volunteering. They had one of those huge tower drop rides right next to it. You know, where they put you in a chair and raise it up a couple hundred feet and then drop you? Well, something malfunctioned and the thing toppled over. A whole lot of people died. It crushed a bunch of tents and landed on the roof of the snack shop. The building collapsed before she could get out. She was pinned under the rubble. Everyone was standing around in shock. Several people were screaming. Amidst the chaos I could hear her screaming for help. Something came over me. I'm normally not the type to do something like this but I ran towards the wreckage. I got inside what was left of the building following her pleas for help. There she was, lying under a huge piece of the rafters. I've never seen someone so scared. She was all bloody and crying, tears streaming down her face. Grabbing the rafter I lifted as hard as I could. I wasn't sure I could even do it but it started to move. I remember thinking I was going to have a heart attack or something. I got it up just high enough that she was able to crawl out. I blacked out. Next thing I know she's the one taking care of me. Turns out she was a nurse. Lying there on the gurney, with her checking to see if I was ok, was the first time in my life that I think I truly felt happy. "

"Awww. That's so romantic!" She says swooning.

I hadn't thought of that day in a long time. Gloria was my guardian angel. She got me off drugs. She helped me become a better man. Everything that she did has lead me to this very moment.

Is this destiny?

"You said you want to give this up but I don't think that's true. From what you told me I can tell that deep down you are a good person. You wouldn't have put on that costume and you wouldn't be here now with me if you weren't." She says. "Now I don't want to push you into doing anything you don't want to do, especially this dangerous lifestyle I have chosen, but I could use you. Things are getting bad out there on the streets. You've got some skills. I saw it tonight but you're rough around the edges. This isn't like fighting in the ring. There are no rules. You'll hardly ever be in a one on one situation and the risk of guns and knives is always present. I can show you how to handle yourself. Buff out those rough edges."

"You mean like a sidekick?" I say.

"A partner."

She hops up and puts her hand out. It's lingering there in space as I wonder if I should really do this. I've done some crazy things in my life but this would be the top of the list. Looking into her eyes I can tell she's genuine.

"I'm in." I grab her hand.

"Radical!" She exclaims.

Her smile is so absolutely adorable. I can't get over it. She has literally in a matter of minutes convinced me to risk my life for complete strangers, nightly, while wearing a costume. She is an amazing person. My emotions are running high and I'm crushing hard.

"There's someone you should probably meet." She tells me.

"Who?" I ask.

"The police."

Oh no. This was a bust. I'm an idiot.

"The police?" I ask, expecting the handcuffs to come out any second.

"Chill out, man. It's not what you're think-ing." She responds with a wink.

I just realized I don't know this girl's name. Not even her fake one, if she has a fake one.

"By the way, I'm Neon Fire." It's like she read my mind.

All of a sudden, I recall seeing graffiti around the city. It was painted on the wall where those kids were breakdancing. I saw it again down near the docks where I work and on the side of a public bus.

"Believe in Neon Fire." I say in a half-whisper to myself.

"That's me."

"I'm Ian." I say back.

"Alex." She says with a smile.

CHAPTER 22

Alex

I'm running late again. I know Tom is going to be pissed. I've been late at least five times in the past month. I'm pretty sure he's getting sick of it. He hates heights and meeting up on a roof is not his ideal situation. I bet he's sitting there, smoking his cigar, cursing up a storm. At least tonight I have a legitimate excuse. I've got someone for him to meet.

Ian. I've have so much to learn about you. A mysterious man drops into my life with a similar passion to mine. When word got out about me I thought there would be copycats, but I was wrong. I honestly can't believe this is all happening but I have to play it cool. I can't let him see me geek out too much. He seems like an ok dude. Kinda homely looking but he said he was a boxer so that explains some of it. He does have nice eyes though, brown like mine, and that story about how he met his wife. God, it sounds like something out of a trashy romance novel I would have read as a teenager between my gymnastic practices. Thinking about it makes my heart flutter.

We finally get to the roof that Tom and I have been meeting up at for years. It's the building right next to the police station. A library. Hiding in plain sight as they say. I tell Ian to hold back for a minute. Just as I expected, Tom is pacing back and forth, smoking a cigar and cursing under his breath.

"Damn girl, where are you?" He says while looking at his watch.

Maybe I'll make him wait a few more minutes. No! I got it.

Creeping around like a weirdo I get behind him.

"Tom!" I yell as I spring out of the darkness.

He nearly leaps out of his skin.

"Girl, I told you not to sneak up on me like that. You're going to give me a heart attack! Or stroke! Or make me seize up! You want that?" He says.

"What can I say? Your face? Priceless." I can't help but chuckle.

"You're going to be the death of me." He mutters.

"I'm pretty sure those cigars are going to do you in first." I retort.

"I know, I know. You're starting to sound more and more like Melinda. That's probably why I put up with you."

Melinda is his wife. We've never met but she seems like she nags a lot. He showed me a picture once. She's very pretty. Caramel skin and long black curly hair. She's got some curves to her as well, a true full-figured woman.

"Anyway... You're late! Again!" He says.

"I know, but I have a legitimate reason this time."

"If you tell me you broke a nail again I swear I'll slap you upside your head. I know you don't care about that kind of stuff. You're tougher than that."

I did once tell him I was late because I broke a nail. He saw right through it. Somehow it seemed like a better excuse than telling the truth, which was that I fell asleep waiting in a tree in the park to see if any muggings would happen. Needless to say, nothing happened.

"You can come out now!" I yell to Ian.

"Who?" Tom asks as his hand drifts towards his sidearm.

Ian comes out of the darkness. Those glowing eyes on the mask really are effective. Damn... Color me jealous. You know what? He does look pretty freaking badass.

"What in the world?" Tom exclaims.

"This is..."

Oh no. What do I call him? I can't say his real name. That would be stupid. He's not The Apparition so I probably shouldn't call him that either. Think, Alex, think. His outfit is mostly gray...

"Rona Gray." I hesitantly say aloud as the two words randomly combine in my brain.

Ian crosses his arms and bows up his chest making a very powerful looking pose.

"Sir." He says.

"Is he trustworthy?" Tom asks as he strokes his mustache.

"You think I would bring someone here I didn't trust?"

Hey. Look at that. I trust him.

"Well, nice to meet you...Mr. Gray. I'm Detective Tom Hudson." He says while extending his hand for a shake.

Ian doesn't move. I elbow him in the side.

"Come on, don't embarrass me!" I say.

He shakes Tom's hand.

"Kids today. Am I right?" I goof to try and break the tension.

Kid? I just realize that Tom has no idea that this guy is like forty years old. The mask completely covers his face.

"Where'd you meet this guy?" Tom asks.

"Oh you know, at the supermarket. We were discussing our love for pumpkins and justice." I joke.

Tom ashes his cigar without even a chuckle. Ian is silent as well. I don't blame him. This is probably even more awkward for him. Who am I kidding? The most awkward for him. I finally speak to fill up the awkward silence.

"Tough crowd." I say.

"Let's get down to business, shall we?" Tom says.

I cross my arms and do my best to put on a serious face, imitating Ian. I can't help myself from chuckling. Tom even giggles a bit.

"Girl, please." Tom says. "Remember how I said I was concerned we have a cop killer on our hands? Well, I can unfortunately confirm that as fact. He struck again and this time we got a witness."

"A witness?" I ask.

This guy's been bumping off some old cops and there hasn't been a single lead to go off of. What were those guy's names? Phillips, Daigan, Carmine. I wonder who bit the big one now.

"Yeah, a fireman. He told me that as they approached a wrecked ambulance he saw a man run off into a cornfield. A very large man. Six foot five. All muscle. His face, get this, a grimacing skull."

"Who was the cop this time?" I ask.

"It was actually four victims this time. The EMT, a rookie named Stapleton, Officer Marsters, and the ambulance driver. He was found later at the hospital with a broken neck. I think Marsters was the intended target as both the EMT and Stapleton died from injuries caused by the wreck. Marsters wasn't so lucky. His head was burnt to a cinder. It looked like someone, or something, held him in place while he burned." Tom tells us.

"Stapleton, Marsters? I saw them earlier tonight. A rundown gone bad. Stapleton took one in the gut. Damn. Poor guy." I say. "What's the motive?"

"I think I finally have some kind of connection. Marsters, Phillips, Carmine, and Daigan were all a part of a drug task force back in the late sixties. They busted some serious drug dealers so I'm thinking this is some kind of payback. Trouble is, all the guys they busted are still in jail or dead." Tom says.

"That leaves a lot of ground to cover though.

A lot of people could have a vendetta against them, and even guys in prison can still sometimes have influence over things on the outside." I say.

"So the skull then. There can't be that many six foot five super muscular guys walking around. He must be connected in some way. He's either a hired gun, or some kind of relative to one of the drug dealers. You said this was in the sixties, right? Any of these dealers have kids?" Ian injects himself into the conversation.

That's a good theory. I'm surprised he came up with it so quickly.

"That's an interesting theory. I'll have to look into that." Tom says, impressed.

"Are there any remaining members of this task force?" I ask.

"There are two left that I could find. One, Officer Crenick. He's been retired for years. Lives in a penthouse uptown. Guess he saved his money."

"And the other?" Ian asks.

"A younger guy, relatively. He was a rookie. Only did one assignment with them and then got kicked off the force. He was in some kind of jet ski accident. He's been in a coma for over a year. Name was... Stevens? Yeah."

"Ok. So Crenick and Stevens are probably his next targets. You got a detail on them?" I ask.

"Girl, do you think I was born yesterday? I called it in just an hour ago." Tom replies.

"Great. We'll get him."

"I hope so. Collateral damage is increasing. I

don't want any more innocent lives lost."

"So what's our play?" I ask.

"I was thinking you guys take it to the streets. Maybe there's a thug or other low life that knows something. You two can get away with things that I can't, if you catch my drift?"

"Time to bust some heads!" I say with a smirk on my face.

"She gets it." Tom says while looking at Ian.

"Now that you mention it, a punk I saw the other night had his face painted like a skull. Another had a similar-looking skull painted on his jacket. For some reason I didn't make the connection till just now. Do you think that's related?" I ask Tom.

"Might be coincidence, might not. I think it's worth checking out." Tom says.

"Ok, got it! Anything else to report?" I ask.

"Nope. Just keep your eyes peeled. If anything unusual happens let me know right away."

"Yes sir!" I reply while simultaneously giving a salute.

I'm such a cornball sometimes.

I grab Ian and go to leave. Tom asks me to hang back for a second. I tell Ian it's ok and that I'll catch up.

"So what's this guys deal? Rona Gray? What kind of name is that? Where did you find this guy, for real?" Tom asks.

"I saved him from a couple of punks. Sound familiar?" I reply while giving Tom a little nudge.

"Just be careful out there. You don't know who you can trust." He says.

Looking over at Ian waiting for me at the edge of the rooftop I give him a little wink.

"I don't know why, but I've got a great feeling about this."

CHAPTER 23

Ian

I can't remember the last time I was out this late. Probably back when I was boozing or sleeping around. Part of me is exhausted beyond words and the other half is on edge. My body is starting to crash just as we get back to Bram's cave.

"I have a lot of questions." I say as I take off my mask.

"Let me guess? You want to know how I got hooked up with Tom, right?" She replies.

I nod then undo the buckles that secure the cape and toss it on the workbench. My body is aching all over but in a good way.

"I'll try to make this brief... A couple years ago when I was first starting out, when all I had was a bomber jacket, torn jeans, and my own sheer will, I saved Tom from a bust gone bad. He was cuffing a prostitute and her pimp came out of nowhere and clobbered him. I was hesitant to help a cop, you know, since what I'm doing isn't strictly legal, but it was the best decision I've ever made. Tom understands why I'm doing this. He's actually a little envious. He told me that if he hadn't blown out his knee years ago he might have pulled on some spandex himself and helped me. But he does help me, in other ways. This protective outfit of mine, he hooked me up with a private contractor who has made custom stuff for the Lochland SWAT team. My design of course. He's also a former karate champion and he showed me a lot of stuff that he used when he was in the Vietnam War. They used to send him in alone for some serious covert mission kind of stuff. The dude's practically a ninja. Anyway, we have a mutually beneficial relationship. He throws me a bone every now and then, and I give him any info I can scrounge up from the streets." She tells me.

"Why do you do it though? What got you into this life? Revenge?" I ask.

I realize I have no idea why this woman would have any desire to go out into the streets at night, risk her life, and fight criminals barehanded. It seems insane. I was barely able to convince myself and I basically have no reason to live. No real future or prospects. No wife, no children. I live alone. I know how to fight and part of me longed for excitement, any excitement. Once I slipped on the outfit I knew I had to try. But her? What could be her reason?

"I just want to. It's that simple." She smirks.

The enigma continues.

"Alright, Charles Bronson, It's time to say goodnight. I'm dead tired. It's way too late or way too early and you look like I feel." She jokes as she touches the side of my face. "Let's get some rest and meet back here tomorrow night? Sound good?"

"Sounds good." I reply.

"Goodnight... Rona Gray."

She walks away and just before leaving she turns and gives me a wink. I feel butterflies in my stomach yet again.

Taking off all the gear proves to be a bit more difficult than anticipated. I stumble and trip all over myself. If Alex stayed behind I'm sure she would have had quite the laugh. Shutting everything down, I head back up. A ladder that is well hidden behind a secret door in the wall in the upstairs bedroom is the way back into the cottage.

In the bathroom I see I have a big bruise on my back. Although the outfit is bulletproof the impacts were still pretty severe. My ribs are incredibly sore and so is my lower back. I crash on the bed and my whole body is throbbing with pain. A voice in my head tells me that all I need is some pain killers and I'll be fine. What's a couple going hurt? I quickly quiet it.

Is this really what I want to do? I could just tell Alex tomorrow night that I don't really want this. Or do I? Being with her sparked something inside me that I haven't felt since I was with Gloria. Her energy and excitement reminded me of her so much. The complete opposite of me.

Gloria, are you sending her to me? Is Alex a message from you? Is this what you wanted me to do all along? I have so many questions without answers.

Lying in bed staring at the water damaged

ceiling I can't help but think of Gloria but her image is slowly replaced in my mind with Alex, and that smile. That infectious grin that woke up my heart. I feel like a little kid with a crush. I've always had a thing for strong women but this goes beyond that. I've never met someone like her. A woman who's both incredibly sexy but also incredibly tough. She handled those two guys no problem at all. She didn't even break a sweat. I can't get her image out of my head.

Alex walks into my room. Her boots slung over her shoulder. She tosses them to the ground. She starts playing with her hair, lightly gliding her fingers through her vibrant purple locks. She climbs on the bed and begins undressing. I help her pull off her nylons and then I caress her thighs. We kiss deeply. A more passionate kiss I have never known. She pushes me back and then climbs on top of me. I can't resist her. Her powerful legs squeezing me tight. I grab her waist and feel how strong her core is. She bites my lip and then whispers something in my ear that I can't quite understand.

The morning sun and the call of a seagull usher me back to the real world.

"Damn..."

I have no interest in going to work today but something that cop said stuck with me. A name. Daigan. The guy I work with. That's his name. Maybe he has some kind of insight into this. I can't just go up and ask him a bunch of strange questions. That would be really odd. I'll have to figure something out. Maybe one of my other coworkers knows something?

Despite sleeping the whole night I'm still exhausted. My body ravaged with pain. The bruise on my back has grown and darkened. My head feels like a jackhammer is going off inside my skull but for some reason I don't mind at all.

I think of Alex and my pain seems to melt away. I can't wait to see her again.

"Neon Fire." I say to myself with a smirk.

My stomach growls. Checking the cupboards I realize I desperately need to do some shopping. I'm even all out of coffee. A lone drop circles the bottom of the pot.

There's a diner I walk by every day on the way to work. I'll stop there.

CHAPTER 24

Alex

Flipping through the air I always feel like I'm flying. The wind kisses my cheeks and the street lights below become a blur of colors. For a moment I feel like I've touched heaven.

Landing on my rooftop with grace and elegance, I quickly pop open the vent that is actually a secret entrance. Climbing down the ladder I enter my "lair". A couple of older outfits that I've retired hang on mannequins. I toss my jacket on the table and press on the far wall. It moves out of place on its own and shifts into the wall. The entrance is hidden behind a mirror in my apartment.

Taking a moment to stretch out always feels good although I really wonder how long my body will hold up under all this stress. It's only been a couple of years and I'm already starting to rack up some nagging injuries. In the bathroom I undress, tossing my outfit in a pile on the floor. In the mirror I examine my naked body for any new injuries. Deep scars from past battles mark my back and arms, and are a reminder that no good deed goes unpunished. Running my fingers along one on my side I recall one of my first nights out and how I wasn't paying enough attention. A thug stabbed me in the side. I completely lost my breath and thought I was going to die. The thugs just ran off and left me there, lying in a puddle of my own blood, trying my best not to cry. Luckily he didn't hit any major organs, and I was able to get to the hospital before bleeding out. The worst part was tossing my outfit before I got to the hospital. I worked really hard on that.

The hot water from the shower feels amazing. The warm beads caress my whole body and momentarily all my pain fades away. Sometimes I never want to leave. And by sometimes, I mean all the time.

My hand slides between my legs and I find my fingers touching myself for the first time in forever but only for a moment.

"Neon... what are you doing?"

If I wasn't so damn tired I probably would have stayed under the water for an hour or more. It's pretty much the only place I feel perfectly relaxed.

Tying my hair in a messy bun, tossing on a tank top and shorts, I crash hard on the bed. Wrapping myself in my sheets I sink into my comfy mattress.

Ian. Who are you?

That godawful alarm wakes me from a dreamless sleep. It's better that way. Most of my dreams are things I'd rather not recall. How long did I sleep? Three hours, tops. I stretch my arms high above me and can't stop myself from making a loud yawn. I wish I could lay back down for just a few more minutes... or days. Part of the problem with this life I have chosen is always being tired.

Putting on my saggy grandma underwear and waitress outfit I go into the bathroom. Before pulling up the top I use the spandex strap to compress my breasts. I slap on a hairnet and attach my red wig. Doing my best to style it in a realistic way it's already starting to itch. Next I take a red makeup pencil and overemphasize a bunch of my freckles. To finish off the look I throw on my huge black-rimmed glasses. I stare deep into the mirror at a person I no longer recognize. It's me, but not me. A shadow of the past.

Every morning I die, and every night I am born again.

"Hello, Alex. Nice to see you again."

CHAPTER 25

The Face Of Grim Death

My true face stares at me. It burrows a hole inside my chest. It knows me better than anyone else ever could. Its pale, porcelain, skin riddled with cracks and fractures. A reflection of myself that I can not deny. Those hollow eyes and twisted grimace give me the strength to do what must be done.

Taking it off the table I slide it over my false face. It bonds with me like a symbiote. I give it life and it gives me power. Such power. I feel it flow through me like a massive adrenaline rush. I can't stop shaking. My veins are on fire. My muscles bulging and contracting.

On the wall. The names and false faces of my enemies. One by one I've crossed them out. It won't be much longer. Not much longer at all.

The fire I have built illuminates the room. Nothing more pure. Its energy consumes all that surrounds it. I am like fire. A fire that will not be put out by anyone. No one will stand in my way. I toss the faces of the false ones in and watch them burn to a cinder. The embers dance for me like a beautiful ballet.

I no longer seek illumination for the things

that have happened.
>There is no rhyme.
>No reason.
>I realize that now.
>No great plan.
>There only just is.
>And time is running out for us all.

CHAPTER 26

Detective Tom Hudson

Melinda read me the riot act last night. You'd think that she caught me cheating on her or something. That fiery spirit of hers is part of the reason I love her so much. She's quite the woman.

Lying in bed this morning I hold her close to me and think about trying to put the moves on her. She moans gently as I pull her close to me but before things get too serious we are so rudely interrupted.

Cara busts in through the door and jumps on the bed. Her hair is a total mess and her pajamas are on backward.

"Hey, wake up! I made you breakfast!" She shouts like she isn't two feet from my head.

"That's great dear! How about you go to the dining room and wait for us?" Melinda says, oh so kindly.

"Ok!" Cara says as she leaves the room.

I resume my position spooning with Melinda.

"Now where were we?" I say.

"Getting up for breakfast." She says.

"Oh, right." I reply.

Out in the dining room Cara has put out a

lovely spread of burnt eggs, burnt toast, and some delicious fruit loops. I make a pot of coffee while Melinda entertains Cara for a few minutes.

Rona Gray? Who was that guy? I have nothing to go off of. I don't know his real name. I don't know what he looks like. Nothing. If Alex trusts him he must be someone special, that's for sure. That tip about one of the dealers having a kid, that was good. I'm surprised it never came up before. I'll have to look into that first thing when I get in the office.

Rona Gray? What the hell kind of superhero name is that? Doesn't exactly strike fear in the hearts of men. Sounds like someone my daughter would be friends with. That outfit was kinda cool though, and those eyes were creepy as hell. Glowing in the darkness with a permanent scowl. I get a chill just thinking about it.

Ms. Faye-Darling is going to have a lot of questions to answer but for now it's breakfast time. Despite being burned the eggs aren't too bad. I choke down a piece of the extremely dry toast and can't seem to finish another.

Cara eats her cereal but can't seem to help herself from making bubbles in the milk. My mouth still has the faint taste of burnt toast so I regret not opting for some of those fruit loops. I try diluting the flavor with more coffee. My second cup of the morning. I'll have at least six over the course of the day. Sometimes eight or more if I'm feeling a little burned out.

After getting dressed I go back to the kitchen

to get myself cup of coffee number three. I find myself drifting away in thought.

The twisted skull...

Who is this guy that's going after these cops? A giant muscle monster who can crush a skull with his bare hands? That's someone I wouldn't want to tangle with. It sounds like he's a real freak of nature. If he is a child of a dealer that was busted in the sixties that would put him at about mid-twenties to mid-thirties. That seems just about right. These cops must have done something really horrible to this guy to warrant such terrible deaths.

Thinking about the crime scene photos of that Sargent Phillips guy makes me gag.

Melinda comes into the room looking sexy as hell in her power suit. She leaves a few buttons of her blouse open just for me. She likes to tease me. Every night, or morning, when I get home we fight, then we make love, and then all is right again. It's been working for years and I know we are both happy. She just worries about me too damn much. I guess she thinks one of those pencils I push might jump out of my hand and pierce my jugular.

"When do you think you'll be home tonight, baby?" She asks.

"I don't know. I just got a big tip regarding a case I've been working. Might be late."

"You work too damn hard, babe." She replies with a hint of frustration.

"Well, unfortunately crime doesn't sleep."

"I hate to tell you this but you're not exactly

in peak physical shape anymore. It might be time to give it a rest." She tells me.

"That's not what you were saying in the shower a few minutes ago." I retort.

She laughs and gives me a light slap across the face.

I love this woman.

"It's fine. Chief hasn't had me pounding the pavement in months. What was it he called me after my knee surgery? 'Insurance nightmare'?" I say.

"Well, *he is* right." She says.

"Right?" I say as I grab her around the waist and give her a big kiss.

"Ewww! You guys are gross!" Cara interjects.

"You're damn right we are!" I kiss Melinda again. This time with the tongue.

Cara covers her face.

"Ok babe. I'm going to drop her off at school and then head to the office. I'll see you later tonight." Melinda says.

We kiss a few more times. I hate saying goodbye to that woman.

Driving to the station I hit a pothole and spill some coffee on my pants.

"Damn, not again." I mutter to myself.

This has become an almost daily occurrence.

Turning a corner I get stuck at a light. A group of kids are crossing the street in front of my car and they look like they are in a heated discussion. I roll down my window a little and eavesdrop on their conversation.

"Did you hear that Neon Fire was on our street last night?" A little girl says.

"That's not true! She's not even real!" A little boy replies.

"She is too! I saw her!" The girl says.

"Oh yeah? Then describe her!" The boy retorts.

"Well, it was dark!" The girl replies.

"See! I knew you were lying!" The boy says.

"Am not!" She replies vehemently.

"Are too!" He replies.

This goes on for a few rounds.

"She is! And one day I'm going to be just like her!" She yells.

I smile to myself thinking about my little superhero team. Tom Hudson, Agent of Justice. The Femme Fatale Neon Fire and... Rona Gray.

Rona Gray? What kind of superhero name is that anyway?

CHAPTER 27

Alex

The subway ride into work was the usual. The same stinky people all crammed into an underground tube. I own a car but my parking spot is just too good to give up in this city, plus I think the battery might be dead since I haven't driven it in over a year. I'd much rather be taking to the air anyway. On the walk to the diner I caught a bum trying to look up my skirt while pretending to sleep. I lifted my skirt and gave him a free show. Wasn't he in shock to see the glorified diaper I'm wearing. His face was pure gold.

Outside the Hot Rod a guy is smoking a cigarette with his big wolf dog. I see him almost every day. All he ever gets is a cup of coffee. His name's John. The dog's name is Courage or something like that. A huge grey and black mutt that looks scary but is actually very friendly.

"Hey John." I say to him.

"Hey little miss Darling." He says while I bend down to pet the dog.

John asked me out one time but he's like sixty, plus he's hideous. Nice guy but damn. Those cigarettes have done him no favors. His face is hollow, sunken in, and pockmarked. He's got about half his teeth and what's left isn't so great to look at. He looks like he might have been handsome once upon a time, but that time is long gone.

"Hey, can I get a drag." I ask.

"Sure thing, little lady."

He passes me the cigarette. I rescue it from his shriveled, wrinkly, discolored fingers and I take one long drag. Its nasty taste fills my mouth as I inhale the hot smoke into my lungs. I hold it in for a moment and my head starts to swim. Coughing out the cloud of smoke, John pats me on the back and asks if I'm ok. I silently nod. I consider taking another drag, but pass the cigarette back instead. What can I say? I'm only human.

"Thanks... let me guess? Cup of coffee?" I ask.

"You know me so well." He says with his gap-toothed stained smile.

We are swamped so I'm running around like a chicken with its head cut off. I'm definitely regretting staying out so late last night. I pound down the coffee whenever I get a chance. Even Tamara, who's usually slow because she's flirting so much for tips, is hauling ass. Part of me envies her energy and enthusiasm. She's bouncing back and forth looking super sexy like she was plucked straight out of a Whitesnake music video. She whips her hair around so much I don't know how she doesn't get whiplash. She went heavy on the glitter today and even I can't help but stare at her from time to time.

"Hey, check out the guy that just walked in."

Tamara says to me.

I look over and see Ian. He's dressed in jeans, a white t-shirt and brown leather jacket. His eye and nose are a little swollen from last night.

"Guy thinks he's James Dean or something, without the good looks." Tamara continues. "I bet I can get a few bucks out of him."

Tamara pushes herself up and pops another stick of gum in her mouth.

"No. I got this one." I say.

"Suit yourself." She replies as she walks off to another table full of some construction workers.

"Now, how are you boys doing this morning?" She asks while leaning over and putting her hands on the table.

She practically falls out of her shirt. The faces of the guys sitting at the table all go flush. One of them even takes off his hat and wipes his brow.

As I'm walking over towards Ian's table I decide I want to test something. I slide my name tag off and slip it into one of my pockets. Approaching the table he looks up at me and smiles. I smile back. It's weird seeing him in the daylight and in normal clothes. He looks like some bruiser from down the block. You'd never guess he was anything special.

"Good morning." He says.

"Good morning. What can I get you?" I ask.

He looks at the menu.

"Just three eggs, scrambled, and an English muffin." He says.

"Anything to drink?" I ask.

"Cup of coffee would be just fine."

I write it down on my pad and turn to walk away.

"Hey, wait a minute." He says.

I stop in my tracks. He must have recognized me. I turn back.

"Yes?" I ask.

"I think I'll have some bacon as well, please."

"You got it." I say as I walk away.

Oh my God. He doesn't recognize me. You know what this means? My disguise works perfectly. If he didn't recognize me then no one would be able to. After dropping off his food I take every chance I get to look at him. He's just sipping his coffee and staring out the window. I wonder what he's thinking about.

Is he thinking about me?

Why do I keep staring at him?

"How's it going with James Dean over there?" Tamara asks.

"I think he's more the Charles Bronson type." I reply.

"The death wish guy? What gives you that impression? He doesn't look anything like him." Tamara responds.

"I don't know. I just have a feeling." I say.

"Are you smiling? You have a crush on that dude don't you?"

"No." I respond. "I don't even know him."

"Yeah, ok, but you definitely think he's cute. And now that I've gotten another look at him I guess he's ok looking, in a kinda rugged way."

"I don't like him!" I yell.

The whole diner goes silent for a moment. I adjust my glasses which had slide down my nose. Tamara tussles with her hair. The chatter amongst the patrons resumes.

"Ok ok. It will be our secret." Tamara says as she dances off.

Do I think Ian is cute? I'm not sure. I hadn't thought about it much. He's for sure older than me by at least ten years, but maybe he just looks that way from all the fights. He said he had a wife and daughter. How old was the kid? Damn. He didn't say. Let's just say he's thirty-five, rough estimate. That's too old for me. Plus I don't even think he's cute. Do I? He did look pretty badass in that costume last night. When I touched myself in the shower, was it him I was thinking of, or was it Rona Gray? Is there really a difference?

I hit a few more tables before heading back to Ian's. He's dozed off. If I'm tired then he must be exhausted. Poor guy doesn't know what he's gotten himself into. I just hope that he can keep up with me. I know that I can be quite the handful sometimes. Tom has let me know that more than once.

"Excuse me." I say.

He wakes up violently.

"You ok?" I ask.

"I just had a bad dream is all." He replies.

"Did you have a long night?"

"You could say that." He replies. "So what do I

owe you?"

He reaches into his pocket and opens his wallet. Catching a brief glimpse at his license I see that he's from Bella Cruz, California. Five-foot ten. Brown Hair. Brown Eyes. Last name: Dempsey. A twenty and a five in the secondary flap. Ian Dempsey. That name sounds kind of familiar but I'm not sure why. I'll have to look into it.

"You know what? It's on the house." I say.

"Wow! Are you sure?" He asks.

"Yeah, My treat." I say.

"Thanks. I really appreciate it."

He looks up at the clock.

"Oh, damn. I'm late for work." He says as he gets up from the table and puts his coat back on. "Thank you so so much... I didn't catch your name."

"Ellen." I say.

"Well thank you very much, Ellen. I hope you have a wonderful day." He says as he exits the diner.

Watching him walk down the street he turns back for a second. He sees me staring at him through the window. He waves. I wave back.

Who is this mystery man who dropped into my life? Meets his wife saving her from a horrible tragedy only to suffer a terrible tragedy himself. Life really isn't fair sometimes. I can't even imagine the pain he's gone through. The pain he's going through. Losing both your wife and daughter. What does a trauma like that do to a man?

Charles Bronson. I joke but it's true. I think he put on that outfit in hopes someone might kill him and he almost got that wish. Suicide by pretending to be a superhero? That's got to be a first. Had I not stepped in he would have been dead. I couldn't have let that happen. I started doing this to help people. Maybe I've helped him already. The way he smiled at me, that can't be the face of someone on the edge.

My heart fills with excitement as I think about the two of us. Working as a team. Taking down all the criminals in this city. Kicking ass and taking names. Making this place a safe haven for all. Just like it used to be.

"Ms. Faye-Darling! Hello? Back to work! These tables aren't going to wait themselves." Sheila yells. "Chop Chop!"

I work a few more tables before Tamara confronts me.

"So... are you pregnant?" She asks.

"What?" I ask.

"With Bronson's baby?" She jokes. "Wait... that sounds like a movie. Tamara Conte in Bronson's Baby!"

"Shut up." I mutter.

CHAPTER 28

Ian

Man, am I thirsty. My hands are raw from all the ropework and I could seriously use a drink. The whistle blows for lunchtime and I realize I didn't bring anything with me. Damn. I ask Eric if he's got anything to spare. He tosses me a bottle of water from his cooler. Part of me wishes it was beer. Old habits die hard. The two of us sit down on a shipping container. I twist off the cap from the water and drink half of it in one gulp.

"Thanks for the water." I say.

"No problem." He replies. "You're not getting a bite of this sandwich so get that shit right out of your head."

We share a laugh.

"Hey Eric, I know I've asked you before but what do you know about Daigan?" I ask as Daigan walks into the office.

"Not much really. Dad was a cop that got killed. Mother's in a hospital upstate I think. That's pretty much it. He doesn't talk all that much. A lot of the guys here like to keep to themselves you know. Why are you asking about him so much anyway? You got a crush on him? Not that I give a shit if that's your thing."

"No." I reply. "You're way more my type."

"I'm just busting your balls man. If you want to know more about him just talk to him. He's a nice guy. Mama's boy, but a nice guy."

Daigan leaves the office and goes back to unloading the crates that came in just before lunch. I hardly ever see him take a break. The guy's a machine.

"What about you? What's your story?" I ask Eric.

"Spent a couple years in Bensonhurst. Armed robbery. The gun wasn't even loaded. I just needed some damn money. In prison I got my GED. Fat load of good it did me. I ended up working at this dump with no way out."

"I dropped out of school." I reply.

"Exactly my point."

"Any family?" I ask.

"I got a woman. Three kids. That's why I was robbing the place. I had no job, no prospects. My dad was a drug dealer and a pimp. I didn't want to get into that lifestyle."

Wait. Eric's a sizable guy. Muscular. Dad was a dealer. He seems about the right age. Works with the son of one of the cops that were killed.

Hold on Kojack. Don't get ahead of yourself.

"What happened to your dad?" I ask.

"Man, you do not let up. He's dead. Or at least dead to me. I don't know. He ran off years ago. Never saw him again. Just to get ahead of you my mom's doing fine. She lives in Florida. Too hot for me down there. I actually like winter." He replies. "You gonna tell me your life story now?"

"Nope... you'd die from boredom." I reply.

"Wait a second. I know that we've been working together for a while now but it just clicked. I knew you looked familiar. Ian Dempsey. That's right. You're the guy who killed The Baron. I lost a lot of money on that fight."

"Sorry to hear that." I say.

"How did you not go to jail for that massacre?" He says. "They'd have to use dental records to identify him after that. If he had any teeth left."

"It was an accident."

"Bullshit." He replies. "I've seen rage in a man's eyes before. You had his number and you punched the ticket."

The lunch whistle blows to end our break.

"This conversation isn't over, my man." Eric says with a grin.

"Yes it is." I mutter under my breath as I walk back to my station.

Seems no matter where I go or what I do I can't outrun my past. Gloria. I did that for you but I did it mostly for myself. The sick pleasure I felt watching him draw his last breath is an unforgettable feeling. It wasn't my intention to kill him, but in the heat of the moment I couldn't be stopped. To this day I'm not sure if I should feel bad about what I did or not. Is it wrong that I don't feel bad? Not in the slightest.

Gloria. My Gloria. A pit opens inside of me and it takes my all to stop myself from falling in. I lean on one of the crates and take ten deep breaths. Hunching over it seems I still can't catch my breath. What is happening?

Gloria's rotting corpse lying in the ground. In her arms, my sweet Rona. They've decayed to skeletons. Their bodies twisted in horror.

"This is your fault." A voice whispers in my ear. "You did this."

I turn and the smashed face of Aaron O'Shaunessy greets me. He smiles at me with a horrible, toothless grin.

"No good deed goes unpunished."

He blows me a kiss. Blood, bile, and other putrified substances pour out of his mouth and cascade down his chest. The stink is beyond belief. Inhaling just the slightest bit of that odor sends my head spinning. I grab and pinch my nose. He laughs. He laughs and laughs and laughs. It makes a wet gurgling noise that brings vomit up my throat.

I fall to the ground and begin regurgitating. All of my organs come spilling out of my mouth in a grizzly display. Grabbing at them I try to shove them back in to no avail.

Sudden darkness, then it's light again.

Looking around I see I am in the cemetery where Gloria and Rona are buried. It's a cold autumn day and the leaves have all fallen. Something isn't right. It's always warm in Bella Cruz. This isn't right. I approach the tombstone. The name is obscured with dirt. Kneeling I brush away the debris with my hand. It feels wet and unusually warm. Turning my hand over I realize it's covered in blood. Looking again at the marker my heart rips. It says my name. Ian Dempsey. Born February 23rd 1951. Died 1986. The month and date are a blur. Frantically I scratch at it but it only gets more obscure. I fall to the ground in the fetal position. I can't stop crying. Pulling my knees in tight I'm just like a baby. Gloria. Rona. Where are you? I need you.

I'm sinking. The ground is pulling me under like quicksand. Four skeletal hands burst out from under me and dig into my flesh. I'm struggling but I can't break free. I'm choking as my mouth begins to fill with dirt. Soon my resistance stops. My hand is all that remains outside of this tomb. The light is failing. With my final ounce of strength I reach with my fingertips. I stretch them out as hard as I can, to the point where it feels like they will rip right off of my hand. Soon there is no more fight left in me. Accepting my fate, I close my eyes.

Suddenly, a hand grasps mine. I'm being pulled back up. Back from under. My eyes are blinded by light. Blinking rapidly I try to clear them to see my savior.

"Not yet." A voice says to me. It's familiar.

It's my own voice.

Finally my eyes are focused. My hero is Rona Gray. It's as if the outfit has come alive. The eyes glow bright like two fireflies in the darkness.

Now I am inside the suit. Upon the hill, silhouetted against the setting sun is a woman. I can't make out who it is. I race towards her but she seems as though she is only getting further and further away.

"Gloria!" I yell.

"Watch out!" A voice screams at me.

Rona appears before me with her chubby cheeks and soft brown curls. She grabs my hand. Compared to her tiny mitts my hands look like that of a giants.

"This way, Daddy!" She yanks my hand.

I'm crashing to the ground. I hear the thunderous sound of metal colliding with concrete. Someone is on top of me.

"What were you doing, space cadet?" A familiar voice asks.

Rolling over on to my back I see Daigan standing before me. His hand outstretched. Grasping his hand he lifts me back up to my feet. A shipping container broke loose from one of the cranes. If Daigan hadn't pushed me I would have been squashed flat.

"Hey, you alright?" He asks.

"Yeah. All things considered." I reply while brushing the dirt from my clothes.

"How did you not hear us yelling for you to get out of the way?" He asks.

"I don't know." I think for a moment. Come up with a decent excuse Ian. "I must have a concussion. I bumped my head pretty hard last night."

"Well you almost just got bumped even harder." He jokes.

"Yeah, no kidding." I joke back.

The boss comes out and starts screaming.

"What the hell just happened?" He yells.

I just realized I don't know his name. You'd think someone here would have said it or mentioned it. I get paid in cash under the table. No checks. I've barely spoken to him since I got hired.

"Nothing. Just a little mishap." Daigan says to him.

"Just a mishap? Just a mishap? This man almost got crushed to death and you call it just a mishap?" He questions aggressively.

"It's really ok. I'm fine." I reply.

"It was an empty container. Nothing was damaged." Daigan says.

"Nothing was damaged? You know how much those containers cost?" He screams.

We shrug our shoulders. The boss tries to get right up in Daigan's face but looks like a child in comparison. Daigan must be at least a head taller.

"Daigan. You're fired!" he screams with spit coming out of his mouth.

"What the hell?" Daigan asks. "What about the guy operating the crane?"

"He's way too valuable to this operation. You? You're garbage. I could find someone like you any day of the week. Get the hell out before I call the cops to escort you out!" The boss exclaims.

"This man just saved my life." I retort.

"You want to be fired too... Hempstead?" He asks me. " That's right. I didn't think so. Daigan, clear out your locker and vacate! Capeesh?"

Turning to Daigan I apologize.

"It's alright man. This was a part-time deal anyway. I have another job at the hospital as an orderly. I can ask for more hours there. No problem." He slaps me on the shoulder.

He smiles. He seems like such a good guy. I really don't want to ask him about his father. Especially now. It seems really inappropriate.

"You want to get a beer sometime? I really owe you one." I say.

"Sure. Just call Saint Maria's hospital. I'll be there."

The boss screams at us to get back to work as he re-enters his office and slams the door. Everyone just goes back to business as usual as if nothing happened at all. Eric was right. It seems like anonymity is the key to success in this place.

What the hell was that? What just happened to me? Panic attack? Shell shock? It was so vivid. More powerful than any dream I've ever had. I roll it over in my mind for the rest of my shift. It's all I can think about. Who was that woman at the end? Gloria? It seems so obvious but inside I'm unsure. I couldn't reach her in time.

The rest of the day flies by. When the whistle blows to end the shift I can't believe it at first. I pack up my stuff and head out the door running into Eric on the way out.

"Sucks about Daigan getting fired. The boss is a serious douchebag." I say to Eric. "The guy saves my life and gets fired."

"He's probably better off. This place will squeeze the life out of you if you let it. I'm sure working at the hospital will be better for him. I don't know why he was working here to begin with." He replies.

"Fresh air?" I say.

"And?" He asks.

"I don't know. It's all I could come up with." I chuckle. "This might seem like a stupid question but what's the boss' name?"

"I don't know man. I just call him asshole." He laughs.

"Hey. Eric! Get in my office right now!" Asshole yells.

"The grinch who stole Christmas is calling my name." Eric jokes. "Catch you later, man." He waves goodbye and enters the boss' office.

Hanging back for minute I look through the window. Seems the boss is asking him something. I can't quite make it out. Eric looks unhappy. The boss tosses some money at him and he hesitantly agrees to whatever it was. Hmm. I wonder what that was about.

Back at my cottage I watch the sunset on the balcony. It's getting chilly. The fall is rapidly approaching. A cool breeze blows by and I see some fallen leaves dance on the pavement below. Popping open a beer I take a swig. I've regained some weight but over the past year I went from being muscular to skinny and bloated, to kinda chubby and average. Although, working on the boat and now at the dock, I was able to retain a good amount of my arm strength. I notice a potbelly starting to form. Disgusted, I toss my beer off the balcony and into the water. The bottle bobs up and down. Watching it drift with the current I'm reminded of Bram and his stupid boat. If he had just let me go none of this would have happened. Is that what I really wanted? At the time it seemed like the only option. Now I'm not so sure. When those thugs had me pinned down and I thought I was goner It seemed like the logical end to my nightmare. But now I feel different. Something has changed.

Alex. You are an enigma. I must know more about you. How can just being in your presence change my mood entirely? Your spirit is just like Gloria's. I feel her in you.

Looking out across the water I think of the tombstone I saw in my dream. It said 1986 on it. That's this year and there are only a few months left. Another cold breeze blows in off the water and I start to shiver.

It's almost time. Alex will be here soon. I need to be ready.

Going down into Bram's cave I power everything on. There's a room off one of the corridors that leads to a substantial gymnasium. It has everything you could possibly need to train. Weights, gymnastics equipment, trampoline, you name it, it's there.

Better than any gym I ever trained at. That's for sure.
     Alex...
     I wonder what you'll teach me.

CHAPTER 29

Alex

Flipping on the lights of the old gymnastics studio I used to train at always sends a chill down my spine. This place was being shut down and sold off. The owner lost all his money gambling and my coach had moved on to bigger and better things. I used the money my mom left me when she died to purchase it. I got it for super cheap. Turns out that old gymnastics training centers aren't really worth a whole hell of a lot. It's my home away from home. I spent many years in this place and I almost prefer being here over being at my apartment. The floor is torn and well broken in. Some of the windows are shattered. The water doesn't work in the bathrooms and at this point I don't have the money to fix it. Something about the smell and the texture of the mat under my feet makes me feel all warm and fuzzy. The ceilings are high and a couple of birds have taken up residence in the rafters.

In my head I hear my father's voice. He's telling me to do better. Be better. Stop making mistakes! Do you even care? Do you want to go to the Olympics? You're a failure! A waitress? That's all you want to be? After all I have done for you? You're an ungrateful little bitch!

I crank the boombox and his voice fades into the background. The last time I saw him was the night of mom's funeral. He didn't say a word to me the whole day. He was gone the next morning. There was no note. Nothing at all.

I stretch out for a few minutes getting my body all nice and limber. Raising my hands to the sky I hear my mother's voice.

"Keep dreaming of Neon Fire." She says.

"Don't worry, Mom. That dream came true."

Rushing out to the center of the floor I round-off, double back handspring to double backflip. I stick the landing. The music flows through me as I enter my next pass. Front handspring to full-twisting front flip. Another perfect landing.

Pointing my toe, I gesture to the crowd. The applause is overwhelming. It showers me like a sweet summer rain. It's cool beads tickle my every nerve. Goosebumps raise on my arms and I smile ear to ear. I'm absolutely glowing.

My final pass. Roundoff, back handspring, full-twisting back to front. In mid-air I feel like I might never come down. My body floats for just a moment and in that moment all the noise of the world, all the pain and suffering, just falls away to nothingness. My feet suddenly grip the mat and I thrust my hands to the sky. The crowd goes wild. They are chanting my name. Neon Fire! Neon Fire! Neon Fire! Love fills me up to the brim and I feel like I'm about to burst.

Dancing to the music I lose all control and let my body move on its own. It's almost orgasmic. The cassette reaches its end and I collapse on the mat staring up at the rafters. A bird flies in through the window and lands in the nest. I can hear the chirping babies. Watching the mother feeding the little ones, I think of my own mother. Without her Neon Fire never would have come into existence. I am who I am now because of her.

Dad. Wherever you are, if you could see me now and know what I'm trying to accomplish, would you be proud of me?

A cool breeze comes in through one of the broken windows. Sitting up I watch the sunset. The sky is streaked with fluorescent pinks and reds. The mother bird leaves the nest and flies off into the horizon. I watch it fade into the distance until it turns to a tiny speck, and then finally disappears.

It's time to head over to the cave. Ian will be waiting.

CHAPTER 30

Ian

Alex is standing in front of me and she looks absolutely incredible. She is wearing a white sports bra and purple short shorts with her hair tied up in a loose bun. Her makeup is immaculate. Seeing her in a revealing outfit like this really shows off all the hard work she has put into her physique. She's got more ab definition than most fit guys. Her legs are thick with clear muscle separations. She even has ever so slightly capped shoulders. Her body puts mine to shame, that's for sure. I look like someone's tough dad in comparison, which isn't that far off from reality.

"Does this place know no end?" She asks as she looks around the gymnasium in Bram's cave touching all of the equipment. Gliding her fingers across the dumbbells.

"I guess not. I'm still discovering secret compartments."

"Ian, listen up! You can handle one attacker, maybe two based on what I have seen, but you're sloppy. I can tell that you were in good shape once upon a time. We need to get you back to that. I can show you the path but you need to be the one to walk it? Understand?" She asks.

I nod.

"I'm going to need verbal confirmation." She demands.

"Yes."

"Ok good. All of this equipment is great but if you can't control your own body you'll never be able to control someone else's, let alone a whole gang who wants to kill you. Every second we spend in here is a second we are not out there. We are letting criminals have their way right now. You must take this seriously. A woman could be out there right now being raped. A child being killed. A small business owner is shot in cold blood over a measly twenty dollars. Do you understand?" She asks.

"Yes." I nod.

"Now that you understand what we are doing here I need you to do something for me." She says.

"I'll do anything for you." I say.

Don't sound so goddamn eager you weirdo.

"Show me how many push-ups you can do."

"Right now?" I ask.

"When else? The clock is ticking, old man." She says as she gestures to her wrist.

Oh Jesus. I can't remember the last time I did push-ups. Must have been when I was still training for my fights. How many could I do then? I think one-hundred.

I drop down and start doing push-ups. Getting to twenty with relative ease I start feeling it a thirty and at thirty-five I have to stop.

"Damn. I used to be able to do a lot more." I say to her.

"I don't care how many you can do." She says.

Wait. What? I'm confused but at this point I'm not going to question her. I feel kinda pathetic. I'm a little gassed. I'm trying to hide it but I'm not doing a great job. Sucking wind like a lung cancer patient.

"It's not the quantity but the quality. It doesn't matter if you can do fifty, a hundred, two hundred in a row. Who cares? Anyone can learn how to do a ton of push-ups. I'm going to show you how to make doing one worth as much as doing a hundred. The secret is control. Here. Watch me." She says.

Alex sits on her butt. Placing her hands at her side she lifts her self up into an L sit position. She lifts her legs into a pike and then slowly starts to move her legs back through her arms. Now she is supporting herself in a handstand with her legs still piked. She then straightens her legs into a perfect handstand. She begins lowering herself down towards the floor and at the same time bringing her legs out behind her into a horizontal position supported only by her arms. She holds in the state for a few seconds. Her muscles bulging and straining. A vein in her neck pops out. She lowers down to about an inch from the floor with her feet never touching. As she comes back up she pops onto her fingertips. She proceeds back into a handstand then into a one-armed handstand. Finally she does a little spin move and lands on her feet.

"That was... amazing to say the least." I say.

Honestly it was. It didn't seem like she was struggling at all. Every movement was precise. Slow and controlled. No jerky motions whatsoever. Truly magnificent.

"I'll never be able to do anything like that." I say.

"That's the exact kind of thinking that I need you to toss the hell out right now." She replies. "You can and you will. Repeat that."

"I can and I will." I'm not sure I believe it but I'll try.

The next two weeks are the most grueling of my entire life. Even when I was training as a fighter I didn't train this hard. Alex pushes me to my limits and beyond. Things I didn't think I'd ever be able to do, like a backflip, I can now do. Well, after many, many, failed attempts. With every new accomplishment she cheers me on. Even in the mirror I can see my body starting to change back to the way it was when I was in my top shape.

Alex has had me working the gymnastics rings. At first I couldn't even do a single proper pull-up but now I'm doing muscle-ups and skin the cats, back and front leavers. She is an amazing teacher. Once I felt something was getting easy she would insist on me doing it again with her hanging on my back. She said I would need to be able to move with an attacker trying to take me down. We would go until I could do it that way too. Every night my muscles felt like they were on fire and many times I wanted to give up, or start popping pills to ease the pain, but her infectious smile and positive attitude kept me pushing. The time has flown by. Work has been a blur. Every minute that I'm there I'm waiting to be with Alex again.

I've been struggling with the balance beam. I blame getting punched in the head so much but she tells me to not give in to excuses. I can finally land a flip on the beam. The joy I feel with each new accomplishment is amazing. Better than any high I had ever experienced from any drug. I wonder if it is meeting the goals or seeing Alex's smile that really fills me with joy? To say that I desire her is a massive understatement, but I do everything in my power to keep our relationship professional. As much as I miss Gloria and Rona, I feel the pit inside my chest close when I am with Alex.

Today we are actually going to fight each other. I've been dreading this day because I would never want to do anything that could possibly hurt her. At the dock I had set up a heavy bag and I had been working it on my breaks trying to get back in the rhythm. I got lucky in that fight with the Tarantula. I need to be better than that as clearly evidenced by my failing against those two street thugs.

At Bram's cave Alex is dressed in a padded helmet and vest.

This should be interesting...

CHAPTER 31

Alex

I feel ridiculous in this get up, but it is in my best interest to not get injured sparring with my partner. The helmet is a little tight. I probably should have tried it on before buying it. Ian is lacing up his boxing gloves. To see the change in him has been amazing. It's like I carved away the unnecessary stone and revealed the statue underneath. His muscles are more defined and some veins are starting to show. I feel proud of myself. He's really come a long way in a short time. He's a natural.

"Ok Ian. I want you to hit me. If you can." I egg him on.

"Are you sure about this? I really don't want to hurt you." He says.

"Oh. Poor little me. I'm a helpless girl. I can't defend myself." I jest.

"That's not what I meant." He says irritated.

"If it's not, then hit me goddamn it!" I yell.

He still stands there hesitating. Better give him some incentive. I slap him hard across the face. He still doesn't fight back. I slap him again.

"Come on! Don't be a pussy!" I continue to poke him.

214 | A DREAM OF NEON FIRE

"Your funeral." He says.

"Oh you're such a badass. Come and get me! Pussy!" I taunt him still.

Going to slap him one more time he stops it and throws a counter punch. I barely get out of the way. Damn. He's faster than I thought. He throws a few more punches but I continue to dodge. He's telegraphing. After a few more punches I can see through his attack. He'll never be able to hit me like this.

"Is that all you got? I thought you were a boxer not a dancer." I taunt again.

Another predictable flurry. I'm starting to get disappointed. Ian stops for a second. He's looking down at the mat. Sweat dripping off of his forehead.

"What's wrong? You want to give up already? I'm up here bozo!" I yell.

In an instant he has changed. His entire face and body language have shifted. His punches are sharper and faster. His footwork more elegant and precise. I'm struggling to dodge. Holy crap! Where did this passion come from? He's like a different fighter.

Before I know it I'm flying through the air. My head rocked back. I crash hard onto the mat and the wind is knocked out of me.

It takes me a moment to assess what just happened. He hit me with an uppercut that even with this padding on sent me to my back. What a wallop! He comes over and helps me up to my knees.

I need a second to compose myself because I'm seeing stars.

"Ian... Damn man. That was one hell of a punch. I'd hate to get hit by that without this padding on. It was like getting hit with a wrecking ball." I tell him.

"Are you ok? I'm sorry. I didn't want to hurt you." He asks apologetically.

"Yeah. I'm fine. No need to apologize. That was great. If you keep that up no one could, or logically should stand in your way."

Now I understand why Aaron O'Shaunessy died. I figured out where I had heard his name before. It was all over the news eight years ago. "Killer Fight! Dempsey Overtakes O'Shaunessy". I tried to bring it up with him once but he got very defensive. I'm a quick learner. Put that in the box of things to never refer to again. It sits alongside Gloria and Rona, plus most of his past. I can tell it pains him to talk about it.

All I've learned is he's originally from Washington state. He used to love going into the forests and exploring. There was a hidden waterfall that he spent time at in the summer. He met his first girlfriend swimming by that waterfall. It was a special place for him. He didn't have much to say about his parents. He wouldn't share much about his life before now. I think it's still too painful for him. There is so much about him that remains a mystery.

"Come on! Let's go again!" I say as I stand up and start tossing light punches at him. "This time I get to hit back."

We spend the next hour sparring. I can tell he's going out of his way to not hit me in the head. I appreciate it. After that one blow I'd certainly had enough. He's got great stamina and he's holding his own against me. I'm impressed. Soon he will be a powerful ally.

While I'm taking off the padding he asks me about Tom.

"So... Have you been in touch with Tom?" He asks.

"Yeah. There hasn't been any activity regarding our skull-faced friend in a while. He still has a couple officers looking in on the two remaining members of that drug task force but so far, zip."

"That's good." He replies.

"Yeah, but Tom did note that more and more street kids are being seen wearing skull paint or skull patches on their clothes."

"Hmm. That can't be a good sign." He says.

"I agree. We need to get back on the street soon." I say.

"Do you think I'm ready?" He asks.

I'm not sure. I want to believe he is, but I still want more time. I need to teach him how to control a situation, especially if he's attacked by a group or if there are weapons involved. I hope we can hold out another two weeks. I just need two more weeks. After that, it's all stuff he'll have to learn out in the field.

"Almost." I say. "Hey, what do you say about

us getting out of here tonight? We've been cooped up in this place for weeks now. It will do us good to get out and mix it up with some randoms"

"What do you mean?" He asks.

"Like, let's go to a club. I know a great place. It's called No Atmosphere." I say.

"Like, a dance club?" He asks.

"Yeah. You don't like dancing?" I ask.

"Not really." He says sounding dejected. "I'm not exactly the dancing type."

Grabbing his hand I pull him to his feet and I start dancing to imaginary music.

"See, it's not that hard." I say as I turn and start rubbing my butt against him.

Well... Maybe a little hard.

"I don't know, I don't want to make a fool of myself." He says.

"You almost died while wearing a superhero costume, and you're afraid of a little dancing? You'll be fine. I promise. Don't you trust me?" I ask.

"Yeah." He replies.

"Good." I say. "I'm going to go home and get ready. I'll meet you outside the club in two hours. It's on 34th and Davenport." I tell him.

"Ok. I'll see you there." He says while mustering up an awkward smile.

"See you in a bit!" I say as I toss my sweaty gym bag over my shoulder and exit through the secret passage.

Boy, is he going to be in for a big surprise.

CHAPTER 32

Ian

Standing outside the club, No Atmosphere, I must have beaten her here. There's a big line to get in. People are all dressed in Halloween costumes. It must be a theme night since Halloween isn't for another week. I had no idea what to wear so I just tossed on a white t-shirt and jeans. It's a little chilly and I regret not wearing a coat. With the line as long as it is and me being, well, me, I doubt I'll be able to get in. I hope Alex isn't already inside. That would be bad.

Turning when I feel a tap on my shoulder I'm greeted by someone I don't recognize. She has green hair to her shoulders with bangs and her face is mocked up like a kitten. She even has false fangs that look quite convincing. Her outfit is a pink frilly crop top with white polka dots. She has a high waisted puffy skirt on with white leggings and black loafers to finish it off.

Holy crap... It's Alex. It took me a minute to figure it out. She looks like a completely different person. Even her perfume is different.

"It's Alex!" She says punching me in the arm.

"I know!" I say awkwardly because I honestly

didn't at first.

"Liar." She says with a smile.

She grabs me by the arm and pulls me towards the front of the line.

"Um. I think we have to wait." I say.

"Don't be such a square!" She retorts.

We go up to the front. The bouncer, a huge black guy in a suit, greets her with a smile.

"Katrina! How have you been darling?" He asks.

"I've been doing real good, Davey. Mind if my friend and I cut in?" She asks.

"No problem for you. Go right in." He says while pushing open the door.

Inside is a barrage of neon lights and smoke. I can hardly see two feet in front of me. The music is blasting. Some techno I don't recognize. Alex is leading me by the hand. We weave through the crowd of people dressed up in all manner of costumes from skeletons to princesses. I bump into a guy dressed as Ronald Reagan.

We find an open table and sit down.

"Katrina?" I ask.

"Hey, what can I say? I like to pretend I'm someone else." She winks.

To be honest she looks super hot. Something about her whole outfit is really doing it for me. A waiter comes by and she whispers in his ear. A few minutes later he comes back with some weird glow in the dark drink and a bottle of water for me.

"I know you don't really drink anymore." She

says.

She's right. I need to stay away from it. Drinking away the pain is what lead to my other issues in the first place. That's a mindset I'd rather not return to. I've been slowly but surely learning to enjoy pain again. It makes me realize that I'm still alive. Still awake.

She takes a sip of her glow drink and her eyes light up.

"That's really good!" She says.

"What's it taste like?" I ask.

"Hmm." She thinks for a second. "Wet pussy."

I spit my drink. She starts hysterically laughing. I'm coughing.

"That was a joke." She says.

She slaps me on the back a few times.

"Are you going to be ok?" She asks.

"Yeah. I'm fine." I say taking a swig of my water to try and stop the coughing.

Now that the coughing has stopped we are just sitting here awkwardly.

"I have to be honest with you. I feel kinda out of place here. This isn't really my scene. I also didn't know I was supposed to wear a costume. I could've at least put a bag on my head." I joke.

She laughs, possibly out of pity for how bad that joke was.

"You actually look really great." She smiles. I melt into my chair.

I feel her foot gently start to rub up the inside of my leg.

The song changes and her ears perk up. She grabs me by the arm and starts dragging me towards the dance floor.

"What are we doing?" I ask, pretending like I don't know the answer.

"I love this song!" She exclaims. "Come dance with me!"

Reluctantly I go along with her. I really don't know how to dance. I'm awkward as hell, stepping back and forth and waving my arms to and fro. Alex is making it look like dancing is her second job. She's moving so fluidly to the music I can't possibly keep up. She turns to me and grabs my arm. She squeezes my bicep as I flex against her grip. She wraps one leg around me. I grip her waist and dip her. I bring her back up and hold her tight against me. Our foreheads touch and I desperately want to kiss her. She slides her hand down my chest and then grasps my belt buckle. She twirls around and pushes her back into me.

I place my hands on her stomach and move them slowly up her taut abdomen. My hands go under her shirt. She isn't wearing a bra. The urge to touch her is nearly insurmountable. I move them quickly back to her waist. Our hips move in unison. She is guiding me. Grabbing my hands she moves them to her outer thighs, then up to her hips.

She leans her head back against my shoulder. I turn my gaze to hers. My desire to kiss her is almost unbearable. Do I do it? I'm conflicted inside. Does she want me too? Have I waited too long? If I kiss her will I ruin everything we have worked towards? Would she forgive me? All these thoughts happen in an instant.

Her hand glides across the side of my face as if she's inviting me in. Our eyes are locked on each other. My stomach is in knots. I'm going for it.

Suddenly, there is a loud noise from the front of the building. At first there is a stunned silence, but then people start screaming. Two guys with pantyhose on their heads and leather jackets appear from the entrance. They are holding uzis. One begins firing in the air. The popping sound of the gun firing almost matches the drumbeat. The music is still blaring but the DJ has already hightailed it out the back exit along with a lot of the other patrons.

"Listen up!" One of them screams at the top of his lungs. "This is a holdup! I want everyone to throw their wallets, purses, jewelry, into the middle of the dance floor and my friend here is going to collect it all. No one does anything funny, and no one is going to get hurt. Especially not this hot little number here!" He says as he grabs some blonde in a skimpy outfit and shoves his gun up against her head.

Alex looks at me. She grins ear to ear. She leans in and whispers to me.

"No one knows who we are."

My heart starts racing. Am I really ready for this? We don't have our outfits and these guys have some serious weaponry.

Looking around the club I realize the lighting

is to our advantage. It's not well lit and the flashing of a strobe is distracting. The neon lights easily distort my image. I haven't talked to anyone but Alex, and the waiter didn't even look at me. Why would he? Also Alex is completely unrecognizable. If you saw her on the street tomorrow you would never know it's the same person.

The excitement coming off of Alex is palpable. I can feel her heat. She is a lioness waiting to strike. Her fists are balled up tight and she's smiling like a psychopath. Her eagerness is starting to affect me. Looking over at the guy picking up the valuables I notice he's placed his gun on the ground. He's ripe for the picking. Before I can even move, Alex is flying through the air and she side kicks the guy with the hostage right in the face. He goes flying back into the wall. He's already out. He didn't see that coming at all. I guess that's my cue.

I rush in at the other guy and belt him in the face. He was distracted by what Alex just did and he didn't notice me walking over. He reaches for his gun on the floor but I stomp on it and his hand. I feel his fingers break under the heel of my shoe. He lets out a yelp and then another quick right hand to his head knocks him out cold.

Well, that was surprisingly easy.

Alex approaches me with that big smile of hers. Just behind her I see that the first guy is getting back up. I signal to her with a subtle nod, she winks and then drops down. Leaping over her I nail the guy with a brutal right hand. Grabbing him by his collar,

I toss him towards Alex who jumps up in the air and catches him in a head-scissor takeover, smashing his head right on the dance floor. Alex does a quick front handspring to get back up on her feet.

Finally the musics stops, just the sound of a record perpetually spinning fills the room.

"Thank you!" The blonde yells as she runs out the front door.

Through the door the lights of a police car flashing can be seen.

Without hesitation Alex and I dash out the back of the club. The voice of someone screaming for us to stop quickly fades into background noise. We run and run until I feel like my lungs are on fire. Alex is a few steps ahead of me with no sign of fatigue.

"Alex!" I yell. "I think we are clear."

She stops running and comes back to me. She is absolutely giddy. Her cheeks are flushed and rosy. She isn't even out of breath.

"Ian. We did it! We worked perfectly as a team. We didn't even need to talk. We were in perfect synchronicity. You are ready. You are totally ready!" She says as she playfully slaps me on the chest.

For the first time in forever I do feel ready. I felt confident and sure of my every movement. My instincts took over and it was an amazing sensation. Adrenaline is coursing through my whole body and I'm simply vibrating with electricity.

The last time I felt this way was when I

fought O'Shaunessy. I knew that I had to win. There was no other choice. That ever-present thought gave me strength. Strength I had never had before and I thought I would never have again.

I thought I would never have again...

Alex touches my arm and I'm brought back down to earth. I fall into those beautiful brown eyes of hers. Something about her hair, the way it's framing her face, triggers a memory.

The waitress at the diner. It was her. I'm sure of it. Clever girl. She is quite literally a shapeshifter. Her body looked different. Her face looked different. She was a different person from the way she spoke to even her body language. She was hiding in plain sight and she even fooled me. She fooled me tonight as well. Katrina. Ellen. Are there others? How many names and faces does she have? Is there anything that this woman can't do? I still have so much left to learn.

I'm falling in love.

Ian... Stop.

"How do you do it?" I ask.

"Do what?" She says with a smile.

I reach over and pull off that green wig. Then I undo her bun and her hair falls down. I wipe away a small bead of sweat on her cheek. She uses her fingers like a comb and drags all her hair to one side. That beautiful purple and pink hair. She looks so silly and cute with that kitty cat makeup on. I can't help but feel happy whenever she is around.

"Everything."

CHAPTER 33

Shock

Toxin told me to meet him at the Bowery Park Tunnel tonight at midnight. That's not our turf and I don't exactly feel comfortable going there, especially in the dead of night. Some tweaker could be waiting just behind a trash can waiting to pop out and stab someone. Toxin, that son of a bitch, is going to get us killed. He told me "Dude, don't worry, it'll be worth it!". It better be. If it ain't then me and him, we're officially done. I ain't putting up with his shit no more.

Approaching the tunnel I can smell burning gasoline and I can just make out some barrels that are on fire. Getting closer now I can see that the tunnel is well lit from tens of burning barrels. There are about fifty some odd guys standing around talking to each other. It's a diverse group. I see guys from the Latin Princes, the Downtown Breakers, and even the Mean Mothers. Black, White, Latino. Even a couple of chicks. I think I've seen one of them before. Carissa is her name, or something like that. She ain't half bad looking with that spiky black hair and heavy eye shadow. I dig the fishnets she's got on. Nice legs.

I spot Toxin with his stupid ass green mohawk. He waives me in like I didn't notice his dumb ass. He's the only guy with a green freaking mohawk. Of course I can see you, you dolt.

"Hey, over here!" He yells.

"Yeah, I see you... Dumbass." I mutter to myself.

It's bad enough that I'm associated with this idiot, he doesn't need to make everyone else aware of it.

Standing next to the barrels, I'm trying to get warm. It's late October and it is cold as a three day old stiff outside tonight. I place my hands so close to the fire that my fingerless gloves start to singe. I'm beginning to lose feeling in my toes. For some reason, no matter how close to the fire I get, I can't seem to warm up.

"So what's all this about, Toxin?" I ask. "I don't know any of these other guys. They ain't from our group."

"Calm down. This is the start of a new group." He says.

A new group? What the hell's wrong with the East Side Clan? Toxin is a little bitch but I didn't expect him to be a defector, and now he's roped me up in it. Great, I'll probably get stabbed just for coming here.

"What do you mean 'new group'? We've got a group!" I say.

"This one will be better. I promise." He replies.

"It better be. I got a bitch back at my place I'd rather be shagging than standing out here in the cold with my balls shriveling to raisins."

Everyone shuts up all at once as a gigantic figure approaches the fires. Everyone is instantly drawn to him. He's gotta be six foot freaking ten and four hundred pounds of solid muscle. Jesus Christ, I've never seen a guy so huge. His biceps alone are bigger than my goddamned head and the veins are bigger than my arms. The creepiest part is he's wearing this twisted skull mask. It's really freaking me out. The more I look at it the more weirded out I get. It's like I'm staring at the grim reaper himself. I'm not sure but it looks like it's splattered with blood. I wonder what unfortunate soul crossed this guy. I'm sure they didn't live to tell about it. I get a chill every time I look into those dark, soulless eyes. The guy is one-hundred-percent pure freak of nature.

"Listen." He says in a deep scratchy voice. "You all come from different backgrounds, different gangs, but there is something inside all of you that makes you strong. You came here tonight for a reason. Look to your brother or sister at your side. Here united with a common goal, that is where true power lies. The time has come to cast aside your false faces and realize who you truly are."

He has everyone's attention including mine. This guy is a legitimate monster. My knees start shaking. Toxin is wide-eyed and grinning. How the hell did he meet up with this guy? I have no clue how this will be worth it to me.

"I only ask this one thing, and then you are free to do as you so choose. On Halloween night go to The 100th street and Paramount block. I'm sure you are all familiar with the one." He says.

I do know the one. It's where all the rich douchebags live. A street lined with nothing but luxury townhouses and penthouse apartments. You won't see a car under sixty thousand parked out front of any of them. I once banged some chick from that area. She was all loaded up on heroin and was spending daddy's money. I was more than happy to play the part of the bad boy in her rebellion fantasy.

"You have my permission to steal anything you desire. Consider it your reward for assisting me. As long as you stand together nothing will be able to get in your way. But I do ask this one thing..."

Now this guy is talking my language.

"When midnight hits...Torch it."

The crowd erupts. Toxin was right. This is a better gang. I've never seen so many different faces, people from all kinds of backgrounds united like this.

I can't wait to see all those rich mothers crying when their castles fall. With this crazy son of a bitch leading the way, I doubt anyone could stop us.

On Halloween night, the world will know who is really in charge.

CHAPTER 34

Rona Gray

Feeling Neon's back pressed against mine gives me strength. We are surrounded by a bunch of skull face paint wearing punks hungry for our blood. Neon told me that Halloween night is a dangerous night and she wasn't wrong. We stumbled upon these thugs preparing to commit some kind of serious arson. They were stockpiling gasoline, kerosine, and Molotov cocktails.

So here we are. Back to back. Punks on all sides armed with chains, pipes, and switchblades. It's ten against two.

I like those odds.

"Are you ready, Mr. Gray?" She asks me.

"Is that a joke?" I retort.

"Thought so." She says.

I drop to my back and put my feet to the air. Neon leans back and I toss her with my legs into a backflip. She twists mid-air and dropkicks one of the punks. His headband goes flying off into the darkness as he collapses to the ground. He's down for the count. Nine left.

Kicking up to my feet I catch a chain as it is swung at me. It wraps around my arm. I use it to pull a punk in and blast him in the face with a strong right hand. Grabbing him by his shirt and belt I hoist him overhead and toss him into two of the other punks. They fall like bowling pins. Watching them scramble is like watching puppy dogs fighting over a chew toy.

Neon gets attacked from both sides, but she drops into a full split causing the punks to punch each other. She then lifts herself into a handstand and spin kicks both of them. One of the punks recovers and she quickly drops and pops up so fast smashing the top of her head under his jaw. His mouth gets slammed shut so hard I can hear his teeth break. He's knocked out instantly. Eight left.

Three of them are hot on my tail brandishing knives. I'm leading them into my trap. Using a fire escape ladder I rush up a few rungs and backflip over them. Landing on one of the guy's shoulders I continue to flip backward with his head between my legs. I send him flying into the wall. He slumps to the ground after his head cracks against the bricks with a sickening thud. Seven left.

Neon is rushing towards me. Without even thinking I drop flat to the ground. She jumps over me and straight kicks a punk in the face. His mouth explodes in a grizzly display. Before he can even recover she hits him with a vicious spinning back elbow. He slumps to the ground, unconscious. Six left.

Three punks all jump me at once knocking me to the ground. I can feel them stabbing at me but the suit is doing its job. I get my feet back under me and with all my might I thrust upwards causing the three punks to splay out. I quickly turn and punch one of them in the nose, shattering his face. God, I do love these gloves. The lead shot in the knuckles makes my punches ten times as effective. Five left.

Another one rushes at me screaming, like that's going to do anything. A swift knee to the gut sends him to the ground. Grabbing the back of his shirt I whip him headfirst into a dumpster. His head dents the side, but I'm not done with him yet. Lifting him high above my head, I slam him down hard into the open dumpster and then close the lid. I get behind it and start to push.

"Time to go for a ride." I say.

I push the dumpster and it rolls right into the back of a guy that was about to attack Neon. He face plants in an almost comical way. Leaping up onto the dumpster I run along the lid and then jump off the opposite side, stomping the punks head on the way down. Three left.

Neon is surrounded by the three remaining punks. I look to her and she gives me a nod to hang back. I wait, ready. I'm excited to see what she does. A punk with a green mohawk gestures with a knife. He thrusts and she easily steps aside guiding the blade into one of the other guy's abdomen.

"Shit, man! You freaking stabbed me!" He yells.

Neon is looking at those two argue when the third man is attempting to sneak up on her. I know she's got this but I step in anyway. I grab him in a chokehold from behind. Neon sharply turns around and punches him in the face. I let him drop.

"Nice one!" I say.

"It's a gift." She smirks and blows the dust off her knuckles.

It's just us and these two. Mohawk man and Baldy. Baldy is bleeding pretty good from his gut. He's putting pressure on the wound, but for his sake I hope he surrenders.

"Get them!" He yells to Mohawk man as he slaps him on the back.

Mohawk man thrusts at us with his knife. This is no longer a fair fight. Not that it ever was. Neon just dodges and dodges his blade like it's nothing. Finally she grabs his wrist and squeezes, causing him to scream like a baby and fall to his knees. A quick knee to the face knocks him out for good. Neon just lets him drop and he smacks his chin off the ground. A couple of teeth come oozing out with his bloody drool. One left.

Baldy is seething with anger and holding his stomach. His face painted like a skull. His teeth gritted. He lunges at us but we separate causing him to fall face-first on the ground.

"Are you thinking what I'm thinking?" Neon asks me.

To say that Neon is creative would be an understatement. Up on the roof she has this guy tied to a chair, it's leaning off the ledge with just two feet on the ground. From the chair, another rope is tied to the chimney. If you cut the line, the guy will go plummeting twenty stories down. Needless to say, he doesn't want that.

"Wake up!" She says as she slaps him upside the head.

Groggy, he shakes his head around and quickly realizes his situation. Looking around he sees that he is teetering on the edge. He lets out a wild scream. He starts trying to fight but the chair shifts. Based on his expression I think he might have crapped in his pants.

"Hey! Eyes over here!" She yells at him.

The punk, although still scared, focuses on her. She has complete control. She grabs his head and pulls the chair forward so it sits flat.

"Let's start with a name." She says.

"Bitches like to call me Shock." He says rebelliously.

"Don't get cocky." She retorts as she bashes him on the top of the head.

"Shit! I bit my tongue!" He yelps.

"Alright Shock, tell me who he is. The guy with the skull mask." She asks.

"I don't know who the hell you're talking about, bitch! Piss off!" He spits blood at her.

Neon casually wipes the blood off her coat.

"Wrong answer." She says.

She steps aside and I know what she wants. I nail the punk with a swift kick to the chest. The chair goes back to tipping off the edge and the line is barely holding it up. It could snap at any moment.

Shock starts screaming as the chair begins to wobble even more.

"I swear! I don't know who he is! I've never seen his face!" He yells.

"Well you better give us something or it's a long way down." Neon says as she walks over to the simple knot that's the only thing holding him up.

She gently tugs on the rope and the knot starts to undo. Shock is really sweating now. The tension is exciting to me. Neon has this joker in the palm of her hand. I can't believe how sexy I find her at this moment.

"Ok, Ok. I don't know who he is. The other guys have taken to calling him 'The Son of Death'." Shock confesses.

"Why do you paint your face? Are you guys organizing?" She asks.

"Organizing? Maybe, in a sense of the word, but I think this guy wants to start hell on earth." He replies. "You know, old testament shit. Fire and brimstone."

"Why cops? Why is he taking out cops?" She asks more sternly.

"Pigs? I don't know nothing about no pigs."

Neon blasts him in the face, knocking out his two front teeth and shattering his nose.

"Damn you, bitch! Shit!" He yells. "I swear he didn't say anything about no cops."

Neon grabs him by the face and squeezes his mouth.

"You are going to tell me where he is or things

are going to get start getting messy." She threatens, oozing with pure confidence.

"The world's going to hell, Bitch. Can't you see it? It's happening all around you. You think you and your friend can stop this. You can't. No one can stop him. The guy's a living, breathing, monster."

"Suit yourself." She says.

That's my cue. I step up to him and grab him by the throat. I start pushing and I feel the tension on the rope getting tighter and tighter. The line is getting thinner and thinner and before long it snaps and now the only thing holding this guy up is me. His eyes are wide and I can see the terror on his face.

"No more games, you pathetic excuse for humanity. It's been a long day and I'm starting to get really tired. My grip is loosening. I'm not sure how much longer I can hold you. So listen to this suggestion and listen well. Either you tell us how to find the monster, or you're soon going to be taking up residence at Breakwood Cemetery."

One of the chair legs snaps. Lurching forward I just barely hold on to him. If I didn't have this mask on he would have clearly seen the panic in my face.

"Alright! Alright!" He screams. "He wants us to set fire to the 100th street and Paramount block. The place where all the slimy, rich douchebags live!"

Lifting him up I throw him down hard onto the rooftop, shattering the chair to pieces, following it up with a stomp to his chest. He lets out a burst of air and blood pours out of his mouth. Part of the chair has pierced him through the leg. He's holding it and wailing like a baby.

"Shit, man! My leg, man! Shit!" He mutters to himself.

"100th street? Why is that familiar?" I ask Neon.

"That's where that retired cop lives, Crenick was his name. He must be planning on taking him out, along with the whole block. But fire? That seems impersonal. Not his style. It must be a distraction." She says.

"But aren't there cops stationed outside that guy's house? I doubt he could sneak in. Especially a giant wearing a skull mask." I say.

"You think a couple coppers could stop this guy? Have you actually seen him? The guy is a legit, steroid-fueled, freak." Shock gurgles.

"What time is this going down?" I ask as I lean in, pressing down on my knee with my elbow, putting more pressure on his chest.

"At midnight! At midnight! Good luck getting there in time." Shock says with a sickening laugh.

A quick, soccer-style, kick to the head from Neon silences him.

"What time is it now?" I ask Neon.

She flips over part of her glove revealing a watch.

"It's 11:45! Shit! I don't think we can get that far uptown in time." She says.

"We have to try."

CHAPTER 35

Detective Tom Hudson

I'm flooring it. Other cars are flying by in my peripheral vision like a giant blur. My heart is pounding out of my chest. I have to get there. I have to get there. I push the accelerator even harder. It's a dangerous game I'm playing as I jump the curb and start speeding down the sidewalk. I'm almost there. Come on. Come on. Come on Tom, you can do it.

The call came in ten minutes ago. A giant, skull face man. He attacked my men outside Crenick's townhouse. Last I heard was screaming and then radio silence. Crashing into a mailbox out front of the townhouse I yank open the glove box and pull out my .44.

The two officers I had stationed outside are both dead. One's head is smashed in a car door. He must have gotten caught while going for his shotgun. The radio is still in his hand. Looking at it I almost gag. The other is impaled on a wrought iron fence. Two of the posts are sticking up through his chest. I quickly check for a pulse but he's gone. It's a grizzly scene. Those poor bastards didn't know what hit them.

Before I can even get my bearings I hear

screaming coming from inside the townhouse. A woman's scream. It falls silent as quick as it came. Rushing up the stairs my adrenaline is pumping so hard I'm moving without thinking. The front door is already open. The lock and door frame have been smashed to pieces. Debris is scattered all about.

Rounding the corner I come across the source of the screaming. A middle-aged woman, her spine is snapped. Her face is contorted into a horrific expression of terror. Her body, a twisted mass. One arm extended out as if she was pleading for her life. This must be Crenick's wife. How many innocents must die? This has to end tonight.

Entering into the main living area I finally get a look at the son of a bitch. Jesus! The guy is built like a brick shit house. Shoulders ten feet wide covered in muscle. Muscle on top of more muscle. Veins exploding out of every corner. There is no way this guy is human. Thumbing back the hammer, I ready my weapon.

"Police! Stop or I'll shoot!" I yell.

He turns to me holding Crenick by the head. Crenick looks like a child in comparison. His head is the size of an apple surrounded by those gigantic hands.

"Shoot him! Shoot him!" Crenick screams.

I hesitate and it's too late. The monster crushes Crenick's skull between his hands. The sound is like someone smashing a watermelon. The blood and brain matter are trickling out between his fingers. I've seen some nasty things, horrifying things, in my time as a cop but holy shit... I instantly gag.

Get it together, Tom! I point my gun again. My hand is shaking wildly. Why can't I keep it steady? My knees feel like they are starting to buckle. My vision is blurring. My heart... beating out of my chest.

"Kneel to the ground and put your hands behind your head! Do it now or else!" I try sounding tough when in reality I'm scared beyond belief.

"Or else what?" He says in a deep, booming, voice.

"I'll pull the trigger and it's lights out! I've got you now, you son of a bitch, and you're going to rot in prison for what you've done!" I yell.

He stomps the ground so hard a floorboard whips up and knocks me off balance. I'm flabbergasted and can't get my feet back under me.

"Pathetic." He says.

Next thing I know I'm up against the wall. My gun flying out of my hand. A mirror shattering behind me. The glass digging into my back through my overcoat. Trying desperately to mount some kind of offense I go for a knee to the groin. He easily stops it with one of his gigantic hands. Now I'm flying through the air. My back collides with the ground and the wind is knocked out of me.

Just barely rolling out of the way, the freak stomps the floor where my head was breaking the boards.

"Jesus!" I exclaim.

If I hadn't moved at the last second...

I manage to get back to my feet. Turning to face him he barrels into me like a freight train and we go through the wall. The wooden framework and drywall flies everywhere.

My mouth floods with blood. I think my ribs are broken. Shit. Look what you got yourself into, old man. A heavy knee lands on my chest. Struggling, I try to move but his sheer weight is holding me in place. He raises his fist in the air. I know he's going for the killing blow and there is nothing I can do about it.

Wait, what's that?

A line wraps around his fist and he is suddenly jerked backward. With whatever strength I have left I sit up. In the doorway stands Rona Gray, in his hands the other end of the line. Alex appears from behind him and rushes to my side. She helps me sit all the way up.

"Tom! Are you alright?" She asks.

I give her a thumbs up and I spit out a huge gob of blood.

"Better now...go take care of that creep." I say and she grins.

The freak stands back up and with no effort snaps the line off his wrist. Alex whistles and he turns and eats a kick to the face.

"Made you look!" She says.

The monster hardly even acknowledges the kick. Alex front handsprings and hits him with the heel of her foot right across the bridge of his nose.

Amazingly it has no effect.

Rona Gray steps into the fight and hits a couple of body blows followed by a powerful upper-cut.

"Is this a joke?" The freak says.

I sit up further, attempting to stand. My ribs are definitely busted. Damn. Where is my gun? Looking around I can't see it anywhere.

The monster grabs Gray and lifts him overhead as easily as he would a baby. He slams him down through the glass coffee table. Oh shit... Gray isn't moving.

Alex leaps through the air and dropkicks the freak in the back but she bounces off like she just hit a wall.

"Nothing but a bunch of pests!" The monster says.

He grabs Alex by the throat and hoists her into the air with one arm. She is dangling in space. She kicks him in the chest several times with little to no effect.

"This effort is futile." He says.

He slams Alex down across his knee. She lets out a terrible scream. My poor girl. I have to do something but I still can't get up. Blood starts pouring from her mouth as she tries to crawl away.

Out of nowhere Gray has recovered. Flying through the air he spears the freak right in the mid-section but it does nothing.

"Where is your passion?" The freak asks.

Grabbing Gray by his cape he tosses him halfway through one of the exterior windows. I'm severely regretting not calling for back up. A mistake that might end up costing me dearly. The monster turns and eats a backhand from Alex. That's my girl! Come on!

"This gnat again." He says.

Alex squares up to him. Her outfit is torn. Her mouth and face bloodied. The monster goes to punch her and she dodges. Come on girl! You've got this!

She dodges another punch and he staggers forward. Alex front rolls, twists around and spinning kicks him in the back of his big stupid head. He lets out an enraged groan. Girl, you got him now!

He rushes at her and she baseball slides between his legs. Popping up, she pushes him from behind slamming him into a half wall.

"You've got him, Neon! Finish him off!" I muster out a bit of positive reinforcement.

Reaching back he grabs a hand full of Alex's hair. He yanks it hard, causing her to fall to her knees.

"Little girls should play with dolls." He says as he rams Alex's face into the edge of the half wall. Her face is a bloody mess. She manages to crack a smile and spit defiantly in his face. He slams her face into the wall again. She's gone limp.

Please don't be dead. Please don't be dead, Alex. Please don't be dead.

"Sleep now. Dream of a better life." He says as he tosses her aside like garbage.

She lands in a heap. Lifeless. God, please let her still be alive.

Rona crawls over to her. He cradles her head. I can tell he's freaking out. His body language says he's terrified. He's looking left and right in a full panic. I've managed to get to one knee and somehow a two by four has gotten into my hand. Now is the time, Tom. You have to do something, anything.

With all of my might, and every ounce of willpower I have left, I smash that freak of nature in the back of the head, shattering the two by four into splinters. The monster falls to a knee. That's right you son of a bitch. Take that!

"Get out of here!" I yell to Rona Gray.

He looks at me confused. The monster is beginning to stir.

"Take her to Lochland Mercy hospital. Ask for Emma. Now go!" I yell to him.

He lifts up Alex and darts out the door. Good luck and goodbye my friends.

"It's just you and me now!" I talk big.

Suddenly, some of the windows blow out and the room is quickly engulfed in flames. What the hell? The room is rapidly filling with smoke. Grabbing a table leg, I go for another blow to the freak's head. He blocks it with his massive forearm and it breaks in half.

My gut explodes in pain. It feels as though he has punched clear through me. I can't breathe. Falling to the ground, the next blow is to my spine. The pain is sharp but over fast. Rolling over onto my back I realize I can't feel my legs.

"This is your fault, old man." The monster says in his booming voice.

Ribs and back broken. Can't breathe. Mind racing. A giant boot lingers just above me.

I hope Cara got a lot of candy tonight. She always eats too much and gets a tummy ache. We tell her every year to slow down but there's no stopping her once she gets going. My little angel. She looked so cute in her little princess outfit.

Melinda and her are probably waiting up for me. I need to get home soon.

CHAPTER 36

Emma

Another long night and I'm dead on my feet. Halloween is always brutal. Crime is way up and so many people come rushing in here with gunshot wounds, stab wounds, burns, and every manner of broken bones. Mercy Hospital is the slum hospital in the bad neighborhood. We have a reputation for not asking too many questions. I chose to work here because I felt like here, we help people who really need it. The downtrodden, the poor.

This place is run down and in desperate need of help but the city says they can't afford it. "It's not in the budget". If people want to go to a good hospital they should go to Saint Maria's. The average person can't afford a bandaid at that place, let alone serious surgery.

We often get criminals in here too. They want to remain anonymous. Unfortunately we have to take in the bad as well as the good. In this case, though, I feel like the good outweighs the bad. Helping out criminals and degenerates is just a necessary evil.

On Halloween you wouldn't believe how many poisoned kids we get. People are sick. Truly

sick. We already lost one tonight. It never gets eas-
ier. Watching a mother cry over their dead child
makes me happy that I don't have kids. If I did have
kids I'd almost consider not letting them go out on
Halloween at all. When I was young we used to run
in the streets, long into the night, without a worry.
What has happened to this city?

I scratch the side of my head with a pencil
and then cross off a name from the sign-in chart. The
sound of the pencil sliding across the paper is like a
needle in my ear.

The rush has died down. Most kids are in bed
by now. There'll probably be another rush around
two or three in the morning. It always seems to pick
up then. That's when the bars close and the drunks
get rowdy. Dangerously so.

Sitting down at the front desk I have a moments peace. I feel my eyes start to get heavy when
a water droplet splashes off the tabletop. Looking
up I see that one of the pipes must be leaking again.
In the waiting room right now are just some parents waiting on their kid to get his stomach pumped
and a few homeless people just trying to get out of
the cold. Even for the end of October it seemed un-
seasonably cold. Almost like it could snow at any
minute.

A father and son come out of the patient
area. The kid was brought in earlier with a razor
blade stuck between his teeth. Blood cascading out
of his mouth, father in full panic mode. What kind
of monster could do something like that to a child?

The father thanks me as they leave, his eyes red from tears. I notice no wedding band on his finger. He's kinda handsome and about my age...

My stomach growls loudly. When was the last time I ate? I can't even remember.

Taking a piss I nearly pass out sitting on the toilet. Working these double shifts is going to kill me. Lord knows the pay isn't all that great. I tell myself I'm doing it for the good people of this city and that gets me through most nights. My head falls forward and I just barely catch myself from slipping off the seat.

Looking in the mirror I see my hair is all pushed up on one side. A bad habit of mine when I get stressed out. My scrubs have quite a bit of blood on them though I can't recall specifically what or who it's from. I look like a hot mess. Skin pale and eyes sunken in. My stomach growls again.

Taking a quick trip to the cafeteria I get myself a cup of yogurt and a coffee. On the way back to my post I pass Dr. Gabriel who's passed out in a chair in the hallway. I step on his foot intentionally to wake him up. If I don't get to sleep neither can he.

I sit back down at the desk and go to enjoy my snack. I get about halfway through my coffee but I'm interrupted before I can even crack open the yogurt. The door flies open and in comes some joker dressed as a superhero but not any I recognize. An all-gray outfit with black trunks on the outside. A long maroon cape and a full face mask. In his arms is a woman... Alex!

"Help us! I need someone named Emma!" He yells.

I run to their side and check her pulse. It's weak but it's there.

"Are you Emma?" He asks.

"Yes. Please hurry!" I tell him.

Rushing past the desk I tell Angela to keep an eye out and that I'll be busy for a while. She hardly even acknowledges it. She just nods and doesn't look up from her crossword puzzle. I lead the two of them into an unoccupied room.

"In here." I say.

He places her down on the bed and gently strokes the side of her face. Even behind the mask I can tell he's panicking. Who the hell is this guy anyway, and why is he with Alex? I get between the two of them. I have to push him back forcefully.

"Alex, can you hear me, honey?" I ask.

Checking her pupils they are responsive but she is in a bad way.

"You need to get out of here and come back in normal clothes." I say to the masked man.

He doesn't move. He's just staring at Alex. Somehow I can feel his pain.

"Hey! Wake up! Get out of here and come back looking like a normal person! You understand me?" I yell.

"But...Alex." He says.

"I'll take care of her. You can't do anything to help her now, so go home or wherever you have to go. Get changed and come back. If someone, anyone, comes looking for you they most likely don't know what you look like outside of that getup. That will keep you safe for now."

He finally acknowledges but still doesn't move.

"You did good. Now it's my turn." I say while touching the side of his face.

He nods and then leaves.

"Ian? Ian?" Alex moans.

Alex has regained consciousness. Ian? That must be the guy that brought her in. I rush back to her side.

"Alex, baby, you're going to be ok." I tell her while saying a silent prayer to myself.

Feeling her abdomen I can tell she has a cracked rib or two but thankfully her protective outfit absorbed most of the damage. Her nose is broken and she starts gagging on blood. Thinking quickly I pinch the sides and snap it back into place. She lets out a scream.

"I know, honey. I know." I say.

"The monster... Don't let Ian..." She mutters as she passes back out.

Checking her vitals I can tell that she is stable for now.

"Rest easy baby, Emma is here for you."

CHAPTER 37

Ian

Changing as fast as I can, I dump the costume on the floor of Bram's cave, toss on a t-shirt and jeans, and fly right back out the door. My head is throbbing and my heart is pounding. I have to get back to Alex. The cab ride back to the hospital is excruciating but will no doubt take less time than the route I took back to Bram's Cave. I followed the rooftops just like Alex taught me.

I can't stop myself from thinking Alex is dead. She was a bloody mess. Her body was limp and lifeless. God, let her be ok. I'm not religious, but I find myself praying for her safety.

"Can we go any faster?" I scream at the cabby.

"Hey man! If you've got a problem, you can walk." He retorts.

Come on, Ian. Hold it together here.

Finally we pull up to the emergency room entrance. In one swift move I'm out of the cab and tossing a twenty through the window. I don't know if I under paid or over paid. I couldn't give a damn either way.

The woman at the desk. Who is that? Where is Emma? I look around frantically but don't see her.

"Can I help you sir?" A middle-aged black woman behind the desk asks me.

"Yes... can you tell me where I can find Alex Faye-Dar..." Emma cuts me off.

"Ahh! Mr. Jones. Come right this way!" She says in a happy tone.

I'm trying to remain calm. Following her into the hall she pulls me aside.

"So you must be Ian." She says.

Is this time to exchange pleasantries? Alex could be dead or dying and I'm standing here talking to some nurse I'm supposed to trust.

"Yeah... That's me. Alex? How is she?" I ask.

"Why don't you see for yourself." She says leading me to the room.

Pushing open the door I see Alex lying in bed. Head bandaged and under the sheets with an IV in her arm. My mind is flooded with images of Gloria and Rona, lying on the slab in the morgue. I feel that pit start to open in my chest again. My knees are weak. The room beings to spin. Collapsing at her bedside I lose consciousness.

It's pitch black. I can't see a damn thing. Slowly a blurry image begins to form. It's Alex lying on the ground. She's a bloody mess. Her hand is reaching out to me. Her eyes are full of tears and she trying to say something but I can't understand it. I'm paralyzed and I can't do anything to help her. Suddenly, that monster is standing over her. He's laughing as he raises his foot over her head. I'm fighting as hard as I can but I can't move. I'm screaming out to her but no sound is coming out. Then it's all over. He's crushed her skull under his boot. I scream so loud it feels as though my lungs are going to burst...

A sharp smell wakes me up. Emma is holding an ammonia inhaler under my nose. I discover I'm sitting in a chair next to Alex's bed.

"Are you ok, big guy?" Emma asks.

Am I ok? I really don't know. I've been rushing around so much I didn't have time to feel. As much as I don't want to, I start to focus on the pain. My back, my neck, my ribs, my head. They all light up. My adrenaline has worn off and my body is throbbing.

"I just got my ass kicked and my partner is dying. So I'm not exactly doing great." I say.

"Hey, drop the attitude!" Emma exclaims.

Come on, Ian. This woman is helping you. Try to relax.

"I'm sorry. So much has just happened. I can't seem to get my head straight." I say.

"Well I have some good news for you. Alex is going to be ok. CT Scan came back clear. X rays show some minor rib fractures but nothing broken. She should be fine in a couple weeks as long as she takes her recovery seriously. She's just resting now. She's exhausted."

"Thank God." I say.

"Knowing Alex, I'm sure she won't take my advice and rest. She'll probably be back on the street before she's fully healed."

"I guess you do know her." I joke trying to relieve the tension.

Emma comes over to my side.

"Ian, would you mind if I checked you out?" She asks. "I want to make sure you're ok too. You gave me a bit of a scare just now when you passed out."

"It couldn't hurt, I suppose." I say.

First she checks my pupils and does a couple quick reaction tests. She doesn't think I have a concussion. Next she makes me take my shirt off. It's actually difficult and she needs to help me. As protective as the suit is a few pieces of glass made it through the armor plates and got lodged into my skin. Emma very carefully removes them and then stitches the wounds shut. She has a gentle touch. Using a freezing stethoscope she checks my lungs. She tells me to take a few deep breaths.

"There's no fluid. That's good." She says as she moves a piece of hair behind her ear.

For the first time I'm actually looking at her. She's my age, maybe older. Forty tops. A little heavy set with a jet black bob haircut. One side is pushed up for some reason. It kinda looks like she just woke up and has bed head. Deep circles under her eyes dictate to me that that isn't the case. I'm fairly certain she hasn't slept in a long time. Her skin is extremely pale, ghost white. She has a bit of acne on her cheeks, but I'm not bothered at all. There is something about her that is very attractive. Our eyes lock and she gives me a soft smile.

"Ok, so other than some minor contusions, bumps, and bruises, you seem A.O.K. to me." She tosses me back my shirt.

"So how do you know Alex?" I ask as I pull my shirt back on, struggling not to groan from all the aches and pains.

"Tom actually introduced us. I met him back when we were both in the army. We served together in Vietnam. I was a medic. He knew I was someone trustworthy. He was worried about Alex's identity getting out, and he knew that I could keep a secret. I don't know if she told you but a few years ago she was a heavy favorite to go to the Olympics. It's a pretty simple relationship. She gets beat up and then I take care of her. But honestly, I haven't seen her in a long time. She's gotten so good at her job that she rarely ever gets hurt, and if she does she patches herself up. When she was first starting out though, yeesh, I could tell you a story." She says as she strokes Alex's hair. "I was married once upon a time, but we didn't have any kids. Alex is kinda like the daughter I never had."

Emma looks at Alex with fond eyes. It's easy to tell that she cares for her.

"Why didn't you and Tom get more involved? You know, put on some spandex yourself?" I ask.

"Are you kidding me?" She laughs. "We are both old and I'm not exactly in tip-top shape. Plus Tom with his family and bad knee." She pauses and touches Alex's cheek. "Alex is an amazing girl. There aren't many people out there who could do what she does... Speaking of Tom, I haven't spoken to him in a while, how's he doing?"

Tom. I completely forgot. He saved us. I have to go back.

Stepping up from my chair I immediately head for the door. Emma grabs my arm.

"Ian... She said don't go." Emma says.

Looking at Alex laying there just increases my anger. I can't stop thinking about Gloria and Rona lying dead. Their cold ivory bodies frozen in time. The rage inside of me is building and building. It feels like I'm a volcano about to erupt.

All of a sudden, the door flies open. Another nurse comes racing in.

"Emma! You have to see this!" She yells as she turns on the TV that's in the corner of the room. The TV clicks on and for a moment there is static. The nurse flips through the channels until she finds the one she was looking for.

There's a helicopter view of a city block, all aflame. Firefighters are desperately trying to put out the fire. A female field reporter appears on screen with big hair and a pink power suit.

"What you are looking at is the 100th street and Paramount block. The whole line of town-houses is completely engulfed in flame. The firefighters are doing their best but it might take a miracle to stop this nightmare! We are getting word right now that there have been several casualties. Among them are police officers who were on this street investigating a recent string of homicides. If this fire is related in any way to that investigation is unknown at this time. If you or your loved ones are still out on this tragic Halloween night the authorities demand that you return to your homes immediately."

"Is that where you were?" Emma turns to ask me.

"Tom was with us." I say.

Emma gets unsteady and then collapses into her chair.

"I'll leave you guys alone, clearly this is none of my business." The other nurse says as she rushes out of the room.

"Oh God...Tom." She says as she places her hand over her face.

Alex stirs from her slumber and opens her eyes. In a blink I'm at her side.

"Ian." She says with a small smile. "You're ok."

"Yeah, I'm doing fine. Just fine." I tell her with tears in my eyes.

"Tom?" She asks.

"I don't think so... Alex, I'm so sorry." I say.

She starts to cry. I do my best to comfort her but the fire inside of me is raging. That freak. That monster. He must be stopped. I will kill him. I swear it. My muscles begin to tense and I feel my strength starting to return.

"Alex. I have to go... I have to stop him." I say.

"He's a monster. He's unlike anyone I have

ever fought before... If you go alone... You'll die." She says with tears in her eyes. "Ian...".

She holds my hand and for the first time I truly feel that she loves me.

"Alex, I have to try."

CHAPTER 38

Alex

It's cold and overcast, my body is aching all over and I can barely stand, but it's Tom's funeral and I need to be here. My purple hair is stuffed up into a black hat, a veil over my face. The November wind blows and the leaves dance at my feet. Just the slightest drizzle makes it feel even colder than it is.

It was a beautifully done sermon, so many people came and spoke about Tom and all the good things he did. He truly was loved. I wish that I could have said something. Anything...

This other cop, Blankenship, he went up to speak but couldn't stop crying. He hardly got a word out. All I managed to understand was "best friend" and "love you, brother". Surprisingly I don't remember Tom ever mentioning him.

The casket was closed because Tom's body was found burned to a crisp with his chest completely smashed in. There was no way they would show the body. I feel horrible for Melinda, seeing her husband in that state. I do the best I can not to cry, to stay strong, but even then a few tears have managed to squeak out. I brush them away.

"Thomas was loved by many and although

his mortal body has died, his soul will continue on and live in our hearts, and in the kingdom of God, forever." The pastor says.

They begin lowering the casket. His fellow officers take turns tossing a handful of dirt on top. Each lump of dirt echoes across my ears like the sound of a distant thunderstorm rolling in. Melinda and Cara are in hysterics, crying their eyes out. I can't blame them. At my mother's funeral I was the same way, but I didn't have someone to hold me. My father wouldn't even look me in the eye, let alone give me a comforting hug.

Turning, I look at Ian. He's been a rock this whole time. Our hands intertwined. I'm squeezing so tight that it feels as though our hands are becoming one. His strength gives me strength. Something has changed inside of him though. He's become cold and distant the past few days. I know he must be focused on that monster and what to do about it, and I know he's worried about me. He didn't leave my side the entire time I was in the hospital. I could tell that he was torn inside between his desire to stay with me and his desire to go and face the monster again. Imagining him going toe to toe with that freak alone makes my heart feel like it's dying.

Emma comes up to my right side. She looks nice in her black dress and hat. It's a very flattering outfit. It's easy to see that she has been crying. Her eyes are red and puffy, her mascara has stained her cheeks.

"His poor family. I can't even imagine what

they are going through right now." She says.

Cara reaches into the hole and Melinda just narrowly grabs her before she falls in.

"Daddy! Don't go, Daddy!" She screams.

Melinda collapses and holds Cara tight. The two cry so loud I can feel my heart breaking all over again. I think of my own mom's funeral and how my father looked. I'd never seen him cry before that day. Even up until the funeral itself he didn't cry. The image of the coffin going into the ground is what finally set him off, I think, as for me, I cried for a week straight. I cried until no more tears would come out.

"We have to stop him. We can't let this keep going." I say with tears streaming down my face. I do my best to wipe them away.

"What are we going to do? We only have the one lead and if he gets to him before we can act we might not be able to catch him... ever." Ian says.

My fist balls up tight. My fingernails dig deep into the palm of my sweaty hand. I want nothing more than to stop this freak but my body is not even at fifty percent. I wouldn't stand a chance against him now. He destroyed me when I was in peak condition. Now I would just be like a rag doll to him.

"I've been thinking about what you guys told me and I think I have a plan." Emma says.

Over lunch at the VFW hall after the funeral, surrounded by all of Tom's friends and family, Emma lays out her plan. She tells us that she's going to get transferred to Saint Maria's and she'll get herself assigned to watching over Officer Stevens. She will stay there, day and night, until the monster is caught.

"That's insane. You might be there for months! Plus I don't want you to put yourself in danger." I tell her. "If anything were to happen to you I wouldn't be able to live with myself."

"It's the least I could do for Tom." She says. " I don't have a family except for a shitty ex-husband. I can handle it. Don't worry."

I reach across the table and hold her hand.

She continues and says that at the first sign of anything suspicious she will contact us immediately. I feel absolutely horrible putting her in harm's way like this but she insisted. In a lot of ways Emma has been a guardian to me. When I was first starting out I got myself into all kinds of trouble and she patched me back up. I can never repay her for all the things that she has done for me over the years. She's like a big sister that I never had. Actually, in some ways, Tom and her were like parents to me.

Now I'll never get the chance to tell Tom how much he meant to me. I look at Ian with longing eyes.

"Why are you staring at me?" He asks.

He's been sitting there silent the whole time and he hasn't even touched the plate of food he got for himself.

"Oh, sorry. I was just spacing out." I lie.

Why is it so hard for me to express how I feel? Ian has been with me for months now and I have started having feelings for the big lug. I don't know what it means just yet. I'm not attracted to him in the strictest sense, but his selflessness, his valor, his unbeatable spirit have turned me on more than once.

That night at the club, No Atmosphere, I would have let him have his way with me. I can't recall a time I was more aroused. I so badly wanted him to make a move but he's such a gentleman and I was too chicken shit to try anything myself.

I want to tell him how much I care for him but I'm afraid of ruining our relationship. We are such a good team and I desperately do not want to do anything to botch that. The best course of action is to leave a more intimate relationship out of the equation, I think?

When I was lying in the hospital bed and he thought I was asleep he told me he loved me. It was so hard to not react to that. Part of me wanted to leap out of the bed, grab him, and give him the biggest kiss, but instead I just laid there with my eyes shut. He wasn't explicit whether he meant love me like a sister, or if he was in love with me. I'm still not certain and I definitely wasn't going to pry. He probably only said it because he thought I didn't hear it, or maybe he did know that I was just faking it.

Oh my God. My head is spinning.

"Hey, are you ok?" Ian asks me as he rubs my back.

"Yeah, I just got a little light-headed is all." I say.

"You need to get more rest. We can talk more about this stuff at a later time." Emma says.

I truly wonder how much time we have. The time between incidents has varied so much. It's either erratic or strictly planned and I don't know which. Is he going off opportunity? So many questions still without answers. Some, I'm sure, we will never know.

"Alright. I think it's time we get going." Ian says.

Ian helps me out of the building and down the front step to the curb. He hails a cab and helps me into it.

"I just need to talk to Emma for a second. Hold on." He tells me.

The two of them are just out of earshot so I can't hear their conversation. Leaning my head back against the seat, I watch them. What are they talking about? Emma is closer to Ian's age and she told me in private she thinks he's kinda cute. Emma's not a bad looking woman. She's got a big heart too. A lot of desirable qualities. This weird feeling suddenly erupts inside of me.

Is this jealousy?

It looks like Emma is arguing with him now but he calms her down. He places a hand on her shoulder and says something that makes her chuckle. I think I see her hand him some kind of package but my head is getting heavy and I'm going in and out of consciousness. I could have easily imagined it.

Ian joins me in the cab but Emma follows just behind and is at the window. I'm pretending to be asleep but in reality I could pass out at any given moment. All of this stress has just been wreaking havoc on my mind and body.

"Are you sure you know what you're doing?" She asks him.

"You don't have to worry about me, Emma. Desperate times require desperate measures." He says completely sure of himself and confident.

"Alright. Well. Please. Please. Be careful." She says as she gives him a playful smack on the cheek. "Both of you... I'll be in touch." She says.

"You be careful yourself, ok? See you soon." Ian replies.

Emma walks away and the cab starts heading to my apartment. I start dozing off for real this time. Reaching over I take Ian's hand into mine.

Ian, what are you planning?

CHAPTER 39

The Monster And His Work

The winter chill has begun. I pull my coat closed to keep out the sharp wind.

100th Street has never looked so beautiful. The sky is still raining down ash from the night before. Not a single building survived. All that remains are the skeletons of a past that should have been long forgotten.

As I walk the street I pass makeshift memorials for those who died. Photos and meaningless religious markers, candles that have died out. More innocent lives lost again for no reason.

When will they learn?

A crying family weeps at the foot of the stairs of a building that was left in ruins. I offer my condolences. Reaching into my pocket I find a lighter. I use it to relight the candles at the base of the stairs. The family thanks me.

Finally, I come to a place I used to call home. Long ago they tore down all the tenements that were here and replaced them with these luxury townhouses. This spot is where my home once stood.

Bypassing the police tape, I wander through

the wreckage. Looking up at the metal framework that surrounds me I feel as though I am in a cage.

    I am trapped in a cage.

    It won't be much longer now.

    Soon I will be free.

    Sifting through the ashes I find a teddy bear.

    Half of it is burned to a crisp.

CHAPTER 40

Emma

As much as I don't approve of it, I gave Ian the drugs he requested. Testosterone and adrenaline that I took from the hospital's stores. He told me that he's used them before and do not worry, but I can't help it. Knowing what he plans on doing I fear that it may be a suicide mission.

I've grown fond of Ian over the past few weeks. He's sweet and gentle but also tough and rugged. I've developed a little crush on him. When I told Alex she seemed displeased. I asked her if she liked him and she denied it but I could tell that she was lying. If she wants him I don't stand a chance. She's younger and way more attractive. Although she is almost like a daughter to me, I still feel jealous of her from time to time.

Alex has been out of the hospital for a couple of weeks now and I've been checking in on her. She's recovering well but it's going to take time. If she jumps back in the saddle too quickly she could get hurt permanently. I always warn her that when you play with fire you might get burned. She always laughs because of the pun on her name. I swear it is unintentional.

I've been at Saint Maria's for a few days. It took a bit for my transfer to go through, and even more politicking to get myself assigned to Officer Stevens. So far it's been pretty easy, I can imagine why the nurse before me didn't want to give it up.

Officer Stevens has been in a coma for a few years now. He's in his late forties with wispy blonde hair. Calling him Officer is a bit of a misnomer. He hasn't been on the force in over a decade. His first name is Martin.

Martin was in a jet ski accident with some escort. She died and he ended up the way he is now. No family to speak of. What a lonely life. I think about my own life for a moment and how I'm being a hypocrite. If I went into a coma tomorrow people could say the same things about me and yet I don't feel unfulfilled. For the most part I'm content with how my life has gone. If I hadn't divorced Oscar and moved back to Lochland, I wouldn't have met back up with Tom and I'd never have met Alex. If that hadn't happened I wouldn't be a part of this super-hero team. Well, a small part.

Today is November 27th and it's already starting to snow. Sitting next to the hospital bed I glance out the window and watch the flurries coming down. Snow is beautiful but I could live without all the complications it brings with it. Car accidents, sledding accidents, snowball fight accidents. It's a busy time of year for a nurse, I'll tell you what.

I decide to pick up the phone and give Alex a

call. It rings a few times before she answers.

"Hello?" She says.

"Hey Alex, It's Emma." I say

"Hey Emma, how are you?" She asks.

"I'm doing well. Nothing to report as of yet." I say. "How are you feeling?"

"A little better each day but it's going to be a while before I can head back out. This concussion really has me knocked for a loop, but it pains me even more to just be sitting around" She says.

"It's good that your getting rest though, you really need it. You push yourself too hard. If you run the engine too long you run out of fuel." I say.

"Is that another one of your sayings?" She asks with a chuckle.

"I just thought of it." I say.

"I bet you were saving that one for weeks." She retorts.

I laugh. She's such a sweet kid.

"How's Ian?" I ask.

"I haven't seen him since the funeral. We've only talked on the phone a couple of times. He told me not to worry about him, but I am. I'm worried sick. I hope he isn't off doing something crazy." She says.

I think of the drugs I gave him.

"I'm sure he just needs to get his head on straight, you know? That was a traumatic thing you two went through." I lie because I know exactly what he is doing.

An orderly comes into the room.

"Hey Alex, can you hold on a second." I say placing the phone down.

He's a heavyset guy, but pretty tall with long hair in a ponytail. This is the first time I've seen him. He shoots me a smile.

"Can I help you?" I ask.

"Oh, yes. My name's Daigan, Walter Daigan. You can just call me Walt. I'm an orderly."

"I can see that." I joke. "What do you need Mr. Stevens for?"

"I'm taking him for a CAT scan. He gets one once a week." He says.

That's right. I did read that. I need to become more familiar with the test schedules for Stevens. It would be bad if they transfer me out of here for not knowing the things I need to know.

"How come I haven't seen you around before?" I ask.

"I could say the same about you. What happened to Amy?" He asks.

Amy was the nurse I replaced. He does have a point. I am the new one to this hospital and I've only been here for a few days, not even a whole week. It is entirely possible that I just haven't run into this guy before.

"Oh, well, she was burned out. I'm her replacement. My name's Emma. Nice to meet you, Mr. Daigan." I say.

"Please. Walt is fine." He says with another smile.

He's actually pretty handsome and he

doesn't seem that much younger than I am. I'll have to remember that name. Walt. I wonder if he likes full-figured gals.

"Ok. Just be sure to bring him right back." I say in a pathetically flirty way.

"You've got it, ma'am!" He says as he rolls the bed out of the room.

Picking the phone up I go back to talking to Alex.

"Who was that?" Alex asks.

"Just an orderly, he was bringing Stevens to get a test done. No big deal." I say.

"Just remember, if you see anything out of the ordinary to give me a call. I'm not going to go back to work for a while so I should be reachable." She says.

"Do you have a number for Ian?" I ask.

"Oh... you want his number?" She asks.

I can tell from the tone of her voice that she thinks I'm trying to put the moves on him but honestly I just wanted to check on him.

"I was just wanting to check in on him. See how he's doing." I say.

"I thought you weren't worried." She says.

I am worried. I am horribly worried. After losing Tom, and seeing Alex in the state she was in, I don't want to lose another person.

"I'm not. What if I call you and you're asleep? It would be nice to have a backup." I say.

After a little more prodding she gives me the number.

CHAPTER 41

Eric

I don't know what has come over Ian but in the past couple weeks I feel like he has doubled in size. His muscles have grown thick, heavy, and lord, all those veins popping out. The man looks like a freak. Even on the coldest days he's managed to get his shirt off. You can see the steam coming off of him, like his whole body is on fire. He keeps insisting on lifting crates by himself, pushing sleds by himself. Eventually you just give in and let the man do what he damn well pleases. He's been so cold and distant, but also focused, and I don't want to step in his way. He's walking with a purpose now, unlike before.

On one of our lunch breaks he asked me to hold the heavy bag in the locker room for him. That motherfucker might as well have been punching me. His hits were so hard It was like I was taking the punches head-on. He didn't even wear gloves. His fists were a bloody mess but the bag looked even worse. It was torn to shreds. My woman wanted to know if I had been in a fight. I felt embarrassed so I told her a palate toppled over on me.

There's this fat piece of shit, Toby, that they just recently hired. Based on how this motherfucker

talks you'd think he was built like Arnold Schwar-
zenegger and had the fighting skills of Bruce Lee. He
claims to have a black belt in karate but I haven't
seen any evidence of this. During a break the other
day he broke a board over his knee like that was supposed to impress us. This loud mouth must think
this place is like prison or something, like he needs
to make someone his bitch to fit in. Ian was not the
one to try.

Toby got in Ian's face and tried to give him
a hard time over some bullshit. Pretending like Ian
spilled some oil on his shoes. Ian straight-up ig-
nored him, which only made him try harder. Next
he started calling him names like "bitch boy" and
"pussy". "Only a fairy would walk around with his
shirt off around a bunch of other guys. He must be
trying to attract another sissy boy". Ian still kept
his cool.

"Tell your wife I said hi." Toby said while
grabbing at his dick.

Well that was it. Ian quickly turned and intentionally missed Toby's head by an inch and
punched a hole straight through the wall behind
him. You should have seen Toby's face. It lit up like
fireworks on the fourth of July. I swear that bloated
piece of garbage shit his pants. As he scrambled
away I could have sworn I saw Ian smile.

I never saw that fat lump again.

Today I decided to get to work early and
Ian was already here. It's a frigid morning but Ian
is standing with his shirt off staring out over the

water. Steam rising off of his shoulders.

"Hey man! What's up?" I yell to him.

He doesn't even acknowledge me. I toss my bag down and approach him. Standing to his left side I can see that he's totally focused on the horizon.

"What's going on, man?" I ask.

He finally notices me.

"Sorry. I was lost in thought." He says.

"I know it none of my business, but what's going on with you lately?" I ask.

"Eric. If someone hurt your family and you could do something to hurt that person, would you?" He asks.

"Is that a serious question? Of course I would. Nobody lays a hand on my family unless they plan on drawing back a stump, you feel me?" I say.

I hesitate but I decide to tell him a story.

"While I was in the joint, my son of a bitch neighbor tried putting the moves on my wife. He didn't rape her but he certainly tried to get her in bed. Then after she rejected him he called the cops and tried to get my wife put away and to have our children put into foster care. That slimy mother... When I got out I wanted to kill him. My wife begged me not to retaliate. She said it wasn't who I was. That I wasn't that type of man. Anyway, he had moved away but it didn't take me long to find out where he was. Even though she begged me not to do anything, I found that son of a bitch and I hurt him. I hurt him so bad that he would never think of doing some shit like that again, but when the moment came when I could have ended his life I stopped myself. A few weeks later he came over and apologized. My wife was so freaking happy. Seeing her face made me know it was worth it."

"But you didn't kill him." He says almost like it's a question.

"No. Killing is wrong, man. If I had killed that guy, how would I be any better than him? It's better to forgive and forget. Killing is something you can't take back. That shit will haunt you forever." I say.

I realize who I am talking to. A man who killed another man, and from what I can tell, it was on purpose.

"Look man, I'm sorry." I say.

"It's true. It is a scarlet letter on your chest forever. A shadow that you can never outrun. But sometimes that is a necessary burden for someone to carry." He replies.

"Can I ask you something? Did you do it, like, on purpose?" I ask referring to the O'Shaunessy incident.

"I did." He replies.

"Do you regret it?" I ask.

"Not for a single second." He says as he turns and walks away.

CHAPTER 42

Ian

I'm not the biggest fan of needles but eventually you just don't feel the pinch anymore. I know I'm wading into dangerous waters with the dosages but I want to get stronger. I need to be stronger and I'm running on borrowed time. When is that monster going to strike again? I have to be ready.

My hits did nothing. Alex's hits did nothing. Is he invulnerable? I've never hit a man before and had them not even react. I've broken men's jaws, busted out teeth, cracked skulls, but this guy took everything I had and more, and he just turned the other cheek.

When I was a boy I had a reoccurring nightmare about a boogeyman living in my closet. At night he would come out and hold me down to the bed. His twisted, wretched face terrifying me down to my very core. My father would come in the room at the call of my screams. He would tell me that there was nothing there. That monsters weren't real...

I need to be stronger. It's an all-consuming thought that pushes me through the pain of every workout. The pain of every injection.

First thing in the morning I run five miles. If I can't beat him in the strength department, maybe I can outlast him. I hate this kind of exercise but I do it anyway. Once I'm done with that I head into the cave.

I usually start with rope climbs. It gets my body nice and warmed up for the coming brutality. Then I hit the rings and focus on the Iron Cross. When I lower into the position I feel like my body is a slab of pure steel that can not be broken. I hold it for as long as possible, which is when it feels like my muscles are about to tear right off the bone. I've told myself over and over that if I can survive this hell there is nothing that freak could do that would hurt me. I whip my body around to gain momentum and backflip to dismount.

Next is gymnastic training. I focus only on the tumbles that Alex taught me. Backflip, front flip. Back and front handsprings. Chaining them together. Nothing too fancy but capable of getting me out of sticky situations. If I am to beat the monster I have to be ready for anything.

Now comes the true test as I rip a barbell off the floor loaded with five hundred pounds.

"Not good enough!" I scream as I slam the barbell back on the ground.

I load it up with six hundred, and it too comes off the floor like nothing. This is the heaviest pull I have ever done and it's still not good enough. I have to go further. I struggle with seven hundred, but I know I can do more.

The clanking metal is music to my ears as I load on eight hundred pounds. Taking a handful of chalk, I dust up my palms and fingers and then the bar. My fingers lock around the barbell like a vice grip. I squat down and take a deep breath. I think about that unholy freak of nature and what he did to Alex. It's all the motivation that I need. Screaming and pulling as hard as I can the barbell comes free from the floor. My shins are cut and raw, caked with blood as I drag the barbell up. At my knees it gets stuck. I close my eyes and see Alex lying in that hospital bed. With one last thrust I get the barbell completely up. Dropping it to the ground it breaks the concrete floor.

I get a sudden head rush and I nearly collapse. I lean up against the cold, bare, concrete wall. The cool stone feels good against my red hot forehead. Sweat is pouring off me and blood is dripping from my nose. I wipe it away.

"Shit." I mutter as I look at the blood on the back of my hand.

I go to the mirror and I barely recognize myself. Steam is coming off of my shoulders and I'm covered in sweat. Since taking the steroids my body temperature has felt elevated and I can't seem to cool off. My body has completely changed in appearance. I thought I looked insane when I trained to fight O'Shaunessy but I'm putting my old self to shame. My muscles are thick and swollen. Veins coming out everywhere. I'm starting to look just like that monster...

Blood begins to trickle from my nose again and I wipe it away once more. My heart is pounding so hard it's like the rhythmic beat of a drum. Tremors begin in my muscles and I can't stop myself from shaking. Finding it difficult to stand I sit on a bench nearby. I look down at my hands. The callouses have torn off and my hands are caked with blood and lifting chalk.

"Come on, body. Hold on just a little longer."

I close my eyes and a vision of all the innocent people he's killed flash before me. Tom... I see the 100th street block on fire. A twisted skull laughing through the flames. Alex lying in a pool of her own blood. Coffins being lowered into the ground.

"No Daddy! Don't go, Daddy!" Cara screams.

It feels as though my heart has torn completely in half all over again.

A rage wells up inside of me.

I stand up, grab a dumbbell, and smash the mirror.

Glass flies all around and then falls back down to the ground like a rain of fireflies. Each piece catching the light, but only for a moment.

My shattered reflection stares back at me.

The doomsday clock is hanging over my head. I focus on what I am going to have to do. I've done it once before, but can I kill again? Won't killing him make me no better than him? I think about Eric's story, about how he restrained himself from killing that guy at the very last second. That something inside of him told him to stop. With O'Shaunessy, I heard no such voice. There was only anger, blind, pure, unbridled rage, and the beat of my own heart. What does that say about me? Do I have more in common with this monster, this freak beyond words, than a good, honest, hardworking man?

My crime was a crime of passion...

Perhaps his is too.

CHAPTER 43

Emma

I've been running on empty. It's been a month now
and I've hardly slept more than a few hours a night.
All I want to do is collapse but I must stick to
my mission. For Alex. For Ian. For Tom. It's almost
Christmas and I haven't bought a single gift, hell, I
haven't even left the hospital this entire time. Men-
tally I feel like I am on the brink of a breakdown.

I have seen nothing suspicious. No visitors.
Nothing. Nothing at all out of the ordinary. Stevens
gets his weekly tests and that's it. I've watched more
daytime TV this month than I have my entire life.
I could tell you everything about every soap opera
on right now and I'm pretty sure I could win at Jeop-
ardy.

Walt comes in to bring Stevens for his
weekly tests. We exchange pleasantries and then he
takes him away.

Staring out the window I see that about a
foot of snow has fallen. It's the most there's been
this year and it's still coming down. Flipping on
the TV it's another soap opera. I wonder what Julia
will do about her cheating husband and his lover
in today's episode. I slump down in my chair. My

eyelids are becoming heavy and all I want to do is sleep...

Suddenly, I wake. I don't even recall dreaming. It's almost as if someone just turned off my power switch and then turned it back on. It's dusk. I look at my watch and it's four o'clock. Oh shit! I've been asleep for over eight hours. Rubbing my eyes furiously I try to snap out of it. The TV is still on.

"Alright Martin... what did I miss?" I ask as I turn to the bed.

Oh no... It's empty.

Leaping from my seat I rush into the hallway.

"What's wrong?" Another nurse asks me.

"Have you seen Mr. Stevens?" I ask.

"I haven't, but you can ask at the nurse's station." She says.

Rudely, I run towards the nurses station while she is still talking to me. Sitting at the station is Katie, a face I actually know.

"Katie!" I yell.

Her head pops up suddenly.

"What is it, Emma?" She asks.

"Mr. Stevens, the guy I've been watching, where did he go?" I ask.

"Let me check." She says as she picks up the phone. "Hey, yeah, it's Katie up on floor fifteen. Yeah, can you help me locate a patient? Great... yeah. Martin Stevens... Yeah. Ok. Thanks. You have been very helpful."

She turns to me as I wait with bated breath.

"Well?" I ask.

"He checked out." She says.

"Checked out? Checked out? The guy is in a freaking coma! How did he check out?" I scream at a completely unreasonable volume.

"They said his son came and got him." She says.

"Son? The guy has no family. Who the hell checked him out?" I ask.

She shrugs her shoulders.

"I guess the guy had everything he needed to transport him." She adds.

I rush back to the room and pick up the phone. My fingers fly fast as I dial the number Alex gave me for Ian. It rings and rings and rings.

"Come on, Ian! Come on!" I mutter to myself.

"Hello?" His voice rings in my ears. Thank God.

"Ian! It's Emma!" I say.

"Hey Emma. What's going on?" He asks.

"He's gone! He's gone! Stevens. He's gone. I don't know who took him." I say.

"Ok. Calm down. Just tell me anything you can. What happened?" He asks.

Waiting a second I think and try to remember what I can. The last thing I remember is seeing Walt take Stevens out of the room. He always brings him back right away. Maybe Walt knows something?

"I'm sorry Ian, I was exhausted and I fell asleep. The last thing I can remember is an orderly taking Stevens out for his tests." I say.

"Orderly?" He says as if he knows something.

"Yeah, Ian, what is it?" I ask.

"What was his name?" He asks.

"Walt. Um... Walter Daigan." I say.

I hear the phone click. The dial tone rings in my ears. My heart is pounding in my chest and I don't know what to do. Ian must know something.

CHAPTER 44

Ian

Walter Daigan. That guy I met all those months ago and worked with, the man that saved my life, he's the monster. I can not believe it. He was so kind and gentle. Besides the obvious name connection, him being that freak didn't really occur to me. He's a big guy but he didn't seem that big. On that Halloween night, no one could have guessed they were the same person. I got so wrapped up in all of this that I never reached out to him like I said I was going to. Maybe if I had... He was right in front of me this whole time. Had I done something, anything, maybe things might have been different. Tom and some of those other cops might still be alive.

Damn!

Damn!

Damn!

I failed. I failed Tom. I failed Alex. I fucking failed.

I won't fail again.

After hanging up on Emma I rushed immediately to the dock. The snow is really piling up and the walk was not fun but nothing was going to stop me today.

I barge into my boss' office.

"Hey, asshole!" I yell.

He pops up from behind the desk.

"Yeah, uh, Hempstead? Right?" He asks.

"Yeah, close enough. Look I need some help and I need it now." I say.

"Well step right up, what can I do you for?" He asks.

"The big guy who worked here that you fired a little while ago. Daigan. I need an address." I say.

"Hmm. I'm not sure I can just give out that kind of information... Maybe if you gave me some kind of incentive I could help you." He says.

A fury begins to burn inside my chest. I don't have time for games. Reaching across the desk I grab this asshole by the back of his shirt and slam his head down on the desk. Hard. He lets out a yelp.

"How's this for incentive? You tell me his goddamned address and I don't bash your disgusting head in. Sound like a deal?" I ask.

"Ok, ok, ok. I'll tell you!" He yells.

I let him up and he goes rummaging through papers. It feels like it's taking forever and I'm starting to get really impatient. Pacing back and forth it feels like my skeleton is going to leap out of my skin.

"You want to hurry it up?" I say.

"Ok. Look, here it is. 142 Carrington Lane." He says.

As I'm going out the door he screams that I'm fired. I couldn't care less. Leaving the dock I run into Eric. He's bundled up tight in a big heavy coat and gloves. His breath is visible and he seems like he's just trying to stay warm.

"Hey man, I just want to say I'm sorry about the other day. It's none of my business what's going on in your life." He says.

"It's ok, Eric. You are a good friend. Maybe I'll catch you around sometime." I say.

"Yeah, man. You too."

We shake hands. Eric is a good guy. I can't believe I thought he might have been the monster. After seeing that freak in person it is no doubt in my mind that it's Daigan. But why did he kill his own father? Now his motive seems so unclear to me, but it won't for long. He's about to face a rude awakening.

I take a cab to 142 Carrington Lane. The whole time I'm clenching my fists and gritting my teeth desperately trying to contain the absolute rage inside of me.

"Is this really the place?" I ask the cabby.

"Yeah, 142 Carrington Lane. Just like you asked for. That will be $11.75 please."

I toss him a wad of cash and get out of the vehicle.

Before me stands a rotting old victorian home. Three stories with most of the windows either boarded up or busted out. It's totally in disrepair. Paint peeling off everywhere, moss has grown over the front porch. It looks like something out of a horror movie. Does he truly live here, or was this just the address he wrote down so no one could track him?

Hesitantly I approach the front door, taking the steps one by one, trying to be as quiet as possible. The boards creak beneath my feet and I wince. Through the windows I see no signs of life. The roof over the front porch seems like it's going to collapse from all the snow.

My hand touches the doorknob. Should I announce myself? I am thoroughly unprepared. Maybe if I just come as myself I can learn something and come back ready to fight? I should have thought this through but it's too late now.

Suddenly, I remember Bram telling me to always look before I leap.

I leap.

"Hey, Walt? It's me, Ian, from the dock?" I say after knocking three times and doing my best to hold off the anger that is on the verge of erupting out of me.

Hearing no response I try the doorknob. It isn't locked. The door opens easily enough and I enter. I thought the outside looked bad... The stairwell is collapsed and there is no way to get to the second floor. The place is completely barren. The only furniture is a classic looking dusty old couch that seems like it hasn't been sat on in a hundred years.

"Great. There's no way he was staying here." I say.

A cold breeze comes in through one of the windows and I start to shiver. Suddenly, my nose perks up. I can smell the faint odor of something burnt. Following it like I'm some kind of blood-hound, I enter into a back room.

"Holy shit." I say to myself.

Painted on the wall are the names of all the cops. Each one has been crossed off, including Stevens, who was the last one. In the room, all there is is a table and a chair. On the other side is a fireplace that is still smoldering. He was here and I must have just missed him. Stevens' name is crossed off. Am I too late? Is this the end of the trail?

I can't let it end here.

Searching around the room I can't find a shred of evidence. In a fit of anger I flip the table over and smash the chair to splinters.

"Shit!" I yell.

A glint of something catches my eye in the fireplace. Rummaging through the ashes I find an old polaroid photo. It's mostly burned but I can make out a woman and child in the picture. She's wearing some kind of jumpsuit. Both of them look so happy although half of the kid's face has been burned off by the fire. Who are these people? Hopefully they are not a victim of Walter's.

Flipping the picture over, on the back in faint pencil I can just barely make out "Candice and Walt". The watermark is much more clear. It says:

LOCHLAND WOMEN'S CORRECTIONAL

It's a lead. A small lead, but it's all I have.

Back at the cave I'm getting suited up. First

the pants, then the top. Trunks next, then boots. These boots have served me well and I wish I could remember the name of the boxer I bought them off of. Gloves, cape, utility belt. Grabbing a roll of athletic tape, I wrap over my gloves to make them rock solid. I punch my own fists a few times to make sure.

One last thing I have to do. Picking up the phone I call Emma.

"Ian! Thank God! What's happening?" She asks.

"Emma, just tell Alex that I'm sorry and I hope one day she'll be able to forgive me." I say and then hang up the phone.

Grabbing the cord of the phone, I yank it from the wall. Tossing it down on the ground I smash it with my heel. This one, I go alone. I pull on the mask.

I am RONA GRAY.

There is one area of the cave that I had yet to enter. It's time to see what's inside. This might be my last chance.

Touching a panel with my gloved hand a sensor reads something embedded in the fingertips. The wall shifts and retracts revealing another exit from the cave, in front of it is a large object covered with a black tarp. Grabbing a handful of it I yank it away revealing a jet black 1965 Ford Mustang Coupe. It shows some road wear and battle damage but otherwise it's in great condition. The tires are caked with mud, the paint scratched revealing the silver metal underneath. As I approach the door I run my fingers across the side. My fingertips trace over the gashes and bullet holes. I'm sure Bram could tell me a story about each one.

Reacting to the same thing in the gloves, the door unlocks. Hopping into the seat the keys are in the ignition. The tag dangling from the key reads "Lady Midnight".

"Please." I say as I turn the key.

The engine roars to life. The lights on the dashboard fire on and illuminate the interior of the car. There is even some gas left in the tank.

"Thank you, Bram." I say.

I shift it into drive and hit the gas. The car flies down a secret tunnel. A long corridor lit only with the occasional swaying overhead light. At the end a door lifts up. I've come out of the passage and on to a cliffside. All I can see is the overcast sky and snow falling down.

"Oh shit!"

The car hits a ramp and I'm soaring through the air. Time freezes for a second but then a dirt road rises to meet the tires. Crashing down I bounce in the seat.

Following the path I realize I'm in the woods that connect to Central Park. It's not long before I get my bearings and I know exactly where I'm headed.

For Tom. For Melinda. For Cara. For Alex. For Emma. For Gloria. For Rona. And for all the people that the monster has hurt or killed...

I stomp the gas.

CHAPTER 45

Alex

A loud knock on my apartment door wakes me from a fairly pleasant dream. Rattled, I shake my head to try and wake myself up. Outside my window I can see that it is snowing heavily.

"Yeah? Yeah? Who is it?" I ask.

"It's Emma! Alex, it's an emergency!" She says.

The tone of her voice instantly wakes me up. Why hadn't she called my phone? I look and see that I had accidentally kicked it off the hook. Damn.

At the door, Emma is in a full panic. She barges in and almost knocks me over. She is completely disheveled. Gobs of snow sitting in her hair. Still dressed in her hospital scrubs. I think this is the first time she's been out of that place in over a month.

"Alex, I think he knows who the monster is and he's going after him alone!" She says.

Wait. I am seriously confused. I must have missed a few steps. How long was I out for?

"Wait, what? How would he know who he was?" I ask.

"This orderly at the hospital. He seemed like such a nice guy. He took Stevens. When I told Ian the orderly's name he seemed to recognize it."

"And what was it?" I ask.

"Walter Daigan." She says.

Daigan... I know that name. That was one of the cops the monster killed. Why would the monster be using the name of one of the cops he killed? Is he related to that cop? That doesn't make sense. Was our hypothesis on the motive so far off?

"I know that name too. Daigan was one of the cops that was murdered by that freak." I tell her.

"That's odd. Are they related in some way?" She asks.

"They must be, although I don't know how or why. Our profile on the creep was way off. If he is related to that cop, why would he go on a killing spree of all of his relative's fellow officers?" I say.

"It might be a fake name. Maybe he needed to use the name as a cover to access information on the other officers." Emma says to me.

"Emma, you're a genius! That makes a lot of sense." I tell her.

"Well I don't know about that." She says modestly.

I pop open my secret closet.

"What are you doing?" Emma asks.

"I have to help him." I say.

"But you're in no condition to fight, Alex. You haven't fully recovered from your injuries." She tells me like I don't know.

Ian is facing the beast alone. I can't let him die like that. Together we might stand a chance against him and if we do die, at least we will die together.

"If I don't go he'll die for sure and I can't let that happen. I just can't!" I say.

Grabbing my battle suit off the rack I toss it to Emma.

"Now are you going to help me or not?" I ask.

Emma is trying her best to help me get this damn thing on but my ribs are still too sore. We finally get it zipped up but I can't breathe. My bandages make it too tight around the midsection.

"Forget this!" I yell as I rip the damn thing off of me.

In my secret closet I pull open the bottom drawer of the vanity. Inside is the outfit I first wore. I slide on the knee-hole jeans, still speckled with blood, then the gray henley shirt. Buttoning each button I leave the top one undone. Finally my brown bomber jacket with my logo spray-painted on the back. All of it still fits.

Tying my hair up in a ponytail I head to the door.

"Emma, stay here or go home. You deserve the rest." I say.

"Where are you going?" She asks.

"To find Ian. No matter what, I will find him." I say to her.

She grabs me and gives me the biggest hug. My ribs hurt but I let it go.

"I love you." She says. "Don't forget this."

She tosses me my utility belt.

My car took a few tries to get started but now I'm back at the cave. Looking for any clues that could lead me to Ian, there is a wall lifted out of the way that I've never seen before. Based on the way it's set up I think it was most likely a garage. The floor is stained with oil. There must have been a car here.

Going back into the main cave area I see that the Rona Gray outfit is gone. Searching through the garbage I find used needles and a bottle of testosterone.

"Oh Ian... What were you thinking?" I say to myself.

Running out of options I sit at the desk and flip on the computer. The password screen comes up. I guess Ian never cracked this. I try a few things but constantly get denied.

"Damn... what is the password? It could literally be anything!" I exclaim in frustration as I slam my hand down on the keyboard.

"Access denied!" The computer says.

Laying my head down on the desk I think back to my bedroom when I was a kid looking through The Apparition comic books. I try to remember if there was anything about a computer password in his secret lair. Even if there was, how would the writers know it? And if they did would they actually publish it?

"Who was the villain again... Wikkid?"

She was a sexy witch character. Her outfit was particularly revealing in the chest region.

A very busty blonde. I could actually see Tamara playing her in a movie. If The Apparition was real, maybe she was too? Although I'm sure the artists embellished a little.

I type it in but I get denied yet again. Come on, Alex, think! For some reason his catchphrase comes to mind. "The spirit of justice will haunt you". What the hell. It's worth a shot. My fingers fly as I type "the spirit of justice".

The voice from the computer tells me "Access granted".

"You've got to be kidding me!" I exclaim with glee.

The monitor lights up with a giant menu of things. Looking through them quickly I have my fingers crossed for some kind of clue.

Database.

Open Cases.

City Map.

Photos.

News Feed.

Radio.

GPS.

GPS. That must be it. As fast as I can I click on it, a map of the city opens up on the screen with a glowing dot moving down one of the streets. That must be the car. I wonder if The Apparition had a sidekick who would guide him where to go. He never had one in the comic books.

The dot is rapidly approaching the Lochland Women's Correctional Facility. That place has been abandoned for years. Something about unsafe conditions for the prisoners. There had been many riots there. A lot of the prisoners got killed. There was also a scandal involving the prison guards accepting sex for favors. Now the women all go to Ludlow Institution.

Why would he be heading there? I don't have time to try and figure out the answer to that question.

I hop out of the seat.

A sharp pain radiates from my ribcage all the way up to my ears.

I ignore it.

"Ian, hold on."

CHAPTER 46

Rona Gray

Lady Midnight slams through an old metal gate going eighty-eight miles per hour. The gate goes flying over the top of the car and crashes down behind it. The long driveway up to the prison goes by in the blink of an eye. The place looks like something that you would only see in a nightmare. Giant stone towers with sharp, angled architecture. It's almost like a medieval fortress. The main lobby area is rapidly approaching. It's mainly made of glass. Not for long.

In a giant shower of debris I smash right through the lobby wall. The car skids and I stomp the brake. Twisting the wheel the car comes to a stop right in the middle of the lobby. Hopping out of the car I take in the sheer size of the place. A huge one-hundred-foot ceiling. In the center of the room is an enormous monument. A slab with a list of names. Must be the names of the ones who founded this place. The last glimmers of daylight shine through stained glass windows. It's like this place was once a church or cathedral.

Off from the lobby area it's dilapidated and practically in ruin. It seems no one has been here in a very long time. Everything is covered in a sheet of dust. At the front desk amongst piles of garbage and paperwork, I find a memo.

As of September 4th 1975 this facility will be officially closed. Any prisoners still assigned to this location will be moved to Ludlow Institution. Please make any necessary arrangements. Thank you.

-Warden Lewis

That was over ten years ago. What could have happened that lead to this place being shut down? If Walter is here I fear I might not even be able to find him in this gigantic place. On the wall is a map of the prison. There is a courtyard in the center. That might be a good place to start looking.

Making my way through the hallways I get a chill down my spine. This prison is seriously creepy, and based on where Walter was living it seems this place would be right up his alley. Finding the door to the courtyard, and using surprisingly little force to break the lock, I enter. Cracked tile floors and dead planters, a couple of benches and tables. No sign anyone has been here recently. Up above me is a glass ceiling with large pieces broken out. Snow is coming down inside the building. The beautiful snowflakes dancing around me almost make this place seem like something out of a fairy tale.

On one of the tables is a deck of cards with two different hands laid out. Brushing the snow off of one of them I flip it over. It's a 2-7 offsuit.

"Bad luck..." I mutter to myself.

Beyond the table I see something horrifying. The body of a young man, it seems he fell a great distance. His body is all but splattered on the tile floor. The blood is fresh, this must have happened recently.

"Ah... I see the pest has returned!" A booming voice echoes from above.

It's Walter. He's standing looking over the edge of a balcony on the top floor. That twisted skull mask seems to taunt me. He holds out his arms to his sides.

"I'm waiting!" He taunts.

Rushing back inside the main hallway I go back to an elevator I passed. Surprisingly it still works. I guess the power hasn't been completely cut or it's running off a generator.

The door opens with a bell and I step inside. I press the button for the 15th floor. The elevator begins to move up and it's shaking violently. It's now or never.

I reach into one of the pockets of my utility belt. Inside is a small syringe filled with the adrenaline that Emma had given me reluctantly. I know she doesn't want anything bad to happen to me. She's a good woman. I think of her acne kissed cheeks and her soft smile. Maybe the two of us... in another life...

I slam the needle into my leg and push down the plunger. A burst of white light flashes before my eyes. My muscles tense and flex and my heart starts pounding a mile a minute. Gritting my teeth so hard it feels like they are about to shatter inside my mouth. Then, a wave of euphoria.

The bell rings and the door opens. Standing before me is Walter. Behind him a hospital bed. That must be Stevens. My mind is racing. Control yourself. Control yourself. My fists clench. I'm bouncing in place, like just before a fight. I'm ready.

"Where is your sweet, little, girlfriend? I fear this will be over far too quickly without her. She was the tough one after all." He says as he laughs.

Aaron O'Shaunessy... Laughing at me. He blows me a kiss.

Moving faster than I have ever before I punch Walter as hard as I can, right in the face. He stumbles back. It's the first time I've seen him affected by anything. I feel my confidence growing.

"A good hit. I see that you have found your passion!" He mocks me. "Let us test your mettle and see if you really have what it takes to stop me!"

Following up quickly I throw another punch which hits him in the eye, then another, and another. I throw a fourth but he catches it. His hand is twice the size of mine. Bending my wrist backward I fall to my knees and I can't help but let out a yelp of pain.

"This is pointless defiance. Soon this will all be over." He says.

Falling to my back I kick him hard in the leg. He falls to one knee with a grunt. I scramble and get back to my feet and follow up with a knee strike right under his chin. He topples over. Leaping into the air I go for a finishing blow but come down to the ground, hitting nothing but concrete.

Walter grabs me from behind and hoists me overhead. I'm struggling to get free of his grip, but before long he slams me right down onto the floor. The wind blows right out of me and my lungs fill with fire. The pain is excruciating. Walter is towering over me. His presence is simply biblical.

"Why are you expecting a different result? I commend your courage masked man, but it's over. Don't force my hand any further."

Thinking quickly, I remember the line launcher that Neon had given me. I yank it out from the back pocket of my utility belt and aim it at Walter's face. I pull the trigger. He caught it! The son of a bitch caught the dart in his bare hand...

Pulling on it, in one stroke, he lifts me back to my feet. I try to pull back but he wraps the line around my neck. Lifting me to the air, I just barely get my fingertips between my neck and the rope as he starts choking me with it like a noose. I'm losing air quickly. I need to think. Think, Rona. Think!

"Do you wish for death?" He asks. "If that is the case, then I will gladly oblige."

He carries me over to the edge of the balcony and dangles me over the courtyard. I'm gasping, choking. It's getting harder and harder to breathe. My legs are kicking but hitting nothing but air.

"Just say the word and I'll release you from this hellish world." He says.

Looking down I see how far the fall is. I see the dead body of that young man. There is no way I'd survive, even in this protective suit. I begin grunting in defiance. It's all that I can manage to get out.

"I see you desire more punishment." He says. "So be it."

Using the rope he whips me over his head, slamming me hard into the floor once again. If I had any breath it would be gone. The adrenaline is still coursing in my veins and I block the pain out of my mind. I get to all fours but I'm met with a stomp to the back. Tears flood my eyes. I scream. I can't stop it from happening. I scream.

One of Walter's huge hands flips me onto my back. He stands over me, his fist raised. The first strike is the hardest I've ever been punched in the head until the second, and then the third. Somehow they are getting worse and worse. If it wasn't for this helmet I'm sure my brains would have been splattered on the floor. Each hit causes me to see a flash of light. The pain is quick and sharp. Desperately reaching around, my hand grasps a pile of dirt. In a weak attempt to do something, I toss the dirt at his face hoping that it will temporarily blind him. He laughs and continues reigning down blows. Over and over again his fist connects. I can do nothing to defend myself. Eventually I just let it happen. The warm feeling of blood fills my mask. A few more blows and it will all be over.

"Gloria..." The only word that seems to gurgle out of my mouth.

It's 1980. I'm in Bella Cruz looking out over the water at the bridge. A female voice calls my name. I turn and see the sunset. Silhouetted against the amazing pink sky is Gloria. She's waiting for me. Walking towards her she seems to change right before my eyes.

"Gloria?" I ask.

She turns and looks at me and it's Alex as Neon Fire. She smiles at me. That adorable, infectious smile of hers. She leans in and whispers in my ear.

"I love you."

I'm in the hospital. In my arms is my beautiful daughter Rona, she's just been born. I touch her nose and she giggles. I'm smiling ear to ear like a doofus. It's the happiest moment of my entire life. I place her into Gloria's arms and the two of them are absolutely glowing. My angels.

All of a sudden, a hand grips mine. It pulls me the other direction. Before me is my sweet Rona, now four years old. With her bouncing brown curls and her rosy cheeks, she looks so beautiful.

"Not yet Daddy!" She says and starts pulling me away.

I stumble into the darkness. I can't see anything at all. Then a light shines and I turn. Now it's a month ago and I'm looking at Alex, lying in a pool of her own blood at the hands of Walter. She's crippled. Dying...

In the hospital, Alex is asleep. I tell her I love her. That I would do anything for her. I would die for her.

"You can do anything you want. Be anything you want to be! I believe in you!" Gloria's words echo in my brain and stretch on for eternity.

It's the night of the fight with O'Shaunessy. In the midst of battle I look out into the crowd and see Gloria. She's cheering me on. Next to her is Alex. She's screaming out to me.

"Get up and fight, you son of a bitch!" She yells.

Snap out of it!

My eyes come alive and my adrenaline surges like never before. Getting my legs up between us I kick as hard as I possibly can. Walter goes flying off of me. He's down, holding his ribs. I feel my second wind building inside of me like a bomb ready to explode. Now is my chance!

Getting to my feet I shake off the cobwebs. Looking at my taped up fists I feel a power surging through them like an electrical current. My cape is heavy, slowing me down. I unlatch each side of the harness one at a time, lift it over my head and throw it to the ground. It lands heavy, kicking up a cloud of dust.

Now the mask. It's full of blood and impeding my vision. In a quick motion I tear it away and toss it to my feet.

My face feels like a wreck but I can't let that stop me. I wipe the blood away from my nose. Clenching my fists tight I get into my fighting stance.

"Stand and face me!" I yell.

He rushes at me faster than I expected he could move. He lands several blows to my abdomen but I don't even feel them. I return fire. Blow after blow to his mask sends him reeling. Pinning him against the wall I blast his midsection with punch after punch. He's on the defensive but I'm moving too fast for him. He's eating every punch at full strength. I can hear his groans from behind the mask. He's hurting and it's beginning to show.

Leaning back I throw my head full force into his face. His head is pinned between mine and the wall. The mask cracks and I can see one of his piercing blue eyes. For the first time I can tell he's scared. Backing off a bit to put space between us, I land a few more shots followed by an uppercut. He has had nothing to answer my attack.

He swats at me a couple of times but I backflip over his arms and then I reel back for the final blow. He moves at the last second and my fist collides with the concrete wall. I hear a snap and a lightning bolt of pain shoots up my arm that I can't ignore.

"Fuck!" I yell.

Leaving myself open he capitalizes. My gut lights up with pain as I eat his knee. Falling to the ground I catch myself but before I can make a move he stomps on my already injured hand. I scream again.

Damn.

Damn.

Damn!

What can I do?

"Time to end this petty squabble." He gloats.

Grabbing me by the back of my outfit he lifts me and starts carrying me towards the edge of the balcony. He intends to throw me off. Suddenly, the ground rushes up to meet me. He dropped me. Doubled over in pain and holding his ribs, blood begins to pour out from under his mask. He starts coughing violently. This might be my last chance.

Up on my feet I start laying into him as hard as I can. He's backing up to the ledge. This is it! If I can just knock him off... Punch after punch he gets ever so much closer. My hands feel as though they are shattering but I can't stop. Just one more hit! Just one more hit!

Push, Ian! Push!

The voices of Alex, Emma, Tom, Gloria, and my sweet Rona cheer me on.

My heart is beating so hard it feels like it's about to burst out of my chest. My head is spinning on my neck and I feel as though I have left my body. The insanity of everything that has happened in the past year... all these thoughts rushing through my brain all at once. Focus! He's just inches away. Come on, Ian! Come on!

A white light flashes before my eyes and a sharp acute pain rockets down my left arm. I grab it as I fall to the ground fighting to catch my breath.

Oh God. Not here. Not now.

"You're sure you know what you are doing

with that stuff?" Emma's voice seeps into my head. She warned me and I didn't listen.

It was too much too fast. It was dangerous and you knew it.

Kneeling before the monster I feel as though I could drop dead at any second. He's steadied himself. Towering over me, his shadow is like a storm cloud blacking out the sun. In a pathetic attempt at defending myself I try to push him away. His giant hand wraps around my throat as he lifts me to the air like a child. It's taking every ounce of strength I have just to stay awake. Stay in the here and now.

I can't give up. Not now. Please...God.

"I can't let you win..." I squeak out with blood frothing from my mouth.

"So close and yet so far." He gloats and begins to laugh. A heavy stream of blood trickling down his chest.

For some reason I think of the waterfall where I met Donna. My first love. We kissed for the first time in the cave just beyond the water. Back then I was scared of the heights. Donna held my hand as we leaped from the top of the waterfall into the river below. I was terrified but her strength gave me strength.

It's amazing what love can make you do...

And so has been my life...

Things are starting to go dark.

This is it...

I must be dying because there she is. Neon Fire. Waiting for me in the distance. I want to go to her. Tell her I love her. Tell her all about how she fixed me and made me a better person. Because of her I became more than just a man.

I am Rona Gray.

CHAPTER 47

Neon Fire

On the opposite side of the courtyard on the balcony I can see Ian being choked to death by that monster. I have to work fast. Readying my line launcher I fire it across the way. The bolt digs into the wall in the distance and the line gets taut. I fling the handle over the line and grasp it with both hands.

"Ian! Here I come!"

Jumping with as much force as I can muster I go flying across the gap. The monster still hasn't seen me. Pulling my legs in, my body accelerates even faster. Letting go of the handle I go hurtling through the air, pushing out my foot. The monster turns to look and I kick that son of a bitch right in the face. His mask shatters into a million pieces.

He's on his knees. Blood pouring from his mouth. Ian did a serious number on him. The freak is in bad shape and maybe now we finally have a chance.

Screaming, he rushes at me. In a quick motion I back kick him in the throat, knocking the wind out of his sails.

"You bitch!" He yells, full of rage, his voice

horse and distorted.

Coming at me again, I go to hit him with an uppercut, but he somehow gets his hand on my hair. My ribs crack as he follows up with a stiff punch to my gut. What the hell is this guy? Is he even human? Blood trickles out of my mouth and speckles the concrete floor.

"Oh, God." I mutter.

Ian seems to have recovered and appears as if from nowhere and tackles the beast. He's going ballistic, landing punch after punch to his face, but it's not enough. The freak tosses him off and gets back to his feet. I rush to Ian's side and help him up.

"Alex... I don't know how much longer I can fight." He says.

"Then we better end this quickly." I say.

Our eyes meet and we exchange a longing glance. I can feel his pain. I know there's something seriously wrong with him beyond even the physical injury.

My Ian...

Hold out a little longer.

The two of us begin our last-ditch attack. We move as one landing blow after blow, pushing the beast back. He's getting overwhelmed. In perfect synchronicity we both jump in the air and spinning back kick him in the chest. He goes falling back to the wall cracking his head against it.

Slumping down, he goes to get up and fails. We finally did it. We got him.

Seeing him like this, doubled over and in

pain, I now understand that he really isn't a giant or a monster. There is nothing supernatural about him at all.

"It's over." I say.

"Walter... why? Why did you do all this?" Ian asks.

Walter spits out blood and looks up at Ian.

"Ian... I thought you looked familiar." He groans. "All I wanted was to be left alone. To finish my work and be at peace. No one would let it be and look at how many people are dead. So many dead and for what? Pointless pain and suffering. But that all ends now." He says.

"But your father was a cop? Why would you kill cops? Explain yourself!" Ian demands

"My father wasn't a cop. I stole that asshole's name so I could access information and track down the others. My father was a good man who got shot down in cold blood. My mother was incarcerated in this shit hole and got killed while she was minding her own business. It's all their fault and there's only one of them left." He laughs as he looks over at Stevens who is lying in a hospital bed at the edge of the balcony. "The one who pulled the trigger and ended my life before it even began."

"Your plan has failed. We've stopped you! It's time you pay for all the lives you've taken and all the people you hurt." I say.

"You're right. I will pay for my crimes. It was my plan all along." He says.

"What do you mean? You planned on turning

yourself in?" I ask.

"Not exactly..." He laughs.

Suddenly, like the sound of cannon firing a huge explosion goes off shaking the floor beneath our feet. Then another and another. This place is lighting up like a Christmas tree.

"We need to get out of here now!" Ian yells to me.

Rushing over to the hospital bed I check for a pulse. Stevens is dead. Another explosion goes off and the balcony is starting to collapse.

"He's gone!" I yell to Ian.

Ian is standing over Walter. Hesitating for a moment, he finally grabs his hand and yanks him up to his feet.

"You're coming with us." Ian says.

"There isn't enough time to escape..." Walter says in a remorseful tone.

I return to Ian and help with Walter. We each take a side and support him on our shoulders. He is one heavy son of a bitch, that's for sure. My ribs are in agony and I'm doing all I can just to keep going.

We get to the elevator door and another explosion rocks the prison. I frantically press the call button.

"Ian... if you were this masked man the whole time... how did you not figure out it was me?" Walter asks.

"I guess I couldn't imagine someone as nice and selfless as you could be..."

"Life is a strange thing, huh?" Walter replies.

Another explosion!

"Come on!" I scream as the elevator finally reaches our floor.

The door opens up and in an instant Ian and I are inside. Walter pushed us in. Before we can figure out what is going on the elevator doors are starting to close.

"Shit!" I yell.

"Goodbye." Walter says with a smile.

"He's getting away!" I say.

"No, he's not." Ian says as he places his hand on my shoulder.

The elevator ride is bumpy and scary as hell. Ian holds me tight to comfort me. The door opens to the lobby and we make a b-line towards the car. Ian is in no shape to drive but I'm not doing so hot myself. One of us has to...

"I'll drive!" I say.

"It's all yours." Ian says.

Approaching the driver side things seem to move in slow motion. The echoes of explosions linger in my ears. Turning I look across the roof of the car at Ian. He's yelling something but I can't hear him.

"Alex! Alex!" He's screaming.

My eyes open and I realize that I am trapped underneath some giant stone monument. If it wasn't for the car I would have been completely crushed. My legs are pinned and I can't move at all. Another explosion goes off and the ceiling is starting to crumble. Tears begin to fill my eyes.

"Get out of here, Ian. Please. Save yourself." I say.

"I'm not leaving you!" He says. Tears pouring from his eyes like a waterfall.

He knows I'm a goner.

I want to tell him I love him but the words won't come out.

"Please... Ian... Just go." I squeak out the words between sobs.

"It's not over!" He yells.

Squatting down he grabs the side of the slab. Letting out a scream akin to a wild animal he begins to lift. His face turns crimson red, veins bulging out of his neck as thick as fire hoses. The sleeves on his suit begin to tear from the stress.

"Move, goddamn it!" He screams.

The slab begins to lift. I can feel my toes. I wriggle them back and forth. Then my hands. I can grip. I start to push myself out from under. Soon I am free. Once I'm out Ian drops the slab. He only moved it a few inches but that was enough. He saved me.

Getting to my feet I grab Ian and give him the biggest hug.

"Ian, you're amazing."

He smiles. Blood trickles out of his nose and his eyes go glassy. He collapses into my arms unconscious.

"It's my turn." I say.

Dragging him as far away from the building as I can, with what little strength I have left, we just manage to get out in time. The whole building crumbles to a pile of rubble in a spectacular show of fireworks. All that remains is a giant, beautiful fire, raging against the snow. Raging against the night sky.

I lay Ian down in the snow. I check for a pulse and I can't find one. Quickly I start performing CPR.

"Ian! Ian! Wake up! Wake up!" I yell.

I continue CPR. Please, Ian. Please wake up! I can't lose you. Not now. Not before...

Pressing my lips against his I breathe hard. One. Two. Three times. Suddenly, I feel his lips press back. I pull away and he has a faint smile on his face.

"Oh thank God you're alive!" I say.

He moves my hair behind my ear.

"Alex... I..." He says.

"I know... I know..." I say as tears of joy trickle down my face.

Propping him up against a tree I sit down next to him. The two of us watch the blazing inferno. The fire rises into the sky and makes a display of gorgeous colors like I have never seen before. It has stopped snowing and the moonlight is showering the whole world in a wonderful white glow. Between the fire and the reflection off the snow it's almost as bright as day.

Sliding my hand into Ian's I lean in and kiss him on the cheek.

"Ian... Isn't it beautiful here?"

"It is." He says.

Turning to look at him I see his eyes have only been on me.

I can't help but smile.

CHAPTER 48

Ian

It's been a couple weeks since the incident and I'm finally out of the hospital. Broken ribs, fractured hand, broken right wrist, severe concussion, internal hemorrhaging, and I also suffered a minor heart attack. Going through the medicine cabinet I take one last look at all the drugs and then flush them. I don't need that stuff anymore. Emma was right all along.

Sitting on the couch I flip on the TV. My body is just one giant ache. I thought maybe they would all just cancel each other out but they definitely don't.

"We hope everyone is having a great new year so far! Can you believe it's already 1987? Absolutely wild!" The talking head on the TV spouts off.

I pop open a can of soda and take a few sips. I haven't drank anything but water over the past month so it tastes like pure sugar, but something is comforting about it. In that vision, or whatever the hell that was, my tombstone read 1986. I'm glad it was wrong. Slumping down on that old dusty couch I can feel my eyes starting to get heavy.

There's a knock at my door so I place the soda

can down on the table. Getting up is a bit of a struggle. Back when I was fighting I thought I had felt the worst I had ever felt or could ever feel...

"Just a second." I say.

My body feels like it's in shambles. I wonder if I will ever really recover from this. Not only the beating I sustained, but the damage done from all the drugs. The doctors told me my heart won't ever be the same. Was it worth it?

Opening the door I'm greeted by Alex. Her hair is about half the length and it's an auburn color. She barely has any makeup on and her freckles accentuate her gorgeous brown eyes. Before saying anything she grabs me in a tight hug. It hurts but I'm loving it at the same time.

"Wow! Look at that hair!" I say.

"I know, right? This is what it looks like naturally." She says looking disappointed.

"I actually like it." I say.

She smiles and starts to play with it.

"You look good." She says.

She is just being nice. My face is a swollen disaster area and I think my nose is even more crooked, but once the swelling goes down I'll know for sure. I always thought that I couldn't possibly get any uglier. Boy, was I wrong.

"It's been a while... How are you?" I ask.

"I'm almost fully recovered. You?" She asks.

"I still have a long way to go. To be honest, my body is a wreck." I tell her, laughing.

"I'm glad you called. I was getting worried

that you didn't want to see me again. The last time we were together... Well... It really took a toll on us both. After I got out of the hospital I went to see you but you were always asleep. I really didn't want to bother you. You looked so peaceful. If anyone deserved the rest, it was you." She says.

I was in the hospital for a lot longer than her. When we first got there I collapsed. Emma made sure to hide our battle suits. The doctor said I was in a coma for three days. They almost lost me once or twice. The whole time I was in there was a giant blur. Even if Alex came to see me when I was awake they had me so doped up I probably wouldn't have remembered. I think Emma came to see me but I'm not really sure. I vaguely remember someone holding my hand.

"It's really ok. I was so out of it. You have no idea." I tell her.

The two of us crash on the couch.

"Can I get you anything?" I ask.

"No... I'm good." She says.

There's an awkward silence that seems to last a millennium. Alex punches me in the arm to break the tension.

"Ow!" I say.

"Come on! That wasn't even that hard!" She says.

"You're stronger than you look, you know." I say.

"That is true." She says with a smile. "So when do you think you'll be able to get back out there, Charles Bronson?"

I had been thinking about it a lot. Did I really want to put that suit back on and go back out there? Fight crime? Risk my life for others? I have literally never been in so much pain in my entire life. Is this what I want?

Looking at Alex waiting for a response, she looks so cute and awkward. She's not her usual confident self. Thinking back, I realize we have never done anything normal together. This is the first time the two of us have ever even sat on a couch together. The awkwardness reminds me of being on a date in high school. It's almost like she already knows what I'm feeling.

The trouble is that I'm in love with her. I want to be with her every moment of every day. Go to bed with her. Wake up next to her. Hold her in my arms and never let go. But she deserves more. She deserves someone better than me. Someone more confident. Someone who can keep up with her never-ending energy. If I continue down this path with her I'll surely be dead before I hit forty-five years old and that's if some monster doesn't end my life sooner.

Looking into her big brown eyes I start to fall. Her nose twitches ever so slightly and her lips part. She makes the cutest little sigh and my heart drops. My stomach begins to fill with butterflies and it feels as though it might burst.

The answer becomes so clear.

"I'm ready when you are." I say with a smile.

Do I regret anything I've done? Without Gloria, without Rona, without O'Shaunessy or Walter, without Tom or Emma, and especially without Alex, I wouldn't be who I am now. Someone I can look in the mirror and be proud of.

So do I?

No.

Not for a single second.

I am Rona Gray.

CHAPTER 49

Neon Fire

It's a cold day, and on days like this I can feel the energy surging in the air, and it feels electric. I shiver for just a second but steady myself. I've let my natural hair color come out and for now I'm really digging it. Maybe somewhere in all this craziness there is a place for both Alex and Neon Fire. For so long I had shut down part of myself but she was still there, just waiting to come back. A person capable of love.

Running my fingers through my hair I tie it back in a bun.

"Punk rock." I whisper to myself.

Standing on the ledge overlooking the city it begins to snow. Sticking my tongue out I catch a snowflake.

My mom and dad are holding my hands as we walk through the park on a snowy day. Kids are sledding and building snowmen. Life was so simple and easy back then. My mom holds me close. She wipes a snowflake off my nose. Her red hair framing her freckly face. She smiles that big infectious grin of hers.

"Keep dreaming of Neon Fire." She says.

The howl of police sirens blare as a chase

begins in the streets below. Gunshots and car horns become a symphony that is playing just for me. My muscles tense and I can't help but feel giddy. The city is like a living, breathing, organism. I am hers and she is mine. This is what I was born to do and every night I am born again.

I turn to Rona Gray.

"Are you ready partner?" I ask.

"Always."

ABOUT THE AUTHOR

Robert William Harms

Robert William Harms is a writer, illustrator, and musician. He has been doing creative things his entire life including recording multiple albums with his bands The Theatre Zombies and The Draculads, as well as drawing comics and character designs. A Dream of Neon Fire is his first novel. He currently lives in Connecticut with his wife, Beth.

You can view his artwork at:
instagram.com/robharmsbelmont

You can listen to music by his bands at:
thetheatrezombies.bandcamp.com
thedraculads.bandcamp.com

BOOKS BY THIS AUTHOR

Neon Gray - A World On Fire: The Strange Case Of Jacob Loomis

A Graphic Novella

www.ingramcontent.com/pod-product-compliance
Lightning Source LLC
Chambersburg PA
CBHW021447240626
47153CB00001B/326